ATTACK OF THE VYPERIANS

A NOVEL BY TIM SAVAGE

First edition.

Copyright © 2015 Tim Savage

ISBN: 978-0692402856

Cover art and design by Mike Wellins — Freakybuttrue.com

VYPERIANS.COM

TIMSAVAGEWRITES@GMAIL.COM

VERY SPECIAL THANKS TO:

TYLER TRONSON
BRANDON S LANSING
JOHN MCCONNELL
JAY LOUIS
VINCE PERFETTO
COREY GRAY
JAMES BENNETT
JIM SWEENEY
BRUCE SPIES
STEVEN KINELL
AARON COVARRUBIAS
DOUG STANZIANO
CHRIS REEBE
ANDY GRANT
MIKE
ARLENE ROBINSON
SKWEEZY FANS EVERYWHERE

FOR MY FATHER.

Attack of the Vyperians

CHAPTER 1

Shallow Space

He stood motionless in the dark room in the starship's bowels. Calm. Collected. Ready. Two of his eight legs supported him. The other six moved akimbo as he unhurriedly rotated his eyes, coolly examining the spectacle on display. Grammeral Q'Shin Zeezak watched the scene play out through the remotescope from the comfort of his cabin, a luxurious fit for the finest Grammeral of the finest fleet in all of known Vyperian space, a fleet respectfully known as "The Emperor's Second Tentacle."

The cabin's opulence was anchored with offerings crafted by the renowned Lowest Slaves in the History of Time cult, a species dedicated to living a life of pain, masochism, and slavery to others, for reasons unknown. Ornate tables and seating, carved out of solid blocks of stone, wood, and bone and accessorized with the rarest of jewels so exclusive most never saw them in the flesh, were at the Grammeral's disposal at any time he chose. Knowing he almost never used the luxuries would probably bring a smile to the Lowest Slaves' mouths, if smiling was something they could even do.

Glowbats illuminated the space, communicating with each other and their master telepathically to always set the right mood. And right now, the mood was dark. As it always was in the moments before the Grammeral made a decision of great importance.

As far as he could scan across the surface of the planet, all the Grammeral could see was endless fire and the shrubs he needed.

And millions of fornicating Garble snails.

He activated the comm on his chair. "Sentlent Bool, I need you at once," he spoke in monotone, abrupt English. And at once, Sentlent Bool entered. He knew better than to keep the Grammeral waiting. Shaped the same octopus way as Grammeral Zeezak, but with a trunk not quite as big as his leader's five feet of body, Sentlent Bool scuttled his way to a position of adherence.

"Yes, my Lord?"

"Have you seen this?"

"The Garble snails, my Lord?"

"Yes."

"Yes, I have."

"What do you make of it?"

Sentlent Bool paused, chose his response carefully.

"I find it repulsive, my Lord."

"Where the snerch did they come from?" asked the Grammeral as he switched out the two tired appendages he was standing on for two fresh tentacles.

"Scanners picked up a drop ship on the other side of the planet, my Lord. They beamed down from there."

"I see."

The Grammeral rubbed a sucker across what could be called his cheek. "They seem to be mating."

"Yes, my Lord. It also appeared to us that the larger creatures have begun to consume the smaller ones."

Grammeral Zeezak clicked his beak. "I wouldn't put it past those perverted creatures to be doing both at the same time."

"Yes, my Lord."

"Sentlent," beckoned the alpha octopus as he turned his tubular body ever so slightly to his second-in-command.

"Yes, my Lord?"

"Do you find their actions repulsive?"

Grammeral Zeezak didn't let Bool reply before continuing. "Or would you say they arouse you."

There was an uncomfortable silence as Sentlent Bool watched Grammeral Zeezak shift his stance while he continued to watch the cannibalistic orgy unfold before him on the remotescope. Sentlent Bool felt his beak quiver and mentally fumbled through potential answers to the Grammeral's query. *Is this one of the Grammeral's psychological traps?* He felt one of his stomachs twist into a knot. The pressure built with every passing sliver of time. Drops of defense slime oozed from Sentlent Bool's pores. His suckers puckered and he was about to spurt out what he hoped would be an adequate response when Grammeral Zeezak eased the tension with a simple change of subject.

"Sentlent, is that drop ship you mentioned within range of our torpedoes?"

"Yes it is, my Lord," Bool replied with a noticeable exhalation of relief.

Grammeral Zeezak tightened his tentacle tips. "Blow it up."

Sentlent Bool straightened. "Yes, My Lord!"

"And since we can assume these creatures thrive on heat,

what do you suggest we do to eradicate them from the planet while not harming the shrubs we need?"

Sentlent Bool knew he *was* being tested this time, and he knew the Grammeral's respect would come with a strong answer.

"My Lord, I would suggest a zero-G bomb with a mid-altitude detonation. The roots should keep the plants down, and the snails should be released from the planet's gravity and float to the upper atmosphere where they will subsequently pop from the pressure."

Grammeral Zeezak rotated his tubular head slowly, and looked directly at his Sentlent for the first time. "Excellent, Sentlent Bool. Execute that plan immediately."

Sentlent Bool knew better than to show excessive emotion in sight of the Grammeral, but in the slimy creases of his stoic face, the glow of appreciation was unmistakable.

• • •

Grammeral Zeezak studied his remotescope while it first displayed the torpedo impacts and exploding drop ship, then displayed the surface of the fire planet as the millions of Garble snails lost their grips and floated up, weightless, toward the stratosphere. He turned a pleased shade of blue at the sight of millions of tiny blobby pops in the upper reaches of the fire planet's sky.

"Send down the harvest teams," he spoke into his comm.

His speaker crackled to life. "Yes, my Lord. Teams launching now."

Grammeral Zeezak scuttled over to a wall panel and

pressed a button. A compartment slid open. Inside the compartment was a thinscreen data tablet. He scooped the tablet from the drawer and powered it on with a cross swipe of his eyes. It glowed to life, and he blinked at the "To-Do" function. He examined his last few tasks.

Finalize Operations Directives: Completed.

Harvest Shebula shrub sap for growth serum:
Incomplete.

With a blink of his eye, he marked that task "complete" as well. He stared at the next objective on his list.

Conquer the planet known as Earth.

• • •

Four Standard Months Later
Washington, DC

The two girls sat at the edge of the bed and played with hair ties and ate chocolate and talked about Zachary the lacrosse player and all at the same time. Katie was blond. Lizzie was blond-streaked. Lizzie suggested Katie had a crush on Zachary and Katie giggled and pushed Lizzie off the bed.

"*Oh my God*, why would you do that?"

Both girls giggled again as their play fighting escalated. Katie tried to pin Lizzie down and Lizzie let loose with a swipe and accidentally hooked on to Katie's shorts and tugged them down an inch. An inch that revealed a tiny neon strap.

"*Oh my God, Katie!* You're wearing a thong? Where did you get that? Does your mom know?"

"I thought I told you. Didn't I tell you?"

"*Noooooooo.* You're *so* lucky! I've been asking my mom for like, a year, and she keeps saying no."

"That's why you have to buy your own underwear. I just went to Victoria's Secret and bought it."

"And you didn't tell your mom?"

"No way! She didn't even know until she did my laundry when I was at practice. I wore it for like two weeks before I threw it under my bed, and then like, the first time I took it off, she goes and does my laundry."

"*Ewww*, two weeks? That's gross."

"It didn't smell till like, day twelve."

"*Ewwww.* Why didn't you just—"

"You can borrow one of mine if you—"

"*Shhh*, she's on! The song's on!"

The girls' attentions immediately focused on the TV as the host exploded through the screen and into the bedroom.

"What's up, everyone! We're about to go live as the one and only Jennica! performs her brand-new song for you, me, and the entire world. It's a Music Television exclusive, and no one has seen this yet. Nobody. Not even me. You guys ready?" Hyperized teenage girls in-studio screamed their lungs out at the cue.

"Well, we shouldn't really wait any longer, should we?" The girls in the studio audience screamed even louder. "We'll get to Jennica! as soon as we come back from this commercial break."

"*Boooo, you suck!*" Katie and Lizzie both hissed their disappointment.

"*Ugh.* I can't believe it. They *always* do that," whined Katie.

"You know why, don't you?"

"'Cause they hate us."

"*Nooo*, 'cause they can make more money with commercials and they know we'll sit and watch them."

"That's crap, I *never* listen to any of the stuff they say."

"Yeah, me too. Gimme another Twix."

"*Hell* no. Two for me, none for you, bitch!"

The two girls resumed their wrestling match but didn't make it far before the commercials ended. They screeched to a halt faster and noisier than a train crashing into a ravine. The host was back on the screen and could barely get his words in over the screaming of the tweens in the room.

"And now here she is, with her brand-new song 'Slit,' it's Jennica!"

Millions of girls around the world screamed in unison as their idol appeared through a haze of smoke, dressed in straps and spikes, and harboring a giant bird on her shoulder.

"*Oh my God*," Lizzie screeched. "She's got ... is that thing a bird?"

It was a pelican.

"She's *sooo* crazy. She just does, like, whatever she wants!"

Jennica! danced and strutted and throatily purred the words of her new song.

Don't (don't)
You (you)
Want
2
Touch (touch)
My bawdy (snap snap)

The pelican flapped once but never lost its balance. It was a true professional.

• • •

Amazon Jungle

The air was thick with moisture and almost as thick with insects. Leaves and branches tangled endlessly on the rainforest floor, preventing all but the heartiest of creatures from passing through. A hot, wet, itchy, miserable green hell.

Deep within the Amazon jungle, up north past the Mato Grosso, lay millions of square kilometers of raw jungle. Right in the middle of the millions of kilometers of jungle were a dozen hearty men. And in the middle of the men was James "Crash" Jefferson, the host of cable television's *Deadly Animals with Crash Jefferson.*

Crash was a beast of a man with a face not unlike fool's gold: hard and pretty and fake. It was a face that had been reconstructed after countless accidents in the line of adventuring duty. Much Hollywood gossip had been bandied regarding Crash's transformation from rugged and average to rugged and dashing over the course of his television career. Officially, it was due to his injuries. Unofficially, Crash had an unlimited line of credit with the top face sculptor in Beverly Hills.

Moving into his twelfth year as a television host, Crash and his men were in the one place they hadn't yet been able to access, the mighty Amazon jungle. Denied one time because of dangerous floodwaters and another because of civil unrest, the Amazon had become Crash's white whale. Weeks had been spent planning the trip, days had been spent pushing deep into the forest, and three men had already turned back because of illness. Yet the remaining men continued on, and had just arrived at the bank of a small tributary. Crash, leading the way, held his fist in the air to signal his men to stop. He looked around and at the jungle. Through the jungle. He twitched his nose. Pointed at the creek.

"A camera there."

A camouflaged man dressed like leaves hustled over to start setting up the camera. "Watch for vipers," Crash yelled, before pointing at a low branch. "Sound there!" Another man hustled over to start setting up the disguised microphones. "Will!" Crash barked over his shoulder to his right-hand man, who emerged from the thickness of the jungle and into the clearing.

"Yo, Crash!"

"Let's set up shop right here. Can you get good shots from these angles?"

"I can get good shots from anywhere. You think this is a good place to find some action?"

Crash knelt and ran his fingers along the indent of a footprint in the mud. The soil was firm, but moisture still leaked from the heel wall onto his fingertips. Fresh. "They'll be through again before nightfall—" A scream broke through the jungle from down near the tributary.

"What happened?" Crash asked, still kneeling in the mud.

"Ray got bitten by a viper!"

Crash stood and yelled, "I told you guys to watch out for vipers."

• • •

Jennica! finished her "live" set and disappeared to backstage safety via a giant cloud of dry ice-induced fog. Within seconds, she was surrounded by an entourage of gigantic men who had one shared goal: Keep the crazy people away. Even backstage, Jennica! was rarely safe from reach of the relentless pursuit of obsessed tweenagers. Or the relentless pursuit of the occasional middle-aged male stalker.

The television studio was sterile, however. No crazies. No drama. Nothing but a quiet march back underneath the set. Jennica! entered her dressing room to the chorus of two tiny dogs yip-yapping.

"Oh my God, I missed you two so much come here come here come here! *Ohhhh*, I love *youuuuuu!*"

Jennica! scooped up her toy poodles and buried her face in their curly fur.

• • •

New York City

The park was crowded with families, friends, food vendors and their hungry clientele, teenagers lying out in the sun (fully clothed and eyes locked on their smartphones), and pigeons looking for responsible partners with hearts longing for commitment. And in between a group of hipsters playing Frisbee and a half-naked man dazzling only himself with metal hula hoops stood a father trying to convince his son that his mother didn't hate him.

"She still loves you."

"Then why is she leaving?"

"Well, because she doesn't, uh, she doesn't love me."

The boy started to cry.

"Oh, uh, no, I didn't mean it like that. I mean I did, 'cause she doesn't love *me* anymore. But it's not a bad thing. It's not a good thing either, though. I'm not happy about it at all, I'm kind of upset really, but ..."

Dr. Frank Faraday had, by this point, entered the vault of his own self-absorption, as he was so often inclined to do, and his son's tears were right in front of his face yet so, so far away.

"Dad?"

"She's a good woman and I'm just so caught up—"

"Dad."

"—and we, huh? Yeah, Trev?"

"Why are we here?" The words dropped out of Trevor's mouth with a sniffle.

Faraday tugged on his glasses and scrunched his forehead.

"Well Trev, that's a real good question. And we don't really know. We aren't even really sure where we've come from. I mean, the Big Bang of course is the main idea, but in the past couple of decades we've been playing with the suggestion in M-theory that states the Big Bang was a side effect of parallel universes colliding—"

"No, why are we at the park?"

"Oh." The scrunch in Dr. Faraday's forehead smoothed out.

"Because it's sunny and warm for the first time in five months, and you've been sitting on my couch all winter and eating my food and getting fat. Do you still like that girl from your class?"

Trevor looked down at the ground. The question caught him by surprise, as most of his dad's randomly asked questions often did. "*Dad.*"

"That's a yes." Faraday grinned as his son blushed.

The father bent over, opened up a backpack, and pulled out two mitts and two balls and gave one of each to his son. Trevor looked on curiously.

"Why do we have two balls?"

Faraday's grin turned to a full smile, and for a moment Trevor thought his dad was going to awkwardly answer him again, and even more embarrassingly this time. But the elder Faraday didn't catch the setup to a sophomoric joke and carried on with his explanation.

"This is really cool. Something I've been working on. Get out there."

Trevor took his ball and glove and wandered about ten meters away from his dad, careful not to go anywhere near the half-naked man with the rings. Faraday fumbled with his own glove and ball, smile still stretched across his face.

"Okay son, now throw the ball!"

Trevor wound up and threw. The elder Faraday made every effort to avoid catching the ball, and they both watched it hit the ground and roll up to Dr. Faraday's feet.

"I don't get it," said Trevor, unamused.

Faraday rolled the ball back to his son. "Throw it upward at an angle. Not straight up, more like forty-five degrees!"

Trevor picked up the ball and threw it higher. The ball made it halfway to his dad, and then orbited around slightly and boomeranged back to him so fast that he almost didn't have time to get his glove up.

"Whoa!"

Faraday smiled again and shouted back. "It's something new I'm working on. Basically catch that plays itself. Pretty cool, huh? Gyroscopes!"

And father and son threw their own balls to themselves in the warm, late spring sun.

CHAPTER 2

Washington, DC

Senator Mike Horton sat down to dinner and reached for the salt. This month's salt and pepper shakers were a fun pair of porcelain kids flying kites. The shakers rotated in and out like substitute players in a lame domestic sport. *Thanksgiving's here, send in the Pilgrim shakers. The Quaker shakers. Huh huh, now that's funny,* thought Senator Horton.

Rebecca Horton was gorgeous. Not gorgeous in the way that many people would describe gorgeous, lazily talking about fake blond hair and dusky eye makeup, but gorgeous in that real way where a woman seems pretty when you first meet her, kind the second time you meet her, and luminescent when you really get to know her. Depth. Strength. Dignity. Class. The power and appeal of both Hepburns.

Horton wasn't always a greedy, snake-tongued politician. He had started out wanting to help people. Hell, he still wanted to help people. But somewhere along the way, he came to his own conclusion that he couldn't *really* help people. And like a ketamine trip that allows a peek into the true futility of life for the inward adventurer, Senator Horton's chosen path showed him the true hopelessness derived from politics and corporate

America, and he figured as long as he was going down with the ship, he might as well get a few kickbacks along the way.

Rebecca sat down to join him for dinner, and she thought about how miserable her life had been for the past few years, and why, oh why, was she still with this man who had become cold as ice?

"Dinner!" she shouted.

Lizzie bounded down the stairs and thumped into her seat at the end of the table. *That's why*, thought Rebecca. *That's why.*

Rebecca spoke aloud, if only to quiet the negativity in her mind. "How's that bill looking?"

Senator Horton was reading emails on his phone with one hand and mashing yams into his face with the other.

"Hmm?"

"That bill, Mike. How's it looking?"

"What bill?"

"That bill. The thing with global warming?"

"The thing with global warming? What are you, fifteen?"

Mike Horton had been drifting further away from the man Rebecca had married and closer to "disrespectful asshole" for a while now, but if he thought he was going to get away with that with Rebecca, well, he wasn't. She was about to light him up. Then she glanced down the table at her daughter, who was looking on with sad eyes. *I need to stand my ground here, but now is not the time to start a war*, thought Rebecca. *Still.*

"Are you kidding me? Don't you dare talk to me that way," she shot back.

Her husband looked up from his phone. "Well, I just figured my wife would be using a slightly larger vocabulary than my daughter when—"

"Apologize."

"What?"

"Apologize now."

Lizzie shifted uncomfortably across her seat. "I think I'm gonna go back to my room while you guys fight."

"You're going to stay right there while your father apologizes. I'll not have that kind of example set in this house," Rebecca said without ever breaking her gaze on her husband. Horton shifted uncomfortably under the unrelenting stare of his wife. He looked at his daughter, and then back to Rebecca.

"I'm sorry."

"Thank you."

Tension dropped, but not entirely, which made for a strange pseudo-normal picking at the dinner by all parties present. Rebecca spoke first.

"So you were saying, about the global warming bill?"

"Well, the money people are finally starting to take notice, and I think we're finally at the point where big corporations are realizing that they just can't avoid the issue anymore and pay their way out of things—" Horton's phone rang.

"Hello. Yes. Are you sure? Okay. I'll be right there." Horton ended the call and looked over at his wife. "I have to go." Rebecca was used to the routine and didn't bother to stop eating to ask questions. She knew she wouldn't get any answers regardless. The patriarch excused himself without actually saying the words and Rebecca felt him leave without ever looking in his direction. She opened her mouth to speak to her daughter, but her daughter left almost as quickly as her husband had. Rebecca Horton's gaze dropped to her shakers, and she imagined the two porcelain children were real, playing without a care in the world.

. . .

The shadowy gray light of dusk darted through expiring storm clouds and leaked into Crash's tent, casting odd patterns on him as he sat on an equipment chest. There was a case of bottled water in the corner, there was the chest, and there was the rugged adventurer himself. And that was it. He liked to keep things simple.

"Crash?" he heard from outside.

"Yeah."

"They're almost set up at the remote site. I'm heading there in twenty. I'll come get you."

Crash didn't respond, just looked down at his hands. His gnarled, calloused, manly hands. He studied the scars. A half-moon jag from the reticulated python in Tanzania. A scattering of healed bites from those barracuda spawn near Bermuda. A slice across his forefinger from that piece of frozen chocolate he tried to cut as a fat, gluttonous child. He winced, then quickly moved on and up his arm. One scar in particular had him transfixed.

Crash traced his finger across a pair of large puncture marks on his forearm, caused by the beast that took him closest to death. Crash always thought it would be an elephant, or king cobra, or even a funnel-web spider that would almost do him in. But no, it was a captive capybara: the world's largest rodent.

A goddamn rodent.

In a goddamn zoo.

Granted, the bite itself was superficial and it was the subsequent infection that almost killed Crash, but it was embarrassing nonetheless. And when his wife and girlfriend both came to visit him in the hospital at the same time, Crash's life began to unravel. Both women left him. Half his assets followed the woman he needed, and his supposed best friend followed the woman he wanted. It took years to recover. Years to build up his wealth and image again. *All because of that filthy animal.* Well, more because of his huge ego and inability to keep his dick in his pants, but his ego had no time for reason. Thus, Crash never thought much about his own possible fault, instead directing all his hate toward the world's largest rodent. And he had been refused his opportunity to get his revenge for years.

Over and over and over again, he had been denied the simple human pleasures of revenge and domination over the inferior species that rendered his life to shambles and condemned him to a hospital for weeks. He'd never forget the morbid, oily stink of that place and the misery he felt there. Even if he did get a new nose out of it.

Crash left his place of rage for a moment to touch his nose and admire, for the thousandth time, the smoothness of its slope and the circular perfection of its nostril holes. But the anger quickly returned with the bite of a horsefly that pulled him back to the reality of being in the middle of the jungle for a purpose, a single purpose. To get his revenge. He slapped at the fly as Will reentered the tent.

"The guys finished early. We're ready if you are." Will tossed a knowing glance at Crash. He was no stranger to

Crash's ulterior motive. But it was his job to keep the big guy on track. "Let's not forget the main reason we're here, and that's to wrap the season with a showstopper and get us all another Emmy."

Crash's pupils constricted as he looked through his hands and into the void. "I'm going to take one of those beasts down. Punch it right in the temple. And I'm going to crush its skull with my bare fucking hands."

"That's not going to look good for television."

"I don't care. You can edit around it. Just like with that penguin I shot," Crash replied. Will winced at the memory. Season three had been a rough one.

"All I'm saying is, let's not get crazy here," Will said. "You can do what you need to do. I'm not going to get in your way. But let's get some good footage first, right?"

Crash didn't answer. Instead, he stood and looked at Will, and the two men talked the kind of nonverbal talk that only those who've been through heaven and hell together could decipher. Will dropped his glance in a moment of shared understanding.

There would be blood that night.

CHAPTER 3

Jennica! sat alone in her hotel room and cried like she did most days while on tour. Her life wasn't miserable all the time, just on the road. Of course, she was sad at home sometimes, but she didn't really show it because her friends were there and she had to look happy for them and keep up her image. Which, she felt, kind of counted as happiness.

Her two bodyguards listened to her sob from outside the room.

"I wouldn't want that life for all the dough in the world, you feel me?"

"No shit, homie. Ay, you know they say the more unique your life is, the harder it is to make friends or some shit."

"No shit?"

"I'd say just ask Michael Jackson, but he dead."

"Yeah, how'd he die again?"

"In some weird fuckin' way that only a weird fuckin' person would. Sleep injections or some shit."

"Goddamn."

"True."

"But I *know* you ain't comparin' our girl in there to Michael."

"Nah, nah. But you know she was famous as a kid, too. Like, her first boyfriend was like a pro hockey player nine years older than her or some shit, know what I'm sayin'."

"For real?"

"An' her first car was a Ferrari."

"Damn! My first car was the bus, homie!"

"Yeah, and you know she had some photogs snap crotch pics and post 'em up online before she was even legally allowed to show the goods."

"Goddamn. Ay, how the hell you know all this shit, Skweez?"

"Wikipedia, dawg!"

The bodyguards continued their conversation on whether or not fame was worth all the trouble given what they knew. It ended in a stalemate. Sure, it was a fucked-up way of life. But then again, Jennica! could walk right in to STK in West Hollywood on a Saturday night and not worry about waiting in line. The guys agreed that was pretty damn nice.

Meanwhile, Jennica! sobbed quietly in her king bed while she looked through pictures on her phone of people who were posed around her like best friends but whose names she couldn't remember for the life of her. *I don't even know who my friends are anymore. Not like, what they're about. Who they are.* Her phone *bing*-ed. A text from her manager.

> Hey doll. Just booked you on Good
> Morning America for Friday. Meet you at
> the airport tomorrow night at 6. Bobby.

Oh yay! They shoot in New York! I get to go home! That'll cheer me up. It always does. Oh, but I won't even be able to stay long enough to visit my friends or even go to my apart-

ment. And then it's back to this crap again. Jennica! whimpered, burying her face into her pillow. *What kind of like, cruel destiny lets me go home for such a short time? I might as well be on another freakin' planet.*

Jennica! sobbed some more and curled into a fetal position. As she tugged at her blanket, the pop star felt a strange tickle in the back of her head.

Maybe you do belong on another planet.

Jennica! stretched straight up in her bed, hands clutching at her blanket. Her eyes darted around the dim room.

She *heard* that voice. But there was no one else in the hotel room. As big as it was, it was still only a single bedroom with a bathroom. Jennica! tried her hand at critical thinking, and the best solution she could come up with was that she had actually thought the sentence she heard, but immediately forgot she'd thought it because she was so tired, thus making it seem like someone else had been talking. Jennica! forced herself to think about different things to see if they sounded weird in her head. She thought of glitter, her poodles, and chocolate, but none of those thoughts felt like someone else was saying them.

Succumbing to ADD after thirty seconds of curiosity, the pop superstar re-buried herself in the super-soft pillows and passed out with a final thought.

Weird!

CHAPTER 4

"Dad, this sucks."

"What? It's only been five minutes." It had only been five minutes. But it had been five minutes of playing catch individually with balls that threw themselves back. Father and son, standing side by side, playing catch, but not with each other.

"This is weird. People are looking at us. The shirtless guy with the rings is staring at me. I think he's a pedophile."

"He's not a pedophile," Dr. Faraday said as he looked over at the man and saw him clawing at the crotch area of his shorts while staring intently at Trevor. His metal hoops were no longer spinning. "Okay, maybe he *is* a pedophile. Let's get out of here."

Faraday gathered his stuff and hustled over to Trevor, and put a reassuring arm around him as they walked across the park and avoided looking at the strange man.

"That guy is creepy. Did they have guys like that when you were a kid?" asked Trevor while he stumbled to keep up. Dr. Faraday hummed to himself for a second. He had no idea how to answer the question. The past wasn't something he had ever been particularly good at thinking about.

"I don't remember, Trev. I spent a lot of time reading indoors. But as far as I know, nobody was watching me from the closet." Trevor didn't even have time to not laugh at his dad's joke before two tall men in dark suits bookended father and son with a casual yet assertive presence. Trevor looked up at his dad for reassurance and saw only anxious fidgeting when the men in suits gently corralled the Faradays to a stop at the edge of the park.

"Dr. Faraday," said the man on his left. It wasn't a question.

Frank's anxious fidgeting abruptly ended as the words froze his movements entirely. He took a moment to gather the words before he spoke. "You know, I honestly never thought this day would come. I really didn't. It's been a long time, Davis."

Neither Davis nor the other suit responded.

"Dad, who are these guys?" asked Trevor as his father pulled him closer.

Faraday looked down at his son. *Honesty first.* "Uhh, these are the guys who are in charge of letting me know they need my help because the, um, how do I put this ... the end of the world might be happening."

Trevor looked up at the men in suits, and then over to his dad. He couldn't read anything from the strange men, but he knew his dad was telling him whatever truth he could. "What? What do you—"

"We have to go," one of the suited men interrupted. "It's time."

Trevor grabbed his father's hand. "Dad?"

Dr. Faraday shook off the shock of the meeting he had hoped would never happen. He squeezed his son's hand and led him out of the grassy urban oasis, men in suits in tow. From across the park, the half-naked man watched the peculiar confrontation and frowned. "Fuckin' weirdos," he said to himself as he picked up his metal rings and whipped them into action.

• • •

Crash was lying prone, belly in the mud, covered in a camou-flaged tarp and directly in the middle of the trail to the water-ing hole. He was mic'ed up and live to his men, and the men were hidden well. But Will was the only one who mattered to him now. He was the only one who had Crash's ear during "go-time." Crash subconsciously switched over to his husky-whisper voice. It kept from scaring the animals, and it sounded cool on television.

"Nets?"

"Ready."

"Tranqs?"

"Ready."

"All right, men. We're downwind and the capybara's eye-sight is poor. We tranq one adult, one juvenile. We tag them, and then you're done. And remember, leave the biggest one for me."

"You heard what Crash said," Will said. "We've all been here before. Let's make it sparkle."

"Thanks, Will. Thank you, gentlemen. Now let's be quiet and wait in this mud."

As Crash lay belly-down in the grime, he thought of all the waiting he had done throughout his life that didn't involve ly-ing in mud. Waiting in line at the bank. Waiting to pick his kids up from school. Waiting to hear back from the doctor to see if the kids were actually his. Waiting to hear if he could actually have kids. Waiting to hear if he could "get a refund" once he found out he had been responsible for the child support for three kids that couldn't even physically be his. Lying in the mud didn't seem so bad.

Suddenly, a rustling. The silence on the earpieces became even more silent. A herd of capybara trotted out from the deep jungle into the slight clearing where most of the men were hidden. An excitement ran through Crash's body and turned his nerves to ice. He was the Kobe Bryant of animal tagging. The white black mamba of black mambas.

Thirty meters out.

"Hold for my signal."

The capybaras snuffled about, slowly traversing the clearing toward Crash's hiding place in the most nonthreatening not-quite-stampede of all time.

Twenty-five meters out.

"Hold."

Twenty meters out.

"Hold."

Twenty-five meters out.

"*Dammit.*"

The capybaras moseyed back toward the jungle in retreat. Not out of caution, as far as Crash could tell, but simply because they had no place to be.

"Should I have Ray throw a stick to scare 'em out?" Will breathed into his radio.

"No. Not yet. Let's see if nature will work with us before we have to force it," Crash whispered in reply. The big rodents started moving again.

Twenty meters out.

Back on track, Crash thought. The animals ambled again toward the trap. And then he saw it. Caboosing the pack of two dozen capybaras was the biggest damn Amazonian river rat Crash had ever seen. "My God. Do you men see that? It must be two-ten, two-twenty." Crash began to tremble at the thought of himself going one-on-one with the monster of his dreams. "You guys are going to have to do a lot of goddamn editing, 'cause this is gonna be a bloodbath."

Fifteen meters out.

"Hold."

"Crash, Todd has a perfect line of sight to—"

"Hold."

Ten meters out.

The chatter went dead. The beasts were too close. The men fidgeted and sweated with nervousness. Will speculated on what Crash's plan could be, but he couldn't figure out what the big man's intentions were. The animals were in sight of all the remote cameras, and the crew had perfect focus with all the manned cameras. The hidden microphones were picking up clean audio. *What the hell is he waiting for?*

Five meters out.

The capybaras increased pace. The closeness of the cool water triggered excitement after a long, hot day, and the musky animals closed the gap to Crash quickly for the last few meters. The moment that the monster of the pack had finished making its way from rear to front, Crash sprang into action. Without bothering to bark orders, Crash pulled his legs up under his body quickly and launched himself out from under the tarp and straight toward the mammoth river rat.

"*Fire!*" screamed Will.

The tranquil riverbank violently smeared into a blur of big rodents, flying darts, trampled greenage, and Crash Jefferson as he flew like a missile toward the trailing pack giant. And, just as he had predicted, right as the beast began to turn around to escape, he collided into it, hitting the animal sideways in a T-bone impact. Wrapping his arms around the body of the beast, Crash tried to wrangle it to the ground. But the beast was much larger than he had planned for, and it wasn't about to go down easily. Barely aware of the rest of the chaos around him, Crash held on for dear life and for sweet revenge while the giant capybara dragged him first around in a circle, and then straight to the river.

This capybara's strength is tremendous, Crash tried to say out loud for his show, but could only mumble due to his mouth being full of matted, greasy fur. He twisted and turned, ripped and rocked, but could only temporarily hinder the animal's progress to the water. It was just too big. And just as the rat was about to drag Crash into the river, the TV host let go with his right arm just long enough to ball up his fist, cock his arm, and hook around into the animal's snout.

Except it didn't connect with the rodent.

Crash Jefferson's fist slid across the side of the capybara's face and body and connected instead with his own temple, knocking him out cold as he fell into the fast-moving tributary.

CHAPTER 5

Dr. Faraday arrived with his son and escorts at Level 7's top-secret building, which looked like any other Midtown Manhattan office building on the outside, and like any other office building on the inside. The main difference was, as far as he could guess, secret things happened here.

He dropped his son off in a hallway and was told the young man would be taken to the daycare room, which was described to him as being the "best of its kind," complete with a state-of-the-art video game setup with giant 3-D projection screen, which seemed to Faraday an odd thing to have for a top-secret organization. *I guess government agents need babysitters, too, though.*

Trevor had stopped sniffling soon after they left the park, and had filled the entire car ride over with incessant questions, asking how the world was ending, why it was ending, if Jesus was coming back, would Jesus be riding a flaming horse, and on and on. Ideas Dr. Faraday assumed were planted by the boy's mother. *Just another reason we can't stay together.* The bittersweet reminder of the ex-love of his life distracted him for a moment, but the scientist's latent observational habits pulled his attention back to the present.

Frank Faraday felt like he should have been taking in his surroundings to remember as much as possible about whatever was about to transpire, but the arrangement inside Level 7's building looked like nothing more than a typical office environment, nondescript and unmemorable. People in suits milled about, shuttling documents around from room to room, and the water cooler swarmed with employees no doubt gossiping about the latest hookup or episode of must-watch television. Faraday wanted to stop and listen, but his escorts kept pushing forward.

"When I was in high school," he said while he and the two men in suits continued down the hall, "my first job was at an insurance company that handled windshield replacement claims." Davis, the suit-in-charge, responded with a weak shrug as they passed an open break room and Faraday briefly overheard two women complaining about dogs pooping on their lawns.

"That place was more exciting than this. Where are the armed guards, or the security checkpoints, or the classified devices? What do you even need me for here?" Neither suit responded, but Second-suit held his arm out to halt Faraday. Davis looked over his shoulders cautiously, and Faraday sensed everything was about to change—that everything he'd so far seen had been a ruse, a façade. There was a sinking feeling in his gut and he held his breath when the suits opened the door and the three walked in together. Into a room with a few folding chairs and not much else. A room even more boring than the boring building they just walked through.

"Please sit," said Davis.

The three men had barely the chance to sit when the door opened again and an Asian woman dressed in a business-casual navy pantsuit entered.

"I'm Commander Rachel Ahn. I'll be in charge of everything you're going to be involved with for the next seventy-two hours." She pulled a small container from her pocket, opened it, and dropped three pills into her hand. *I don't like the look of that*, thought Faraday. Before he could voice his concerns, however, Commander Ahn spoke again.

"If you remember the paper you signed when you accepted your position as you first met our organization, you then also remember that you agreed to follow through with whatever Level 7 judged to be in your best interest when the time came. And Dr. Faraday, the time has come."

"I assume you're going to fill me in on whatever is going on?" Faraday said. The idea of swallowing mystery pills was not appealing to him in the least.

"Yes," responded the woman.

"Will it be before or after I swallow those?"

"After."

"Am I at least allowed to know what these are before I take them?" he followed.

Commander Ahn returned a glance that could not have been mistaken for anything other than a stern "No." Her actual words were more polite.

"I'd like to tell you, but I can't. Not until you swallow them. We need to know you're committed. And you need to be ready."

"Oh, I'm ready." He chortled.

"No, you aren't."

"Uh, yes, I am. I'm here, right? I'm ready."

"No, you aren't. Because you can't be. You can't mentally be ready to understand what we're dealing with until what is in those pills *helps* you to be ready."

At that bluntness, Faraday realized he should have just swallowed the goddamn pills before asking so many questions. He had wanted to rationalize what was happening, and in a sense, he did. He rationalized that he was in the middle of a building, surrounded by people who could easily enforce whatever they chose. He let his gaze wander around, across, and past the men in suits and the Asian woman and sensed urgency from them, but no ill intent. Still though, he hesitated, to the perturbation of the woman in front of him.

"Dr. Faraday, I assure you, time is a factor here. The quicker you swallow the pills, the better. You've had a decade and a half to do as you pleased. Now it's time for you to help *us*."

With a look of concern he didn't consciously realize his face was showing, he took the pills from her and clenched his fist around them, rubbed his forehead with the back of his closed hand. He lowered his hand to his lap and once again looked around the tiny room he was in and at the few people staring at him. Beads of sweat budded on his upper lip. He grimaced and gulped and the sweat shook free from his lip and splashed the floor. No one said a word. Everyone just stared. Them at him, and he at them. Finally, sensing no significant threat other than that of lost time, he shook off the nervousness enough to swallow the three pills.

And almost immediately started vomiting blood.

"Oh God, what ... what's going on?" Quicker than he could comprehend, he felt himself being strapped to a gurney. Commander Ahn stood over him.

"Try not to worry," she said casually while he spit blood

down the front of his shirt. "This is what's supposed to happen."

As more and more blood erupted out of his mouth, he began to lose consciousness. Words drifted in and out.

"... keep ... tight."

"... spilling blood from his ears now ..."

"... get him to the transport ..."

"... liquefy the brain ... gray matter ... almost completely dissolved ..."

Oh shit oh shit oh shit.

His cognitive ability melted away but he could still feel, and he felt pure terror. And as he was rolled on the gurney up the hallway, still no one paid much attention to the newcomer. Not even the dog ladies. They continued to discuss their neighbors' shitting canines, even as a team of people maneuvered past them with a man violently spewing blood every which way.

CHAPTER 6

Heather Gray loved Disneyland and her two little girls loved Disneyland even more. Heather took her kids as much as she could afford, and each had her own special treat she liked most when they went. Heather's oldest daughter, Jessica, loved getting hugs from Minnie. Elle, the youngest, had a sweet tooth for the giant caramel apples she could barely get her mouth around enough to bite into. Heather loved the cleanliness. It was hard being a single mom, and it was especially hard keeping her house clean for more than, it seemed, a few minutes at a time. But Disneyland, despite its size and despite all the people old and young who poured through its gates, was always clean. Always tidy. Always sparkling.

Every time Heather made the trip with the girls, she played a little game with herself, to see if she could spot a piece of trash. She couldn't. But even crazier, she thought, was how she never actually saw anyone cleaning anything up. *Spotless. Always spotless. There isn't even litter when there's no trashcan in sight. Amazing. What I wouldn't give to have a full-time cleaning staff that stayed behind the scenes. Spilled food— wiped up instantly! Dirty clothes—straight in the hamper! Litter box—always fresh!* An excited yelp jostled Heather away from her fantasy.

"Mommy! I see Goofy!" Elle yelled out between chews of

caramel. "I wanna go hug him!" Elle squealed as she bolted toward the big, friendly dog.

"Wait!" yelled Heather while she fumbled around, hands full of bags and gift-store goodies. The bag-burdened mother swung her hip so her carry bag flipped back around behind her and then she turned toward her oldest daughter. "Go with her, Jess. I'll be right there." Jessica needed no extra prompting and raced to meet Goofy with her sister.

Being a warm spring day, even for sunny Southern California, Disneyland was filled with smiling people from all corners of the globe, many of whom hadn't felt warm sun in months. Pasty legs peeked out from shorts and burnt noses shined bright on the faces of tourists in line to meet the characters, but by the time Heather had adjusted all her bags and caught up to her kids, the line to meet Goofy had dissipated to the Grays being the only three people left. And while the two little girls hugged Goofy just beyond the line to Thunder Mountain, no one noticed the light rumbling at first. But as the shaking grew stronger, Heather looked over her shoulder to realize there was no roller coaster passing by. Only then did a certain thought creep in.

Oh my God. An earthquake.

Heather pulled her kids out into the open and away from the Thunder Mountain safety wall as the ground rumbled beneath them. Goofy looked on in involuntary amusement while confused people of the world shouted phrases of surprise in dozens of languages.

The three Gray ladies hugged, hoping to wait out the rolling waves of tectonic rock beneath them. But the shaking didn't ease up. It intensified.

A rumbling louder than any roller coaster Heather had ever heard boomed from east of where she stood with her family. A young father and mother ran past, cooperatively pushing a stroller as fast as they could, when an abrupt jolt shook so hard that the stroller dropped and then popped, launching their infant child a meter into the air.

Oh my God, thought Heather as she looked on in horror.

The baby's father snatched the toddler at the apex of its flight in one deft move, and the family continued their escape.

Windows shattered, scaffolding fell, and a man running from the direction of the Magic Kingdom castle pushed through the crowd screaming, "The whole thing is collapsing, the ground is collapsing!"

Heather took her girls by their hands and fell into the crowd running away from ... she didn't know what. She just knew they were all running away from something, and wherever they were going was probably better than where they were. So Mom and Jessica and little Elle ran and ran and ran as the center of Disneyland collapsed behind them while people screamed for their lives, convinced the end of the world was at hand.

As the façades crumbled into rubble, Disneyland became messy and unkempt and dirty for the first time since it had been built up from a rat-infested orange grove decades earlier.

CHAPTER 7

Halfway through the flight to JFK, Jennica! dozed off. She dreamed of her childhood in Ft. Lauderdale, of the warm Atlantic Ocean and the seagulls that always stole her sister's food, and of her parents who pushed her into a spotlight she never really wanted to be in. She also dreamed of a five-foot-tall space octopus that kept trying to rip off her bikini top.

Eww, she thought in her dream. *That's kinda gross.* Yet she wasn't *afraid* of it. It was more like an annoyance, like all those nerdy boys who wanted to be near her because she was so pretty before she became famous enough to afford ways to keep them far enough away so she could pretend they didn't exist.

On the warm sandy beach in her dream, Jennica! kinda sorta learned to like the big space octopus that seemed to be obsessed with her. She even giggled a few times at its persistent attempts to seduce her with gentle strokes of its tentacles and when it rapidly changed the colors of its skin, she gasped. *It's like a rave!*

All at once in her dream, the space octopus stopped being a space octopus, and instead was a man standing before her. He was a dashing man with dark eyes, a shaved head, and a piercingly intense presence. Something about him was so comforting, even if he happened to be wearing a flowing purple and gold cape. Nevertheless, she melted into his arms and he nuzzled her neck and whispered, "You've lived a hard life."

"It's been *so* hard. I'm *so* lonely."

"You've given them everything. Your heart, your soul, your talent. And they've sucked you dry."

Tears welled up in her eyes. He *understood* her.

"Yes."

"And yet they still demand more and more and they'll keep demanding more until you're dead. You deserve so much better. You are a princess among peasants."

Jennica! started to cry in her dream as she clutched the dashing man ever tighter.

"All I want is to be loved," she said. "I have everything else, but they won't give me the one thing I truly want. Life isn't *fair*."

The man gently pushed her back just enough to be face-to-face with the pop star. Gaze-to-gaze with the blond beauty. "Maybe you belong on another planet."

Jennica! searched the man's eyes and found truth, comfort, warmth, passion. She wrapped her arms around him and pulled him in close and they kissed long, hard, and deep. She became one with the man and didn't even care when, in the mind's eye of her dream, she realized the man had turned back into an octopus and its two lower tentacles were tracing their suckers up her legs.

• • •

Crash came to and found himself, for the umpteenth time in his life, stuck in mud. His whole body ached and was stiff and swollen. He thought back to what had transpired to get him to wherever he was, and all the memories rushed back, right up to and slightly past the point where he had attempted to tackle a massive capybara but instead punched himself out. Conveniently, Crash did not remember being the one who caused his own unconsciousness.

On his back in the mud, the adventurer held his hands in front of his face and saw absolutely nothing. No moon, and not enough starlight to see even shadows of movement. Crash didn't panic. He might have been a television host with an immaculate face, but he also had real skill and wilderness experience to back up those city slicker traits. And he could fuck like a wolf. Although he was relatively sure that skill wouldn't be needed in his immediate future.

He took note of his injuries as much as he could in the darkness. Wiggled various body parts enough to know he wasn't seriously injured. Tasted the fluids on his hands. No blood. That was good. He tasted mud, capybara musk. *That son of a bitch.* Anger welled within him. *But now is not the time to lose my cool.* Deep breath.

He stood up, slipped in the mud, and fell back down. *That didn't hurt too much. Good sign.* He tried to get up again, stumbling and sloshing around in utter confusion. After a few minutes of trying, he gave up on going anywhere far.

He crawled like a soldier, dragging one limb at a time up from the edge of the water into a dryer, more stable patch of soil. The sounds of the jungle filled his ears. He also felt something else filling his ear, and whatever it was had a lot of legs, and then he remembered that the jungle floor was pretty much a living carpet, and it was either going to be up in a tree or back in the mud for the night if he didn't want to get eaten alive.

Crash touched, tasted, smelled, and listened his way toward a thicket to crawl up in ... *shit, what was that? Something big just slithered across my hand. Okay, I can't see anything, I need to get back to the mud. Wait. Leeches. Goddammit. The mud'll be full of leeches. If I could just see something. Shit, I woke up in the mud. Who knows how long I was in there. Jesus Christ, my whole body is probably covered in leeches.*

Crash felt up his body like a desperate, sexually curious teenager, but everything was slimy and Crash couldn't tell leech from muck.

Fuck. Shit fuck shit. Okay, maybe I didn't get washed that far down the river. Maybe Will is close!

"Will! Will, can you hear me?"

Crash waited for a response. All he heard was the buzzing of insects and a blood-curdling bark-yelping. *Christ, this jungle is loud. Can't it just shut up for a minute? How is anyone supposed to hear me with all these damn crickets and shit.*

"Will! It's Crash! I'm over here!"

Nothing but the jungle, and the jungle didn't care. There was no other choice, he'd have to wait till dawn. Tired and drained, he slumped to the ground and plopped his legs back into the mud, keeping his torso in the grass. *The leeches can have my legs, but everything from my dick up belongs to me.*

• • •

Senator Horton arrived home just as his wife was about to doze off. Her eyes fluttered open while he removed his shoes at the side of their bed. She wrinkled her nose.

"Are you wearing dirty underwear?"

"What? No. I thought you'd be asleep by now."

"You smell ... funky."

Can she smell the sex on me? I told him not to make a mess. "Hmm. I don't smell anything, but I'll tell Maria to use a stronger detergent next time she does laundry," Horton said, hoping his mindless passion hadn't gotten him caught.

"What was the meeting about, or can't you tell me?" Rebecca asked.

Senator Horton smiled in the dark. "I can't tell you."

"Well make sure you smell your clothes before you leave next time. You don't want to show up someplace important with smelly trousers."

• • •

Forks clinked on plates, toasted English muffins scraped with knives spreading jam, and sips of coffee and juice orchestrated a comfortable breakfast soundtrack for the Horton family. Then Lizzie spoke.

"Can I get a thong?"

Senator Horton dropped his butter knife and shook his head in annoyed disbelief like a cat that had just been squirted with a spray bottle.

"I'm *sorry?*"

"No, you can't. Stop bringing it up," Rebecca said to her daughter while ignoring her husband's shock.

"You've talked about getting a thong with our *daughter?*"

"It's been brought up. What was I supposed to do, tell her

thongs don't exist?"

"Dad, I've already worn them plenty of times. I just want my own now."

Horton inhaled so sharply he could have plucked a bird from flight.

"You—what? Whose thongs are you wearing if you don't have one—never mind, I don't want to know." He stood up from the table. "You know what, you handle this, Rebecca. I, I can't even—I'm not dealing with this."

"Perfect. You can handle the most powerful people in the world on a daily basis but you can't talk with your own daughter at breakfast."

"She's not asking me about policy and economic development, she's asking to buy lingerie!"

"Dad," whined Lizzie as she rolled her eyes. "It's just panties."

"Just panties," Mike said without looking at her. "Furthermore, if Hilary Clinton started talking about *panties* and *thongs*, I'd react the same way."

"Oh, stop blowing things out of proportion," Rebecca said.

"I'm not blowing anything out of proportion."

"Good, because you have to take Lizzie to school today."

"What?"

"I have an early meeting. It's perfect timing. You can catch up with your daughter in the car. Maybe she'll ask you for bra advice."

And the faces of both father and daughter turned brighter red than the coils that had toasted their English muffins.

• • •

While the Lexus sedan rolled through the Washington, DC suburb, Mike Horton silently cursed the way his luxury car was just so damn good at blocking out exterior noise. It was stone-cold silent inside, and he even thought about putting down the windows before deciding against the idea, since he had never once put down the windows of his car and that would just have been too obvious a ploy to keep from having to talk to his daughter. He looked over at her, and his looking over caused her to look over, and Mike and Lizzie almost looked at each other before both looking away.

Shit. Eh, fuck it.

"Nice spring day," he said as he lowered all four windows. *Ah, much better.* The suburban neighborhood sounds of early morning landscaping filled the car and killed any awkward silence that might have forced father and daughter to bond.

The car pulled up to the school and Lizzie hopped out without so much as looking at her father. She was sure he assumed it was because she was still embarrassed. It was because she was sad. *Why doesn't my dad give a shit?* She shut the car door behind her without a word between them.

I can't believe the longest talk we've had all year was about my underwear, she thought.

Thank God she's out of the car, he thought.

Horton pulled away and started back to the house. He raised the windows and turned on his satellite radio to the Sinatra station and played an awful set of dashboard drums while he drove. As he pulled up to a stoplight, he thumbed through his smartphone's calendar app, its hourly columns streaked with colorful through lines of nonstop meetings. And then his radio spoke to him.

"Senator Horton. Your assistance is required."

Mike Horton almost jumped off his leather seat. He stared down at his radio in confusion. "What the hell?"

In his distraction, Horton didn't notice the dark van that had pulled up behind him. He did, however, notice the second dark van that roared through the intersection and skidded to a stop directly in front of him, boxing the Lexus in between the two vans.

A handful of men in suits exited the rear van, and before Horton knew what was happening, had thrown open his car door and yanked him out. The politician opened his mouth to scream, felt a slight tickle in his neck, and lost consciousness.

All but one of the men carried the senator into the rear van and slid the door closed, and the man who stayed behind jumped into the empty Lexus. The three vehicles left the intersection and the entire episode was over before the light turned green.

CHAPTER 8

The filthy, oily water had been deceptively still before betraying a hint of the giant life it supported. Smooth, precise vibrations undulated through the stagnant liquid. The creature that generated the tiny waves knew better than to move more than what was absolutely necessary. And yet, as a creature of considerable size, even the tiniest of actions had noticeable reactions.

The creature's feeding system had run empty of nutrients so distantly in the past it had forgotten what it was like to have its hunger satisfied. Tons upon tons of fat reserves kept it alive, but had it had the option to kill itself efficiently, the creature would have. Alas, it was a species evolved to live long and slow, and trapped in a barren, watery tomb left it with no resources to end its anguish, unless it wanted the hell of a long, tortured death by starvation.

The behemoth hibernated when it could, awakening every few years only to call out with its mind, and only to hear nothing in return. Again and again the cycle repeated, driving the creature further to the brink. Hope was almost gone. Sanity was sure to leave next. The creature longed for death and cursed its hearty biology in the recesses of its consciousness. With its final slivers of optimism it slept and awoke and called and slept and awoke and called but never did it once hear back.

Until one day it did.

• • •

At 6:41 a.m., Jennica! was having a meltdown in her dressing room. "I'm *performing*? No one told me I had to perform. I'm not performing. You're out of your *mind*!"

Her PR agent, Tully, tried to calm her down. "J, listen, I don't know how this slipped through, but think of how it will look if you back out."

"I'm *not* backing out. I'm just not performing. I'm not singing. I'm not."

Tully shooed everyone else out of the room with wild gestures that contradicted his soothing tone. "It's fine. I'll handle it. We're fine."

"We're *not* fine."

"Sure J," he said to her while continuing to shoo. "Guys, we're fine. Give us ten minutes. Thanks." The last person left, and only then did Jennica! start to cry.

"Tully, I'm not doing this. I can't do this. No one told me I was going to have to sing."

Tully waited till Jennica! dropped her head in between her hands before rolling his eyes.

"Jen, girly, what did you expect?"

"No one told me I was going to have to sing!"

"Since when do you sing on these shows? It'll be tracked—"

"Perform! You know what I mean. No one bothered to frickin' tell me! I just want to talk like the other guests do!"

"Jen."

Two sniffs and a pause before she answered, "What?"

"Since when has anyone ever invited you on a show to

talk?" Tully said bluntly, aware that his reply might not have been the most sensitive response, but Jennica! didn't hear him or didn't understand or didn't care.

"I'm just not ready right now," she said before changing her tone to a frantic plea. "Where's Bobby? I need Bobby!" Bobby was her manager.

"I'll get Bobby."

"Please get Bobby. Get Bobby and tell him we need to work this out."

"I'll get Bobby," soothed Tully as he hurriedly walked to the door.

Jennica! wiped her eyes, looked up, and called one final request. "Oh, and Tully?"

Tully looked back. "Yes, J?"

"Do you know anyone that has any pills?"

Uh-oh. "What kind of pills, dear?"

"I, uh, I don't know. Never mind."

Tully walked out and shut the door behind him. *Well, at least she's not far enough gone where she knows* how *she wants to get fucked up. And at least I know I've got about three months to find myself a new A-list client.*

CHAPTER 9

Frank Faraday opened his eyes. *Something is different.*

He knew where he was and what was happening, even though he had no memory of anything after the gurney trip through the hallway when he had thrown up blood on people who cared far less than they should have about a random man puking blood onto everything.

Their regard was far different from the people around him twenty-five years earlier. Most of his fellow Cornell graduates were a foot taller and a dozen years older than he was. He was used to always being "the kid," programming code at two and scoring near perfect on the SATs at five. Yet, as nine-year-old Frankie Faraday heard his name called to pick up his bachelor's degree in Physics, a thought ran through his mind for the first time.

I don't think I like living like this.

It took time, during which Frank Faraday was showered with awards and grants and earned multiple degrees (including a bachelor's in Automotive Marketing and Management that he earned in seven months just to win a bet). But then it happened. A switch in his brain flipped, and he was simply *over* living a life that had been planned for him since before he could form memories. After telling those he cared about that he was going to think about his options, he packed a bag, bought a plane ticket, and left it all behind.

And now, another switch had flipped. The scientist sat up and stretched his limbs, grimacing preemptively for pain that didn't come. He looked around. There was nothing in his room but the gurney he was on. He looked around again, this time with more attention to detail.

Wait. The walls were made of concrete set nine years earlier by a local construction company that had recently been shut down for violating building codes to save money in the recession. He looked at the gurney. It had been manufactured by a medical supply company in Turkey within the past eight months.

A sharp tinge of nervous fear spiked along his spine.

How do I know these things?

A door slid open and Commander Ahn walked in. Faraday took one look at her and smiled. "Your sister," he said confidently, "has amazing breasts."

Staring at the commander's shocked face, an unbidden memory came. Fifteen years earlier, six months into traveling across Europe, just as he'd entered Sweden, he hated it immediately. He didn't know *why* he hated it—it was more of a gut feeling—but as soon as he crossed the border, he had a remarkable dislike for the country. As he had come to learn in his life, however, those deep intuitions often indicated some sort of truth that sooner or later would come to the surface.

That truth came while cruising across northern Sweden and headed nowhere in particular when he entered a small pub, intending to get a beer. He drank one, but then another, and another still. Nine beers and a couple hours later, he'd made fast friends with some rogues whose English was rough but who were warmer and more gracious than anyone he'd ever met. They paid his tab, he said goodbye, and left the pub triumphant.

He stumbled through the street, drunk and happy, pirouetted onto the sidewalk and caught the reflection of his own silliness in a barbershop's window. He kept spinning but kept his eye on the reflection. He had never been allowed to be silly before. He laughed and laughed and laughed. And then he fell over and passed out, facedown, in a pile of trash.

Commander Ahn stopped in her tracks. "My sister has *what*?"

Faraday couldn't believe what he had just said. And he *really* couldn't believe what he saw. He was looking at Rachel Ahn's sister, Cora, and she was naked and doing jumping jacks while a young man poured water down her chest and she screamed like she had just discovered that ripping her shirt off would cure world hunger and then she ripped her shirt off with that same ferocity and ...

... and then there was no topless Korean woman in front of him. Only a very serious clothed one. Shocked by the instability of the delusion, his body trembled, and then tremored and then quaked, and he fell violently off the gurney onto all fours.

"What is going on? What is happening to me?"

Head lowered, he puked straight down his arms. Warm, sickly-sweet-smelling vomit flowed through his fingers to the cold floor as he struggled to catch his breath.

Two men in suits walked in and helped him back up to the gurney. They strapped him down without resistance. Commander Ahn didn't know if he wouldn't or couldn't resist at this point. She knew what the nanobots did to a person. In theory, anyway. She stood over him and waited for the scientist to settle down enough to attempt a conversation with him. Finally, he calmed, save for the occasional gasp for air.

"Dr. Faraday, do you understand me?"

He nodded while licking the spittle from around his lips.

"May I ask you a few questions?"

Still slightly wheezing, he turned his head a bit to look at her, but didn't answer. She spoke again.

"I promise you'll be able to ask anything you like in a moment."

He looked away again, nodded slightly.

"Recite pi for me, please."

Faraday hesitated. His pause was one of exhaustion, not lack of an answer. "Three-point-one four one five nine two six five three five eight nine seven nine three two three eight four six two six four three three—"

"That's enough, thank you," she said. "Do you know who Charles Finn was?"

This time, no hesitation came from her strapped-down subject. "American water polo player from the early 20th century."

"Was he any good?"

"His team won the bronze in 1932."

"They certainly did," Commander Ahn replied without surprise.

The scientist furrowed his brow and took a breath. "Can I ask my questions now?"

"One more from me, if you don't mind." Faraday had calmed down considerably and his tester decided on one more challenge. "Which Star Wars movie was the best?"

"*Empire Strikes Back*. It was the best. No it wasn't!" he

yelled fervently back at himself. "What?... Yes it was.... Don't even fucking *tell* me that you think it was *A New Hope*, because that was *good*, but it was simple. Actually, *Return of the Jedi* was the best." Faraday's eyes rolled back and forth as his self-arguing escalated. "What the fuck? What is *wrong* with you?"

Confusion poured over his face as he realized he was having a heated debate with himself about something he didn't even know he had seen, since pop culture had been forbidden to him as a child. He knew of Star Wars, but hadn't watched the movies, yet as he thought of them he saw them playing in his head in real time. The bodily shaking resumed, as did the argument with himself.

"Well, can we both agree that the prequels were shit? No, we can't, because the last twenty minutes of *Sith* was right up there with the originals in intensity! You can't count part of a movie, are you insane? Where'd you learn to debate, you moron!"

His face flushed red with intensity and one of the men in suits jabbed the raving man with a needle to calm him down. The tranquilizer didn't take effect quickly enough to keep Faraday from rolling off the gurney one last time while screaming "Jar Jar Binks is *shit*!" at the top of his lungs.

As his head hit the floor, scrambled thoughts of Star Wars blurred together and then gave way to the memories of Sweden from fifteen years earlier.

"*Shit!*" Young Frank Faraday had awakened in the same pile of Swedish trash in which he'd passed out. He remembered little from the night before, but he had a nagging feeling that before he'd lost consciousness there had been more in his possession than just his pants.

"Shit," he'd said. *Shit* was right. He felt like shit, his mouth tasted like shit, he looked like shit, and he was in deep shit. Pants aside, everything he had on him the night before was gone. His shoes, shirt, wallet, backpack, passport—gone.

And now, as he clutched his head on the floor inside Level 7, it seemed his mind was gone too.

• • •

The gurney had been replaced by a folding chair, and Faraday sat motionless and thought about how this was the first time his feet had been on the floor voluntarily since he first walked into the damned building. He also thought about sea slugs, gingerbread cake recipes, and nude pictures of Brett Favre.

At least I'm not visualizing multiple *dicks.* And before he realized his mistake and stopped his train of thought, a million cocks invaded his mind. Small penises, big penises, ugly gnarled dicks and beautiful rods. He mentally screamed in frustration while slapping his head repeatedly as if trying to knock all the dicks out.

"The empty beaches of Costa Rica."

Instantly, Faraday felt peace as he took in serene images of the whitest sands and crystal-clearest waters of the most immaculate, untouched beaches of Costa Rica. For a moment, he was calm. Then he thought of a monkey. Then lots of monkeys. And then great apes, and then King Kong screaming in his face, and he started freaking out all over again.

"The empty beaches of Costa Rica," said Commander Ahn again as she crossed the room. And again, he calmed.

"What is happening to me?"

"First, keep your thoughts where they're at. Take a deep breath."

He did.

"Good. Self-immolation."

Faraday's thoughts switched from the peaceful beach to images of people lighting themselves on fire, and then video feedback loops started playing in his mind, and just as he started to lose himself again Commander Ahn spoke with a firm voice, "Pull yourself back, Dr. Faraday. Find your peace again on your own," and he listened to her words and thought again of those wonderful Costa Rican beaches. He sucked in a deep breath and closed his eyes.

"Can you hold that thought for now, Doctor?"

He nodded.

"Good. I'm going to go into detail about some things, and your mind is going to want to wander. You will need to keep pulling it back. For now, I recommend you use the beach I suggested. Later, you might find other things that work better for you. Ready?"

"Yes."

Commander Ahn put a gentle hand on his shoulder as he sat, cradling his head in his hands.

"Your brain, as it was, no longer exists. The pills you swallowed were filled with nanotechnological devices: microscopic robots that broke down and—for lack of a quicker explanation—ate your brain, and then reconstituted the matter into a hybrid device that is everything you were, but combined now with technology that gives you a ..."

Ate my brain. Dr. Faraday began to shake as his fear tuned out the woman's words.

"Pull yourself back for me, Frank," said Commander Ahn as she reaffirmed her grip on his shoulder.

His body calmed. Peace came quicker this time. *I'm learning.*

"Good. Shall I continue?"

"Okay."

"You are directly connected to the Internet, and are, to put it basically, a living search engine. You have complete and instant access to all the information available online, and there are software and hardware filters in place to actively provide you with information on almost anything that your physical eyes perceive, your mental capacity can conjure, or your emotions can dwell upon. You are plugged into the entire public web, as well as many parts of the deep web including multiple secure websites that remain unindexed and inaccessible to most. There is some nasty stuff there. I suggest you tread carefully."

Faraday remained calm, although he felt an excitement he hadn't felt before in his life. *I've had, quite literally, my mind blown.*

"We weren't sure how you'd react, since you will essentially have to relearn how to use your own brain, but it really didn't take long comparatively to get to the level of control where you aren't still vomiting and throwing yourself around into walls, so we have confidence you'll have a complete handle on things soon enough. Obviously, there are some filtering concepts you'll have to learn for yourself."

Faraday thought long and hard about what all this meant, and it was no simple task to think long and hard. His mind wandered every which way, and he found himself having to quickly bounce from image to image to keep from falling into "obsession traps" and getting stuck in feedback loops of whatever he was thinking of. If there was a hell, surely endless clips of late-20th century boy bands all singing at once was it.

"The greatest part about this, Dr. Faraday, is that I don't really have to explain much more to you than this. You'll already know the rest of the answers yourself just by referencing them."

And Dr. Frank Faraday, with his newfound mental power, understood completely.

"You'll see," continued Commander Ahn, "that this allows you to make detailed calculated assumptions as well. As much as it pains me, let's take my sister's, um, endowments for example. In a split second, you knew every public record about me, including the fact that I had a sister, and you saw the profile picture of someone who had her name on a social networking site. Then you made the unconscious correlation that, even though there are many people with her name, she was the correct match because of our facial resemblances. How you found whatever video you found, I'm not sure, but somehow your fancy new brain made that connection."

Faraday wasn't about to announce that Commander Ahn's sister's video had been one of the hottest amateur uploads to the porn sites that year. But he did watch it all over again in his mind.

Commander Ahn noticed his distracted state. "You seem pretty calm still. How's that beach working out for you?"

Faraday pulled himself out of the wet t-shirt video just long enough to reply. "Uh, great. The coconuts are round. Perfectly round."

"Not funny."

"I wasn't—"

"Half the people on Earth will be dead or dying within the next seventy-two hours unless you get your shit together and keep it together."

Faraday gulped and his sweat pores opened like faucets.

"Let's get to work. No pressure."

CHAPTER 10

When he heard that Jennica! was throwing one of her tantrums, Bobby came running down the hall of the television studio. He'd thought they had an agreement. Tantrums were for small towns, not big performances. Especially not TV performances. He tapped on her door and heard sobbing. "Jen. Jen, it's Bobby. Jen, open up baby." He heard a muffled "Come in," and opened the door.

Clothes were everywhere. Garbage was strewn about. Boxes of Godiva chocolate that had been in her gift bag had been torn open and smashed onto every surface he could see. He glanced over at the mirror and held back a loud sigh. I HAVE NO SOLE had been written in chocolate across the glass. *Why couldn't I have Beyoncé as a client?*

"Why should I do this, huh? Like, they just take from me and give nothing back," Jennica! warbled out through sniffles.

Tully had reentered the room as well. He looked around. "What the hell happened in here? I just left to find Bobby a few minutes ago! What is going on with you, Jen?"

Jennica! cried into her hands and Bobby and Tully shared "I don't know how the hell much longer I can do this" glances.

Tully had left the door to Jennica!'s room open, and a production assistant poked her head in. "Five minutes till showti— Holy shit." Tully hurriedly shuffled the PA out of sight and Bobby shut the door behind them. Jennica! was moaning the word "no" over and over again, peppering her rambling with "I have no *soul*" from time to time.

With her head buried in her hands and her constant sobbing, she didn't hear a word her manager was saying. She thought of that dream from the plane. She found herself on that beach again and thought of the gorgeous man who knew exactly how to comfort her, how to hold her. He was so beautiful, and so gorgeous, and so handsome. Everything she figured a man should be. And he seemed to know exactly how to hold her to make her stop crying. *The perfect man! Why can't he be real? Oh God, why can't you be real?*

I am real.

Jennica! gasped.

I am real, and I love you.

Jennica!'s heart skipped at the sound of the haunting voice. She questioned her reality, but didn't want to open her eyes, didn't want to leave the comfort, even if it was just a fantasy.

You're so gorgeous, she thought to him. *And you know how to hold me to stop me from crying. You're everything I want.*

I will come to you shortly.

When?

Soon. But I need you to do something for me.

What? Anything!

I need you to perform for me on your show. Perform for me like I took you away to paradise and it's our wedding night. Perform for me Jannica, and I will come to you soon.

Jannica?

Jennica. My apologies. I am so caught up in your love

that I—never mind. The point is, I need you, my love. And I need you to perform for me. Go onto your show and create the best performance you've ever done. You've been using your talents for 'them' your whole life. Now use them for you. For me. For us.

Jennica! sniffled once more and let a grin wash across her face. *Okay, I will!*

I love you. Now go.

Bobby had been trying to stop Jennica! from moaning and crying for five minutes when abruptly she did. Seemingly out of the blue, the pop star stood up with a smile and then proclaimed, "Let's go do this!" while charging out of her dressing room. Incredulous, Bobby watched her walk out. He couldn't decide whether to be happy she was doing her job, or be miserable she was ruining his life. He decided on both. And then he cursed loudly and threw an Evian bottle at the mirror and followed his mercurial client to the soundstage.

CHAPTER 11

On the far side of the moon, a spacecraft held steady against orbit. It was a perfectly round saucer, hundreds of meters in diameter and milky white in color. Floating alongside it was an exponentially larger, needle-shaped battle cruiser from which the saucer had just detached.

Grammeral Q'Shin Zeezak emerged from his cabin in the saucer and took the anywherevator directly to the command deck. All officers saluted upon his arrival. He knew he had been born for this, born for command. One day he would be leader of the entire Vyperian fleet. He *knew* it. Ever since he had been a youngling and could count to eight on his tentacles, he knew it. He was spawned to lead.

"Remotescope on," the Grammeral ordered as he took a seat on the ergonomically fitted command chair. The room's lighting softened to prevent glare on the deck-wide monitor. Softened, but not enough. The Grammeral preferred a relaxed combat deck and longed for the personal glowbats of his cabin.

"Channel seven," he ordered.

The image on the remotescope changed from the looming dark side of the moon to the hosts of *Good Morning America*.

"And coming up, in just a few moments, Jennica! will be performing her latest song for us, live in our studio!"

The human male's pretty, appropriately idealistic representation of a privileged Earth female cohost beamed and added, "You won't want to miss this!"

Grammeral Zeezak stared intently at the screen. "No, Earth, you won't."

All across the western US time zones young women were glued to their television sets, which marked the first time in history that many teenage girls actually woke up earlier than they had to on a school day. The network predicted record ratings for *Good Morning America*, and that people who couldn't watch the performance live would swarm to the website and spread the segment virally across the globe. The network execs knew how it would work, how effective it would be, and so did Jennica!'s people. It was a kind of transcendent media saturation that had happened before, but never on the scale predicted for her performance. If the Beatles were more popular than Jesus in the 20th century, then in the 21st century Jennica! was more popular than the Beatles and Jesus combined and with sprinkles on top. If the trendsetter's predictions were correct, thirty percent of women under the age of thirty-five would be exposed to the performance one way or another within the following seventy-two hours. And not just in the United States. *Across the entire planet.*

Grammeral Zeezak knew the potential as well. And that was why, as soon as the broadcast of Jennica!'s performance started, the transmission was intercepted, recoded, and spliced in a matter of microseconds with a custom subliminal message strong enough to reprogram the suggestive minds of any Earth female who watched the video, "live" or otherwise. And so, in between the cuts of latex-ensconced backup dancers, suggestive thrusting, and Jennica!'s bubblegum smile, images of eight-tentacled otherworldly creatures mixed with emotional anchors of comfort, safety, and lust flashed and embedded themselves into the psyches of young women from Bakersfield to Barcelona to Bali.

The seeds are now planted, thought Grammeral Zeezak as he watched Jennica!'s pelican miss a step during the chorus and lose its balance ever so slightly. *And soon shall come the harvest. The sex harvest.*

CHAPTER 12

Crash Jefferson did his best to keep along the riverbank as he followed it upstream, hoping to spot the location where he and his men had set up their camp the night before. After spending most of the early morning in complete darkness trying to fight off bugs instead of getting precious sleep, progress was slow and painful in the already unforgiving jungle.

Even more bugs had taken residence. Hundreds, millions, billions, even trillions of bugs. Ants, flies, wasps, spiders, moths, beetles, mosquitos. Tick bugs, stick bugs, crawl-up-on-your-dick bugs. Crash hated bugs. They never ruined his life like that goddamn capybara did, but they were small and capable of crawling into holes without invitation. *They're all over me. They're in me.* And they never stopped. *Bzzzzz.* Slap. Slap-slap *slap.* No matter how much he slapped, he never stalled their attacks for more than a split second.

Slap-slap. *Bzzzzzz.* Slap. *Bzzzz.*

Crash rounded a slight bend in the river. Still no clue where he was. Slap. *Bzzzz.* He was lost and severely dehydrated in the largest, most unforgiving rainforest on Earth. *Probably going to die in the jungle. Bugs everywhere. Capybaras laughing at me. Bzzzzzz.*

Palms sticky with sap, forehead greasy with grime, eyes burning with dirt and sweat, the man with the perfect nose slapped a palm frond out of his way and let his mind wander to relieve the grinding monotony of green and misery. Crash started thinking about his life. His successes. His failures. His regrets. *I wish I hadn't choked that giraffe in front of the Make-A-Wish kid.*

I also wish I could get with a hot brunette one more time. I'd do anything for some sweet ass just once more in my life, Crash thought while flicking an ant off his forearm. *Maybe that freaky tattoo artist I met at the wrap party last season. What was her name. Raven something. Raven Von Mon-Dragon. Yes. With those stocking tattoos up the back of her leg. Oh God, she was hot. If I ever make it out of here I'm gonna call her up and tell her I want a koi tattoo or some-thing and get her back to the Crash pad and show her some real freaky shit. I just want one more chance at that. Bzzz.* Slap-slap-slap. *Bzzzz.*

And I want a sub from Bay Cities Deli.

Crash's mouth would have watered at the thought of freaky sex and cured Italian meats had there been any saliva left in his glands, but instead the thought of food just made him sad. *Bzzzzzzzz. Bzzzzz.* Slap-slap-slap-slap-slap. He stopped stum-bling through the foliage, exhausted and drained. It was too much. His brain couldn't distract him any longer and his body couldn't push any farther. The weary TV host reached out to brace himself on a massive tree trunk and immediately a bat-talion of insects crawled off the bark and up his arm while a swarm of small, flying, biting flies settled around his head. Crash yanked his hand back from the tree, but it was too late. Bullet ants stung his fingers. A centipede crawled across his forearm. Biting flies attacked his face.

Bzzzzzzzzzzzzzzzzzzzzzzzzzzzzzzzzzzzzzz.

"*Aaaahhhhhhhhh!* Shut the fuck up!"

The tortured man snapped and swung wildly at the flying insects and tangle of vines and giant leaves and thick, humid air. He spun in circles, screaming, spun and flailed and twisted and turned and tripped and fell. Gravity dropped him onto a slick pile of rotting leaves, and they dislodged just enough to send him sprawling over a rock and right into the mouth of a small cave no more than a few feet beyond what he could previously see in the thick green wall of tangled fauna.

Crash spun around on the dirt floor of the cave for a moment, and then snapped out of his frenzy and gathered his senses. It was dark inside, but not black, and the cave was shallow enough that he could see the back wall. Except there was no back wall. There was a metal door. And the door had a glowing button.

What the hell did I just find out here in the middle of nowhere?

Crash stood perfectly still while the adrenaline pumped through his body.

This has to be a drug thing. I've found my way to a cocaine plant.

Moving cautiously as if squaring up against a predator, Crash owled his head to the left and looked back into the jungle, and was reminded of how itchy, filthy, lost, and miserable he was. He turned his head back to the door and took a breath. He pressed the button, pushed the heavy metal door, and walked into whatever lay on the other side.

The door slowly closed on its own with a sealing *pwoooof*, and Crash covered his eyes when blinding light lanced to the back of his skull. Slowly, he peeked. The first thing he noticed was everything was shiny and clean, and that he was at the beginning of a long, metallic hallway.

The second thing he noticed was the glowing red light of what appeared to be an oddly shaped, circular security camera pointed at him.

The third thing he noticed was the small cloud of gas that sprayed directly into his face.

The fourth thing was that the floor *really* hurt when his head hit it as he earned the tenth concussion of his life and was knocked out for the second time in twenty-four hours.

• • •

Crash awoke in a cell. It took him some moments to come to. Once he did, he sat up and again took in his surroundings. He rubbed his sore, dirty head. *How long have I've been out? Minutes? Hours? Days?* The cell's walls, floor, and ceiling were made of metal. The bars were glass. *Maybe acrylic.* The oval cell was empty except for him. There wasn't much of anything outside the cell he could see, either. Just more metal.

Not feeling up to standing just yet, he dragged his muddy body to the front of the cell and peered around as far as his peripheral vision allowed. The entire room was about ten meters square, and as far as he could guess, there was another cell on each side of his.

"Hello? Anyone else in here?"

He winced and rubbed the back of his head. Talking hurt.

"Anyone?"

Nothing but silence. *Silence. Beautiful silence.* Crash leaned back and smiled. Wherever he was, it beat hanging around those goddamn bugs. Even if it involved being in a prison.

He felt a tickle on his arm and looked down. A lone black ant skittered erratically through his arm hairs. He pinched it between his fingernails and severed it in two. *Back on top of the food chain.*

CHAPTER 13

Jennica! was on fire for her showing on *Good Morning America*. She didn't know what she had heard in her head, had seen in her mind, but he seemed so real and so positive and so gorgeous it inspired her to reach the greatest heights of lip-syncing in the history of pop music. Every choreographed move was spot-on. Every thrust was meant for someone special. Even the pelican couldn't keep up.

And Jennica! had the biggest, cutest, most adorable smile plastered across her face the entire time. The performance was immaculate, a courtship display of the most intricate and intimate of rituals. It was the kind of performance her fans would watch a hundred times over, until they ultimately became so saturated with those three minutes and forty seconds of sensory overload they would see Jennica! in every short blonde who walked down the street and hear the synth and drums in every patch of white noise that drifted into their ears—all without realizing that coded within the video was a message designed to speak to the deepest parts of the fertile, female mind and persuade them toward one quite particular idea.

The mission to harvest Earth's resources had long been in place. The mission to harvest Earth's females, that was a recent development. A species more scientific than romantic with its procreation, the all-male Vyperians weren't known for their sexuality, leaving most of the process to spawning labs. That was, until preliminary Vyperian reconnaissance teams started beaming back data streams of Earth women, sending all who laid eyes upon them into a frenzy and causing the conquering of Earth to be bumped much higher on the Vyperian's "To-Conquer" list. Many officials balked at the change of plans, but the argument rarely lasted once they, too, experienced first-hand the sight of human female beauty. Even the Emperor was rumored to have taken an extreme liking to the "Earth females with their exquisite chest-fat deposits."

Grammeral Q'Shin Zeezak had never been to Earth, but he was not the type of conqueror to embark to a new land unprepared. And from the research provided to him via data streams from those of the Vyperian race that explored before him, the Grammeral knew the toughest thing to break in a human was its will. His species had tried and failed with test subjects repeatedly, but an effective breaking point was never found. Human beings were stubborn. More stubborn than the undomesticated giant planktons of SergeSei.

The harder the Vyperians tried to force humans to bend to their collective will, the worse the results. Yes, the humans always ultimately submitted. It also destroyed their minds to the point where they became useless. Test after test failed until a moment of clarity when it became obvious to Grammeral Zeezak what his dagger move would be. *If I can't break their women, I will do the next best thing. I will bend them. We must control the females without them ever realizing they are being controlled.*

And so the recon team spent its time and energy for the next few Earth years learning human patterns and rhythms, and somewhere along the way, the Vyperians learned enough about human psychology to understand if they could get their hands on a highly influential person just long enough to plant a psycomm chip, the time would come where direct psychic communications could be made at just the right times to nudge that person in just the right direction to suit their needs.

Much to Grammeral Zeezak's disappointed surprise, the result of the recon team's multi-year testing on the most influential humans was upsetting. It wasn't a president of a nation that topped the list, or a wizened elder, or even one of their revered religious figures who held the highest esteem among the fertile young females he needed. No, it was an empty-minded pop culture figure groomed from an early age for the purpose of reaching out to the shallow cravings of young Earth women everywhere for nothing more than a monetary profit. At first, none of the Vyperian council would believe so much influence could be exerted by such a pointless source. But evidence piled on to support the findings, and as abhorrent as it was, data was data. And as much as it bothered the octopus, he found himself struck by a strange feeling. One that he had not felt before.

Halfway through her "Proud To B A Grrl" US tour, Jennica! was given a new purpose in a truck stop bathroom in rural Nebraska at the age of seventeen when she was unknowingly gassed, implanted, and memory swiped before she had a chance to sit down and pee.

Jennica! became the biggest piece Grammeral Zeezak needed for his puzzle. And as he had sat and talked with her—mind to mind—from the dark side of the moon to her dressing room, he knew she was the right choice for the Vyperian task of brainwashing the human female masses. All she had to do was perform the snerch out of her song. And she did. She did it so well that no girl watching could tear away. Perhaps it was that thrusting, or that magnetic smile, or her trained pelican.

Or perhaps, just perhaps it was the psychological magnetism embedded in the video that burned deep into the cortexes of those hundreds of millions of fertile young Earth women worldwide.

The seeds had been planted. The beliefs would change. The Vyperians were coming to rape Earth's resources. They would stay to make love to its women.

• • •

Lizzie stared at her quiz. No question unanswered, and all answers probably correct, as they often were. Another forty minutes before pencils down. She stared at the backs of the heads in front of her. Counted the number of ponytails. Seven. The teacher turned around to the whiteboard, and Lizzie pulled out her iPhone and hid it just below the surface of the desk.

OMG. Three texts from Katie about the new Jennica! video. *How did she see it already?* Lizzie read the first message.

> my sis in Cali got 2 see new jennica!
> song live on tv. she texted the vid to me.
> it's soooo good. u HAVE 2 watch!

OMG. Lizzie glanced up at the teacher just long enough to feign interest, and then touched on the link to launch the video. She stifled a gasp. Even with the sound off, she could tell it was the best Jennica! video of all time. Lizzie watched half of it before becoming cautious, and stuffed the iPhone into her pocket. But half a video without sound was enough to get her excited for the moment. Really excited. Something was good about that video. It made her warm and tingly all over, but she couldn't quite put her finger on why. And she was hungry for shrimp.

Weird.

CHAPTER 14

Crash woke up in the exact set of circumstances in which he'd fallen asleep, right down to the bisected ant on his arm.

Have I been out long?

He couldn't see a light source in his cell, or in the room beyond, but the atmosphere held a steady glow. After the night he'd been through, he could have slept in the cell for twenty hours and not known the difference. He did feel better, though. And he was still happy about not being swarmed with bugs. But goddamn, was he hungry. And thirsty.

He dragged his body upright, lurched to the front of the cell, and looked around again. The looking around took about four seconds, since the room was still empty.

Walls, ceiling, floor, and bars. Got it.

Crash always got cranky if he didn't eat, and the familiar foul attitude crept up on him as it was prone to do.

"Anyone out there? Can I get some food and water?"

Crash heard his own echo and nothing more.

"Hey out there. I'm hungry."

He grunted and snorted like a bull, a bad habit he picked up in television that usually led his staff to drop whatever they were doing to accommodate his wishes.

"*Hellooooo?* You trying to torture me? Is that what this is about? I know you don't want to kill me, or you would've done it already. *Hellooooo?*"

Crash paced up and down the cell, spending twice as long at the front glaring at nothing before turning heel and pacing to the back before once again, anxiously returning to the front. "Hey. *Hey.*" Nothing. "*Helllooo.*"

He snorted and sniffed and grabbed the acrylic bars and— they dropped to the floor so abruptly he fell achingly back in surprise before realizing he could walk out of the cell to the larger room, and then he did so quickly before the bars could rise up again.

Eyes darting to every suspicious shadow, he walked with calculated steps into the outer room and confirmed there was in fact another empty cell to the right of his, but to the left was the entrance to the brig. He looked around one more time at his holding area, took a deep breath, and walked through the passage to the unknown of the facility beyond.

What the hell else am I gonna do. At least there aren't any goddamn bugs in here.

CHAPTER 15

Head cradled in hands, Faraday thought about the beginning. Thought about the two strange men in suits who had found him, somehow, in a rural Sweden police station fifteen years earlier.

The young Dr. Frank Faraday stood to greet the two men. *Why would they come all the way from the embassy?* They all shook hands and the first suit led them out of the building.

"Dr. Faraday, my name is Davis," the first suit started as the three men made their way down the street on foot. "I'm going to give it to you straight."

Faraday shifted his hands in his pockets, grasping for something to fidget with at the sharp turn in conversation.

"We're not from the US Government," Davis continued. "And we're not here to replace your passport. We're from an organization called Level 7 and we've been searching for you since you dropped off the grid. We'd like to make you an offer...."

Faraday rubbed his temples as he thought of that day fifteen years ago. He cringed. *I should have walked away. Should have walked away when they made the offer. Walked when they wouldn't give me details. I should have just. Walked. Away. But they knew what I wanted and they sold it to me.*

"We'll fund your travels, your experiments. You can go

anywhere. Do anything. Learn and create by your own rules."

Young Faraday stared off to the horizon. His mind was electric with fanciful possibilities.

"As a showing of good faith, we've already made the first deposit into your bank account. All you have to do in return is lend us your brain one day. Until then, you're free to do as you please."

How could I have known they meant 'lending my brain' in a literal sense? Faraday winced as his head throbbed.

But he was young and in love with his new freedom and naive to the reality of the devil's deal at hand. The word "yes" slipped from his lips before his better judgment could stop it, and the deal was made.

Faraday half expected to never hear from Level 7 again. Aside from the occasional anonymous deposit into his bank account, there was no contact from the men in suits. Months turned to years and he spent his money and time well, finishing his travels, earning degrees for fun, and tinkering around with his inventions. He even got married and had a son. But all good things end, and so it did for him on that exceptionally nice and warm spring day in the New York City park.

"Don't worry, Dr. Faraday," said Davis as they got into a dark sedan at the edge of the park, "you made the right choice."

Faraday thought of Davis, and his words, while he threw up so hard he burst a blood vessel in his eye, making it look like someone had just punched him in the face. All things considered, however, he'd begun to get the gist of his new brain. He was able to filter thoughts and access information with more stability. The hardest part about being an active search engine, he learned, was getting the hang of being selective. *There is so much worthless data out there.* The pointlessness of Davis's woefully inaccurate assurance aside, he'd come across more pictures of people having sex with animals than he ever knew existed, though the more he'd seen, the more he felt and understood the rhythm of the information, and the easier it was to filter out the bad stuff. *Like living with my ex. She never stopped nagging, but after a while, I just didn't hear it. Same with horse porn.*

Although he hadn't quite tuned it out completely.

"Blllleeeaaarrggh."

But even with a flashlight to all the dark, hidden corners of the Internet, alone and locked in his room in whatever building he was in and separated from his son, Frank couldn't uncover the two answers he really wanted. *Where exactly am I?* and, *How the hell did I end up with this ability?* He searched and searched, but the earlier mention of nanobots wasn't enough information to search with; the rest of the world still saw nano-technology as a pipe dream of the future. As far as locations went, everything about the room he'd spent all morning in did little to provide clues. Things were just too generic in his prison.

Faraday wiped the puke from the corner of his lips and dropped his gaze to the chair he was sitting in. IKEA. Shipped from a distribution center in Southern California. Aluminum frame, origins unknown. Fabric woven in a Swedish plant, dyed with an indigo color from Barrington DyeCo, based out of Southampton, England. *Fascinating. I could spend the rest of my life inside my head.* Then he frowned, realizing he was more disconnected from the outside world than ever. *I am never getting laid again.*

He had been told there was "plenty of work to do" because "billions could die," then had been locked in the room and left alone. Granted, it had only been five minutes, but time was a factor. *These people have been telling me since Sweden they're on my side. But then they pull shenanigans like this. How can I help when I'm abandoned in a room with no explanation?* He'd had enough.

The room door opened. Commander Ahn entered, alone. *Good, perfect timing*, Faraday thought. *It's time to make a stand.* So he stood, and he did his best to look enraged. Commander Ahn caught on that he was upset. She saw him throw his best glare toward the door, and then at her.

"You know, the door was unlocked," she said.

"Huh?"

"Yep."

And with all his power and access to information, he hadn't caught on to that piece of information or even investigated his possibilities.

"You mean, I'm not locked ... wasn't locked in here?"

She smiled. "No. What gave you that idea? Did you even check?"

He hadn't. He had spent so much time in his own brain he didn't stop to question his own situation. *How did that happen?*

"How did that happen?" his lips parroted his thoughts.

"Well," she said, "let that be a lesson. Just because you have access to all the information known to man doesn't mean you're going to know what to do with it."

Faraday felt his face go tomato red. "I guess not." *I'm an idiot.*

"Perhaps we chose the wrong person for this project," she said.

Faraday looked down at the floor in embarrassment.

"I'm kidding. Let's go."

CHAPTER 16

Crash took one step into the new room and the door swooshed shut behind him. The new room was much darker, duskier. He squinted hard as his eyes adjusted. There was a stink in the air that struck him as oddly familiar, and as he took another step, he noticed a different surface under his feet. The new floor wasn't metal. It seemed to be dirt and straw. *Like in a barn?* He kneeled and ran his fingers through the soil.

As his eyes further adjusted, he could see the room was circular, about a hundred meters across and shaped like a dome, so the room's direct center had a ceiling roughly fifteen meters high, but near the walls it was closer to ten. The room seemed empty, except for what looked like a large trough on his left side, and a giant pile of hay on his right.

A series of lights flashed, and chaotic noises sounded from hidden speakers. *What the hell is this?* In the faint light, he saw the giant hay pile on the other side of the room shift, and then stand on four legs, and then turn and look directly at him.

That is not a giant pile of hay.

Chapter 17

Faraday and Commander Ahn walked the corridors of the Level 7 headquarters, passing people doing mundane things, which once again struck Faraday as odd. Before he could ask, Ahn steered him back on track.

"We have high hopes for you, Frank."

"You know," he replied as he was snapped out of his thoughts, "I almost gave up on this day ever happening. I figured I'd just collect your money and run my own little experiments for the rest of my life."

"Well, now that you're here, what do you think so far about your new ... abilities?"

He took a breath as his mind's eye blasted through data stream after data stream. Census statistics, world records, the latest water harvesting methods from sub-Saharan Africa.

"It's incredible. It's like ... like I was blind my entire life up until an hour ago. This is absolutely—I have no words. It's incredible. Aside from the whole puking my guts out part."

"Well at least we didn't put a chip in your head. Your brain was just too important to risk that," replied Ahn with a wink. Faraday couldn't tell if she was joking or not.

"I have three questions," he said.

"Give a man access to more knowledge than any human has ever had before in history, and what does he want? More!"

Faraday chuckled. "That said, it shouldn't be too hard for

you to guess what I'm going to ask."

"True. I'll give you the honor of asking, though," she said as they continued side by side down the hallway. As pleasant as Commander Ahn could be, Faraday was still uneasy with his circumstances and his heart palpitated as he asked his first question.

"Where is my son?"

"He's safe. He's been playing video games in the playroom. Greatest childcare in the world, remember?"

"When can I see him?"

"Technically you could see him now if you wanted, but I'd suggest waiting to establish a bit more stability of that new mind of yours, which shouldn't take more than a few more hours of practice."

"Fair enough."

They passed a man sorting pencils.

"How did this happen?" continued Faraday as he cast a lingering glance at the pencil sorter. "I've been through all the public information there is on nanotechnology, and there isn't the slightest hint of this … project. Which makes it completely classified."

"Indeed. As I've said, your brain was 'eaten,' processed and reconstructed in your own skull by nanobots that were in those pills you swallowed. You could even say you've now got shit for brains."

Faraday didn't laugh. "How could that even be possible? There's no technology on Earth that comes close to being able to do that, and I would know."

"And you would be right."

Faraday caught a glimmer in Commander Ahn's eye as she

spoke, and he knew. "It's not from Earth," he said, his own eyes widening.

"And your final question, Dr. Faraday?"

Faraday was awestruck. His brain had been completely rewired to handle massive amounts of data, but he had retained the same emotional capacity. And this was some heavy shit. The last time he was this dizzy with a new excitement, he was seventeen, and Lisa Macon's hand was down his pants. *I wonder what she's doing these days?* A flood of information soaked his mind. Commander Ahn saw the faraway look return to her experiment's eyes.

"Where'd your mind wander this time, Dr. Faraday?"

"Salem, Oregon."

"What's there?"

"My teenage crush."

"And how are things with her?"

"Well, she's been in jail three times for a cocaine problem, she's a stripper at the Platinum Club, and her boyfriend Todd is the lead singer of a local band called 69Mustang."

"That's very sad."

"It is. Their music is terrible."

Commander Ahn and Dr. Faraday ended their walk in front of a door marked "Priority Access," and Ahn swiped a keycard and reached out to allow her hand to be scanned on a panel.

"Your final question?" she asked again while waiting for the scan to complete.

"I was going to ask what this is all for, but you're leading me to the answer, aren't you."

She smiled. "Right this way, Dr. Faraday."

CHAPTER 18

Senator Horton's eyes were open, but he saw nothing. Pitch black. He couldn't move. Hands bound, feet bound, either tied or taped to a chair. Wherever he was, it smelled like cleaning chemicals. A male voice spoke in front of him.

"Senator Horton." Ten, maybe fifteen feet away.

At first, Mike Horton wasn't sure he should say anything. But after careful consideration of the fact that he saw, felt, and knew nothing and couldn't budge an inch, he figured a few words would do more good than harm.

"Yes?"

"My name is Davis. You're wearing a hood because we cannot allow you to know more than what I am about to tell you."

"Okay. Why am I tied up?"

"What would be the first thing you did if you woke up with a hood over your head?"

"I guess I'd take it off."

"That is why you are tied up."

"Okay."

"Right now, there is a spacecraft on the far side of the moon. On board are tens of thousands of creatures belonging to a race of beings far more advanced than humans are."

Senator Horton laughed in sincere surprise. Then he shut up once he realized he was probably being held hostage by lunatics that might pull his fingernails out or chop off his balls or something terrible of the like. In hindsight, laughing was a poor choice. Senator Mike Horton then got fake serious real fast.

"Spacemen. I see. And who might you be?"

"We are members of a faction called Level 7. We exist for one reason."

"To save Earth from the impending conquest attempt?"

"To save Earth from the impending conquest attempt, yes."

"Oh." Senator Horton had no idea what to say anymore. He only knew that he was in danger, and he was still convinced someone might try to chop his balls off. He'd heard about these kinds of crazies before. *There must be a comet coming into orbit.* He wondered if his shoes had been replaced with Nikes and if the blanket on his head was purple.

"We've implanted a chip in your head that will allow us to communicate directly with you when the time comes," the man who called himself Davis continued.

Horton felt a twinge of fear, but nothing seemed strange inside his head, so he let the panic wash past him. "Okay."

"That is all, Senator. We will return you to your car."

"Wait."

There was no response. Horton took that as a sign to continue.

"Uh. Why me?"

"We like your style. One last thing. Do not talk to anyone about this. We can't risk for you to become compromised."

Like my style? What the hell is that supposed to mean? But before Senator Horton could prod further, he felt a prick in his neck and thought it would be a really nice time to close his eyes for a second.

He opened his eyes and was back in his car, at the same intersection from which he'd been abducted. The light was red. No signs to indicate anything had happened except for a dull metal box, a six-inch cube on the seat next to him. In etched lettering it read, "DO NOT OPEN UNTIL."

Until what?

He stared at the box until he heard a honk. The light was green.

CHAPTER 19

Crash barrel-rolled deftly to his right just as the giant creature charged past him. *The fuck is going on here?* was all the critical thinking he had time to muster while the giant beast corrected itself and again headed straight at him. In his attempt to dodge the beast's assault, Crash had scuttled toward the middle of the dome-shaped room, leaving him wide open for an attack. He realized his mistake too late. The furry behemoth galloped on all fours with a full head of steam, lowering its body as it blitzkrieged the TV host. Crash did his best to dodge again, this time jumping to his left, but there was too much open space for the beast to move this time, and it bucked its head and knocked Crash's legs out from under him, causing him to spin end over end before landing on his face.

What did I get into this time? Facedown in the straw, he groaned and pulled his head up enough to look at the beast in the dim light. The creature was still bucking around like an angry steer, not realizing it had already hit Crash and he was twenty feet away in the dirt.

What is that thing? He squinted harder, and made out a shape. He gasped and felt his face go numb.

Capybara. It can't be.

But it was. A fifteen-foot-long, multi-ton capybara. The world's largest rodent had just gotten larger. And the sight of it filled Crash with pure rage.

"*Aaaahhhhhhhhhh!*" Crash jumped to his feet, and the capybara saw him and realized it had been bucking at nothing. It continued its bucking, but now drifted in the human's direction. Crash's fists balled up as anger took control of his body. With the fury of a man with a thousand bullshit child support payments, he ran straight at the supercapybara. And got clobbered.

The beast's swinging head connected with Crash's torso, swatting him through the air without effort. The adventure host landed near the water trough, shook his senses back, and felt his nose. It was intact.

Gotta get control of myself. Gotta think. Crash looked around, but saw little in the poorly lit room, even as his eyes adjusted. The domed room seemed entirely empty except for the trough, him, and the beast, which was now trying to circle around to get on the other side of the watering bin. Crash ran straight back to the wall, keeping the trough between his body and the animal as long as he could. As he backed up, the beast stamped a couple of times, and then settled back down onto the straw, leading Crash to believe it had the same short memory and poor eyesight its smaller cousins had.

At least it isn't genetically superior in that way. That piece of shit.

Fighting the anger building up anew, Crash kept his course. *Maybe there's a way out.* He eased slowly around the outer edge of the circular room, keeping sure he didn't move fast enough to startle the supercapybara, although it seemed perfectly content with sitting on the ground at the moment. He didn't increase his speed at the animal's placid demeanor. Better to be safe.

Just when he thought he would be trapped in the room forever with the giant, stupid rodent, he came upon an opening in the wall he hadn't been able to see from more than a few feet out. His spirit was optimistic as he gave a cautious peek around the corner. He was looking into what looked like a smaller anteroom. *Maybe the beast's sleeping area?* The light was darker in there. And the room was far, far smellier. Crash maintained his deliberately slow pace and moved in, then toward the back of the room. He suddenly realized that if the beast came back, he'd be cornered with no way out. A decision made, he continued, but listened even more carefully for signs that the creature might be moving in his direction.

At the back of the smaller room there were some piles of straw and another, compact version of the larger water trough. He looked behind it and saw, cracked and broken in the dirt ... a camera. Next to the camera was something round and hairy the size of a basketball. The light was especially faint all the way in the back of the anteroom, so Crash bent down to look closer. Will's dismembered head stared back at him.

No.

Crash's rage took control. He stood up, fists balled.

You took my women. My money. My dignity. And now, my friend. He wanted to say goodbye, but he couldn't look at the disembodied face again. When he looked away, deeper in the straw, a soft glint caught his eye. *Will's machete.* He reached down and picked it up. The machete had been on every adventure of theirs since the beginning. It was nigh invincible, its steel true. That blade had cut through the toughest jungle vines, countless bamboo stalks, and the neck of the world's largest eastern diamondback rattlesnake.

Now it's time to see how much you can really cut through.

He slunk back out of the anteroom. The supercapybara was still minding its own business where he had left it. And as much as he wanted to charge at it in a full-on assault, he knew he had to be tactical. He maneuvered around the side wall again, circling until he was about forty feet away, directly behind the giant creature. He started toward the monster, slow at first, and then broke into a full sprint.

Before the beast knew what had hit it, Crash ran up alongside it and swung the machete with everything he had, slashing it open all along its left flank. It screamed a horrendous rodent scream and flipped around, trying to grab Crash in its mouth to gnaw him to his demise.

But Crash had slowed the monster considerably and was able to dodge its attacks this time. He feinted left, then right, and barrel-rolled, all the while sneaking in hard slashes and soft jabs; each one weakened the furry bastard further and further. Like a matador, Crash knew he had topped the beast and was in full control. He played with it, allowing it to think it had an open bite or buck or stomp, but Crash would always move away just in time. He thought of the moments that led him to this point, and thought about how what had seemed to be an incomprehensibly bizarre turn of events in the middle of the Amazon had in fact turned out to be the chance for a greater revenge than he imagined.

The adventure host drew blood and sliced flesh, and when he grew tired of his deadly dance, he parried the creature's final, exhausted move and spun around all the way to its rear, where he grabbed the fur and pulled himself to the top of the supercapybara's back. With a final scream, he grasped the machete handle with both hands, the blade pointed down, and plunged it between the monster's shoulder blades. It wailed and wailed, and tried to buck, but couldn't buck hard enough in its weakened state to shake Crash off.

Crash hopped down to the beast's head and spun off, so he was flanking the creature, and with a giant, final swing, severed the head from the body. Both the monster's head and Crash fell to the ground, the head relieved from its body and Crash relieved from his demons. Crash, on his knees, dropped the blade and screamed.

"I *win*, motherfucker!"

CHAPTER 20

"*Kidnapped?*" Rebecca Horton gasped. Her husband was shaking as he told her the version of the story he figured she could handle: loonies kidnapping him and giving him a box. The black vans. The chip they said they put in his head. Horton had at first no intention of even telling his wife, but she had pulled into the driveway the same moment he had, and he was too shaken to come up with a good cover story that fast.

"And you woke up in the car at the same intersection they grabbed you, and the box was on the seat." They both looked down at the matte metal box. The box that had "DO NOT OPEN UNTIL" inscribed on its lid.

"Yes."

Rebecca stared at it, and then at her husband, and then back at the box. "Until wh—"

"I have no idea," Horton said before she could get the question out. "I have no clue. They said they would contact me."

"Through the chip in your head."

"Through the chip in my head."

Rebecca wanted to roll her eyes, but nothing about her husband's state suggested he was okay. His face was sweaty. His eyes, sunken. *Something* had traumatized him. He reached for a glass to fill with water and it tumbled out of his hand and into the sink. She walked over and put her hand on top of his at the edge of the counter.

"So I guess the real question is," she said softly, "who are these people, and what do they want with you?"

"You mean, provided what they told me about the space-ships and creatures and the chip in my head is all a bunch of bullshit?" Horton replied while staring at the glass in the sink.

"Well, yes."

Husband and wife looked at each other and, for the first time either could remember, laughed together. It wasn't a hearty laugh, but it cracked the tension nonetheless. Finally Horton was calming down from his horrifying ordeal.

"So what are you going to do about it, Mike?"

He thought for a moment. "I'm going to contact the feds and get some security."

You will not contact anyone.

Rebecca saw her husband's eyes open wide in terror. "What's wrong?"

He shook his head. "They—I just heard a voice."

"What?"

"In my head. It said not to contact anyone."

Rebecca's eyes opened just as wide. "We need to get security over here right now," she said as she hurriedly walked to the kitchen phone. "I'm going to call the school and arrange to pick up Lizzie and we're going to get someplace safe. And I want that, that damn box out of our house immediately."

The box stays. Tell your wife to calm down.

Horton's hands started shaking and he pushed his palms down into the kitchen counter to steady them. It didn't help. *I am losing my mind.* He pressed so hard into the counter that his knuckles flushed to white, all the while his mind being compelled to keep his wife calm no matter what. He relaxed his grip. Let his hands drop from the granite countertop.

"I'm sorry, dear, I'm just exhausted." He smiled the same smile he smiled when he lied to her about his illicit affairs. "Post-traumatic stress," he added.

Rebecca didn't look convinced in the least. "So you didn't hear a voice?"

"Oh, I heard a voice all right. It was something the leader of the group told me earlier, and it just now came back to me. Just remembering it, I guess."

Rebecca searched her husband's eyes, but she couldn't find his lie. "So we'll get rid of the box?"

"Yeah, we have to get it out of here," he untruthfully agreed.

"And you'll get us some security?"

"As much as they'll give me."

"Okay." Rebecca's shoulders dropped and she wrapped her arms around her husband and they hugged.

"Go pick up Lizzie," he told her, trying to hide his anxiety. Rebecca walked out of the kitchen and he stared at the wall, becoming more and more stressed at the thought of another unwanted, uninvited message stabbing deep into his mind. But nothing came.

• • •

All of Lizzie's friends had been freaking out about Jennica!'s new music video. It seemed every girl in her high school had seen it at least twice, and there wasn't a single girl who hadn't sent it along to multiple friends. The song was an epic hit, and the video was making its way virally across the globe.

School was only halfway over for the day when Rebecca came to pick up her daughter, but even by then Lizzie had memorized the entire chorus and bridge of the song. She was humming it as she followed her mom into the SUV, but stopped when she realized something was off.

"Mom, why are you picking me up? Is anything wrong?"

"Yes, well ... yes, but nothing big. There's just some stuff going on, but your father is taking care of it." That was all Lizzie needed to hear to move on. Her father was high profile enough where this hadn't been the first time she got pulled from school, although she was surprised her mom had come for her instead of some kind of man in a suit. *Some of those guys were kinda cute though*, thought Lizzie. *But they'd be cuter if they had eight arms.*

"Huh?"

Lizzie was so startled by the odd thought that she had responded to herself aloud as she rode along in the passenger seat.

"What's that, Lizzie?"

"Nothing." *Weird.*

Lizzie pulled her iPhone out, hit play on the queued-up video, and mumbled along as the chorus played. "*Don't. Don't. U. U. Wanna. Wanna. Touch. Touch.*"

Rebecca glanced over. "Whatcha singin'?"

"*Ohmygod* Mom, it's the newest Jennica! song and the video just came out this morning. It's *so* good."

"You've seen it already?"

"Everyone has, Mom."

"Is that what you girls do instead of your schoolwork?"

"*Mom*. You don't understand! This is the best song I've *ever* heard."

Lizzie searched the glove compartment for an auxiliary cable. "Here, plug it in and listen!" she practically shouted as she handed her mom one end of the cable.

"Maybe later, Lizzie, I'm not really in the mood right now."

"Well you gotta see the video when we get home," Lizzie pleaded, unable to tear her eyes away from the screen.

"Sure," replied Rebecca as she continued the drive home. *God, was I this bad when Cyndi Lauper came out?*

CHAPTER 21

The manifestation of all of Crash's hatred and revenge had been destroyed. The man sat, emotionally and physically drained, at the side of the monster he had taken down.

I did it. He rubbed his bloody fingers together. The blood had started to dry and his hands were sticky. He took his first deep breath of the day and thought just for a moment about his revenge.

I won. What now? The hollowness of avenged loss didn't last long before his survival instinct pushed it back down.

I need to get the hell out of here, that's what now.

He wiped Will's blood-soaked machete in the straw on the floor, and did the same with his hands. He got up and walked toward the anteroom, and turned back a last time to eye what was left of the beast. He wanted to smile but couldn't. *Will deserves a better burial than this.* He took his shirt off and wrapped up the head of his good friend and slung it over his shoulder.

He saw a door in the rear of the anteroom, standing open. *Was that open before? Nothing in this place makes sense.* The adventurer moved to exit the dome-room for good, and then thought of something. Quickly, he turned back into the anteroom and jogged over to the other side of the trough where he had found Will's head and the machete. And Will's DSLR camera.

Crash picked it up, turned it on, and hit play. He watched enough footage to see that Will had filmed the giant capybara—and an empty laboratory that Crash hadn't himself seen. *Whatever's going on down here isn't going to be secret for long.* The screen went dark, the dead-battery light flickered, and the camera felt like a thousand pounds in his tired arms. *No good to me now.* He took the memory card from the camera and dropped it into a cargo pocket, and headed off bloody, shirtless, and holding his friend's head in a makeshift satchel in one hand and the giant machete in the other. James "Crash" Jefferson was the picture of ruggedness as he finally left the stinking, dirty, den of death and walked through the open door into the next unknown.

CHAPTER 22

Grammeral Zeezak sat packed in his human fleshsuit at the edge of his second bed, his land dweller bed. It wasn't unacceptably more uncomfortable than his liquid bed, however. *If I must practice living as a human, I will do it in luxury.* The bed's sheets were woven with living microworms, and the subtle movements lulled even the harshest insomniacs quickly to sleep. Their interwoven bodies wrapped the sleeper with a comfort so incredible, it was thought to be taboo on some planets.

The Grammeral glanced across his quarters to the holosculpture jutting from the far wall. An amazing piece, it had taken three generations to craft. It flowed with the trapped spirits of creatures so pure that to gaze upon them was to embrace the most brilliant visual spectacles imaginable. The holosculpture danced like a supernova, exploding again and again for the octopus's pleasure.

Grammeral Zeezak's bed was big enough for a half dozen, yet slept only him. For the time being. A deep, primal lust had awakened within the Vyperians, triggering intense desires that few had been faced with in their lives, and Grammeral Zeezak was not immune to the new impulses. He could not put his tentacle on it, but there was a hunger inside him for the touch of a female that became more real the more he let his mind dwell on it. Worse, not feeding that hunger almost left him ...

sad?

No. I cannot allow myself to drop my guard. Now is not the time for self-pity. Self-pity is not the warrior's way. I must stay focused. Still, something about Jennica! stirred feelings inside the octopus. He closed both his human eyes and his natural eyes.

Through the moon and across space, Grammeral Zeezak reached out to the Earth female who sat in her hotel room, anxiously awaiting a touch from his mind.

Soon we shall be together, he projected.

• • •

It startled her, even as she had expected him. Jennica! tuned out whatever Tully and Bobby were passively trying to tell her about her latest behavior.

Soon we shall be together.

And magically, everything was better.

Please come to me, she thought.

I will be with you soon.

When?

Soon.

How soon?

Two days.

Two days!

While Tully explained to Jennica! that she was going to have to be more reliable and agreeable if they all were going to keep making her tour work, Jennica! squealed, lost in her own little world, and Bobby looked at Tully as if he knew they weren't getting anywhere and maybe he should straight-up ask

Jennica! if she was already deep into hard drugs, and Tully looked back at Bobby as if he needed some hard drugs himself just to stay sane.

• • •

Yes. Two days. Two days and then—

Grammeral Zeezak's concentrated communication with his Earth crush was rudely interrupted by his beloved but ill-timed Sentlent Bool, who had rolled in brusquely on the flats of all eight of his tentacles.

"What do you want, Sentlent?"

"My Lord. Another breach in Zeta Base."

Grammeral Zeezak snapped out of his trance. "I was under the impression Zeta Base had been planted in the midst of terrain undesirable to human occupation."

Sentlent Bool didn't have time to reply before the Grammeral continued. "Was it in relation to the first breach?"

"We don't know, my Lord. It was another single human. Another male. The automated system incapacitated the earthling and then led him into the feeding cage, as it had done with the first."

"And did mutation experiment one-zero-one take care of the new intruder as well?"

"*Errggg.*"

"'*Errggg,*' what, Sentlent?"

"It was being cared for with automatic maintenance, but the intruder destroyed it."

"The intruder destroyed automated maintenance?"

"The intruder destroyed mutation experiment one-zero-one."

Grammeral Zeezak unnaturally furled the brow of his human head and found it hard to make additional facial expressions. Although the fleshsuit was adequate, creating human faces took a tremendous amount of energy, and he and his men had only recently been practicing facial shapes. He tried again to show a look of displeasure. His short lapse into the travails of not being able to arch his human eyebrows menacingly was broken as Sentlent Bool, not understanding the attempts to look angry, prodded for further instruction. "My Lord?"

"He killed the mutation," said the Grammeral as he gave up and allowed his human face to relax. "With what weapon?"

"Only a blade, my Lord."

Grammeral Zeezak unconsciously ran his human finger across one of the many ceremonial sucker caps that draped from his bed stand. "Interesting. And where is the human now?"

"In one of the mutation's exercise tubes."

"Lead him to the transport room."

Sentlent Bool's tentacle tips betrayed the slightest yellow color of curiosity. "And then, my Lord?"

"Transport him directly to the ship. Have a pod's worth of soldiers waiting. Begin in fleshsuits, so as not to frighten him into shock. Question the human. See if you can get him to answer willfully. If not, dispose of him quickly. We have a schedule to keep. Oversee it yourself."

"As you wish, my Lord."

• • •

"*Hellooooo!* Where did you go? Come back to me!" Jennica! said aloud to no one in particular after not receiving any replies from the mystery man in her head.

Bobby and Tully stared at the singer blankly. In a split second the pop star had gone from being unexplainably happy to having a serious breakdown. When Jennica! banged on the hotel room television and tried to talk to it, Tully pulled Bobby aside and whispered hoarsely to the manager, "I'm done with this. No more. If you don't get this nut job some fucking valium, I'm canceling the tour."

CHAPTER 23

Crash didn't feel like traipsing down a dirty tunnel just to find another monstrous creature to fight. He had barely handled a big rodent. *What if there's a giant piranha waiting for me?* He didn't have to find out. The ceiling above him swooshed open and he watched, amazed, as a thin, circular, metal pad a meter across floated down from the hole. He was so dumbfounded by the levitating circle he almost didn't get out of the way when the disc whooshed past him and settled on the floor with a small flash of light. He looked up through the hole in the ceiling. *Looks like another room.*

Crash stared down the dirty tunnel where he stood. He could see no end to it. Looked back up through the hole. *What's the worst that could happen?* He stepped onto the disc.

The transport pad was anticlimactic; it simply took Crash up to the level above where he'd been. He was in another tunnel now, but this one was much shorter, and without any dirt on the floor. A row of lights illuminated in succession, signaling him to go left. He did.

While he walked, he took account of the technology surrounding him. The lower level was mostly bare, but up top were monitors, wires, and pipes. Opaque vats four meters high lined the walls, and chemistry equipment was scattered about. *Someone put a lot of work into this,* he thought as he passed by. Some of the equipment looked familiar, some of it didn't.

Crash wasn't sure if that was because he was someplace alien, or simply because he knew jack shit about this kind of science.

The environment had a sickly smell to it, and Crash had a distinctly different feeling about this new part of the building. Down below felt lonely and cold, but here, up top, left him feeling spooked. *I don't like this.*

A door slid open to his right.

Crash, for lack of a better option, once again obeyed the suggestion and walked, machete at the ready, through an open passageway into a room filled with what seemed to be futuristic telephone booths.

The first stall lit up. Crash paused. *I* really *don't like this.* Second thoughts bombarded his mind and he backed away. The door he had entered the room with closed with a *schwoooof.* Crash dropped Will's head and leaped to the door. Pried at it. But it was too late. He was sealed in. He turned to look at the strange booths, and the first one flashed again.

Well shit.

He took a breath, scooped up Will's head, and walked into booth one.

One moment he was standing in a room full of futuristic telephone booths, the next he was standing in ... another room full of futuristic telephone booths. But this time, he had company.

Standing around Crash in a semi-circle just outside his booth was a handful of strange-looking men. The TV host stared, taking in the scene.

The hell is this shit? The men wore purple jumpsuits, and all looked eerily similar. In fact, Crash couldn't discern any difference between them at all. They were a bunch of short, bald, Yul Brynners dressed like Prince.

There the two factions postured, sizing each other up. A half dozen identical, small, bald, purple-jumpsuited fellows surrounded a tall, shirtless, bloody man with a machete in one hand and his friend's severed head wrapped up and slung over his shoulder.

Crash took notice of a different man in the background. *He watches like he's in charge. But he's not the main leader, just the right-now leader.* The right-now leader spoke from the back of the pack.

"Identify yourself."

"Never mind me, who the hell are you?" Crash snarled.

Sentlent Bool, the "man" in the back, hesitated. He had momentarily forgotten that some "Earth types" were prone to noncompliance. *Pity,* thought Bool. *Answers would have been preferred, but we don't have the time for this.* Sentlent Bool projected an order to his soldiers. The men drew handheld firearms. *Shoot the earthling,* he commanded with his thoughts.

But not quite before the machete came down.

Schlick.

Crash swung so mightily that the little man in front of him was cut cleanly in two. The other small men were stunned just long enough for Crash to make his move.

These assholes have no idea who they're fucking with. Crash didn't have time to further analyze, or to see that the man he had severed had dissolved into a pile of tentacles and slime. It was go-time. And in go-time, there were no rules. There was no time to over-think. Giving over completely to instinct, he swung Will's head like a mace and made solid impact with the closest man to him that wasn't already in two separate, quivering, oozing pieces. The makeshift club landed with a thud, knocking the little guy back a few feet. *Game on.*

The little bald Princes attempted to shoot their pistols, but before any of them could fire off a shot, Crash hit them pre-emptively. He was taken aback at how slow they were. *These guys move like they just woke up.*

He swung the machete with one hand and Will's head with the other, like two windmills of punishment for anything that came within range. Stunned by his rapid movements of testosterone-infused masculinity, the aliens began losing the ability to hold their fleshsuits together. While Crash slashed and swung, the strange little men burst at the joints as their true octopus selves popped out of the humanoid bodies in a flurry of tentacles.

It was Crash's turn to be stunned. "What the hell?" he yelled.

Three of the creatures remained uninjured, but the only one left in human form was their leader, who was frantically hitting buttons on a panel in the back of the room. The two octopuses near Crash moved much more quickly without their awkward fleshsuits to hinder them. They snaked their tentacles out at Crash with lightning speed.

This is a whole new fuckin' ball game, Crash thought while he swung the machete at the closest octopus, hoping to chop off a tentacle. But it deftly slapped the blade aside with another appendage that appeared to come out of nowhere. Crash felt a tentacle swipe toward him from his left flank, so he side-stepped and swung Will's head at the bulk of the beast, but again his attack was slapped away. With eight tentacles and the ability to balance perfectly on only two, that left six on each octopus with which to fight. Crash cringed at the math. Eight plus eight minus four equaled *I'm about to get my shit kicked in*— Three tentacles came at him at once.

He spun and dove, but was caught midair by a tentacle so strong it held him upside down and entirely off the ground. The memory card he'd swiped from Will's camera fell out of his pocket and dropped to the floor. Crash looked down, but before he could do anything, the card was smashed by yet another tentacle that flew in with tremendous speed and power. *Dammit!*

Crash struggled and wriggled and swayed and swung, but the tentacle held strong. The second octopus slithered closer, and they both eyeballed him closely from right-side up. He swung the machete, but it was snatched and yanked from him. The one who was their leader walked cautiously over.

Crash's whole world was upside down, and so was he. Blood rushed to his face, and he was helplessly dangling while trying to hang on to his friend's head, which was now bursting through the seams of its fabric sling. The leader, still in human form, stayed far enough away from Crash to keep safe. He spoke.

"Tell us who you are, and how you found us."

"Why don't you tell me something?"

"I'm not going—"

"Like how your buddy here is going to wear an eye patch on that ugly earless head of his." In one quick movement, Crash whipped out his pocketknife, sprung it open, swung his momentum forward, and plunged the knife into the big left eye of the octopus holding him. It shrieked and dropped Crash on

Will's head, and before the monsters could stop him, Crash grabbed the bloody satchel, dove back into the transporter booth, and slapped the control panel.

And was instantly inside a small room.

He dove out of the booth quickly to make sure he wasn't zapped back to wherever the hell he'd just been, and strode over to a panel on the wall and pressed a glowing button. The wall in front of him slid open, and he walked out from a hidden door into a grungy bathroom stall. Rays of daylight leaked in. Crash hadn't seen actual daylight since he'd fallen into the cave a lifetime earlier. Enraptured by the lure of sunshine, he hustled out and into the afternoon glow and found himself in the middle of an urban park.

Scores of people bore witness to the scene of the pocketknife-wielding, blood-soaked, shirtless man who emerged from the public park men's room with a severed head hanging from a few threads of cloth wrapped around his knuckles. And all of them, jaded New Yorkers as they were, screamed or gasped or freaked the hell out.

CHAPTER 24

Mike Horton knew Rebecca would return with their daughter before too long, and he knew he had to do something about the box. But he couldn't do anything. He was petrified. The mystery people were reading his thoughts, and knew what he was going to do before he did. They talked to him inside his own mind, and every time Horton even *thought* about that, thought about people being *inside his head*, he felt pangs of panic. Everything kept compounding on everything else in a tortuous spiral of anxiety-ridden thoughts.

I promised Rebecca I would keep us safe, and I promised her I would get rid of this damn box, and I can't do either of those things. Horton started feeling guilty on top of feeling afraid, and for a moment thought he was going to have a breakdown when his hands started to shake. *Get control of yourself, Mike.* He slowed his breathing and steadied himself.

If I can't actually get rid of this box and call for help, at least I can pretend to. Horton scooped up the box, climbed upstairs, and found an adequate hiding place in the bottom of his dresser drawer of war memories. He buried the box under some certificates and awards. *No one said I had to keep the damn thing on me at all t—* His inner ear tingled.

Keep the box on you at all times.

"What! Why?"

You will need it soon, but the exact time is not known. You

120

must remain with it.

"The hell am I supposed to tell my wife? I promised her I'd get rid of the damn thing."

The voice didn't answer.

Horton heard Rebecca's car pull up and the doors open and slam.

"Shit."

• • •

Rebecca opened the front door to the house with Lizzie in tow to find her husband standing in front of them, holding the box. She swallowed her shock for Lizzie's sake. "I thought you were getting rid of that thing?"

"Yeah. I mean, I called the, uh, agency, and they told me to, uh, keep it."

"What? Why would they do that? Lizzie, could you grab me a water from the fridge?" Rebecca waited until her daughter was out of earshot before continuing in hushed tones. "Wouldn't they want to investigate it? What if it's dangerous? Are they coming over, Mike?"

Horton broke a sweat. He was as skilled as a person could be at keeping cool, but this was ridiculous. He had no idea what he was doing. *What the hell do I tell her?*

"I didn't call the agency."

"What?"

"They told me not to."

"Who told you?"

Do not tell her about us. It will only complicate things.

"The voice in my head."

You are making a mistake, Senator.

Horton looked at his wife and read the fear in her face. "I can't let them win."

This is not about winning. I am in control now. Submit and make it easy on yourself, Senator.

Lizzie returned from the kitchen just in time to see her father break down, screaming at nobody and swatting aimlessly in the air while Rebecca watched in terror.

"You will not control me!" he shouted. "I am in charge! I am in charge here!"

Rebecca frantically maneuvered past her husband to her daughter and pushed her toward the front door. "Lizzie, honey, go wait in the car."

"Mom, what's happening to Dad?"

"I don't know. *Go.*"

With those words, the story Horton had told earlier fell apart in Rebecca's mind. Aside from a nondescript metal tin, her husband had no proof that anything had happened as he said it had, and now he was having a mental collapse in front of his family.

Rebecca pushed out to the front steps and turned her daughter to face her. "Listen to me. Go wait in the car." Lizzie took one more look over at her dad, just long enough to see him collapse to his knees, and then she silently walked to the car, got inside, locked the door, and peered out through the windshield.

Horton stopped screaming, suddenly aware and present. He pulled himself up and leaned out the front door toward his family, bracing himself on the frame.

"Becky, get Lizzie inside. It's not safe out there!"

He stumbled and motioned for his wife to come into the house, but she didn't budge from in front of the car, staying in between him and their daughter. Horton was shifting uncomfortably, on his feet but shaky. The voice plowed through his head again.

You're failing your task, Senator.

He clutched the side of his head with his free hand and forced words out to Rebecca. "I know this is hard to believe but I swear everything I've told you about this is true."

Mike Horton's eyes welled up with tears, and Rebecca could bear it no longer. She walked back to their home, reached out to her husband, and helped him up and inside to the couch while Lizzie, crying, watched through the windshield and open house door.

CHAPTER 25

Workers in lab coats weaved around tables covered in test tubes, microscopes, burners, and robotic arms. If there was a playground for scientists, Dr. Faraday was standing in it. He was giddy as he walked to the closest table. On it, dozens of rats crawled around in a bin.

A lab tech pulled out a thin touch computer from his pocket and swiped a few gestures. The rats stopped their random scurrying, turned toward the center in unison, and crawled toward a focal point. They stood up, climbed on top of each other, locked legs, and within seconds had assembled into a single unit a meter tall. They walked fluidly together as one toward the edge of the table where Faraday stood, and as he bent over for a closer look, the unified creature jumped toward him. He fought back the urge to shit himself in surprise and instead caught the writhing mass as if it were a dog jumping into the arms of its owner.

"Cute, huh?" said Commander Ahn.

"I don't know if 'cute' would be my description of choice. You're experimenting with controlling the actions of living creatures." A chill stabbed the back of Faraday's neck as he observed the rat-thing still cradled in his arms. "And sentient beings as well?"

Commander Ahn said nothing.

"I'd like to know," he pressed while gently releasing the rat mass back into the pen.

"All in good time, Doctor. Let's go."

"Where are we going?"

"It's time to show you why you're here."

• • •

Faraday and Commander Ahn sat on opposite sides of a conference table in a room with one other man, who was seated at the head of the table. Frank scanned and searched with his super brain, but could retrieve no information about the new person. Strange that the man wore the markings of a generic military leader, yet there was no country of origin attached to his medals and uniform. In the center of the table was a most peculiar piece of equipment.

Headgear? thought Faraday.

The new man motioned to Frank and spoke.

"Dr. Faraday. I've heard much about you. My name is Jordan. Hopefully you can help us as we teeter on the edge of global chaos."

Global chaos, echoed Frank's thoughts.

"If you would, put that on," continued Jordan as he waved to the strange device on the table. Faraday stared at the thing for a moment.

"I'd rather not until I know what it does."

"Put it on now," said Jordan without hesitation.

Faraday felt his throat tighten as he reached out to the bulky helmet overlaid with bumps and wires. He stopped. *No. Enough is enough.* The scientist slammed his palms to the table.

"No," he called out, much to his own surprise. "You've been stringing me along blindly for years now, thinking you could buy me off. Maybe you thought I'd be a puppet and never question anything, but I deserve to know what's going on, and I deserve to be treated with respect. In the past twenty-four hours I've had my brain scrambled with ... with alien technology, I've vomited out my guts—my own guts for chrissakes! And I've been more terrified than I've ever been in my life. And," he looked down, "I haven't seen my son since I got here."

"Your son is fine," responded Commander Ahn. Jordan remained silent.

"I want to see him," said Faraday. "I want to see my son."

"You can see him anytime you like."

Instantly, a live video feed of Trevor's playroom popped into Faraday's head. Trevor was napping in a large bed in the corner.

"You won't be able to physically see him for a couple of days, so for now, this will have to do," added Commander Ahn.

"Why can't I see him in person?" Faraday asked while his mind stayed with the image of his son.

"You can't see him right now," replied Jordan, "because everyone on Earth is in danger and we need you here right now. So please pay attention, Dr. Faraday. You need to listen carefully to everything I'm about to say."

Frank remained with his son in his mind's eye, took a breath, and settled himself. "Fine."

A holographic projection of Earth appeared above the center of the table.

"Here's what we know," said Jordan. "Three days ago, we detected an anomaly on the other side of the moon. Using our scanners, we discovered that the disturbance was caused by a propulsion technology that could only come from a spacecraft, and it became quickly understood that this vehicle was from somewhere else. It is, in fact, an alien spacecraft, and they have come here to destroy us all."

"How do we know they want to destroy us?" asked Faraday.

Jordan looked at Faraday as if he had just asked to pull down his pants and shit on the table. "Well, what else would they be coming halfway across the galaxy to do, *Doctor* Faraday," the man spat.

Faraday scrunched his forehead. *Is this guy serious?* "Um, how do we know they came halfway across the galaxy? Do we know anything about them at all?" He started rubbing his temples. "Actually, forget them for a minute. I want to know how you guys came across alien technology in the first place. Obviously, you've already had some sort of contact if you're utilizing it. I want to know more about *that*."

Jordan's face all but blew apart with bursting blood vessels at the contention. "You've been on this project for one goddamn day! We give you the greatest power known to man and you come in here all half-cocked and asking questions. Who the hell do you think you *are*?"

Faraday was momentarily stunned to silence. *Who the hell is this guy? He's like a stereotype from a bad movie.* "Just answer one question for me," he said, voice cracking with frustration. "Why did you do this to me? You give me access to what you say is 'all the world's knowledge,' yet I obviously don't know anything about what you're talking about and you don't seem to give a damn about my opinions or questions. How am

I going to help anything?"

"Because, Dr. Faraday," replied Jordan, "when the shit goes down, we're going to need you to be able to give us instant reports on information from wherever in the world the shit is going down."

Faraday laughed a laugh of surprise and dismayed understanding. "You're kidding me." He shook his head. "So essentially, you've just turned me into a human Twitter feed."

"That's a great way of putting it," Commander Ahn answered. She was met by an unamused look from the scientist.

"You were our best hope," said Jordan. "From an early age, your mind was capable of handling massive amounts of information. We needed someone who could do it without having a mental collapse. And so far, you've far exceeded the others."

"Others?" questioned Faraday.

"We tried this with other subjects who weren't as capable as you are," Ahn said. "They were exposed to too much too soon, and ..."

"And? What happened to these others?"

She didn't answer. Jordan stepped in. "We might as well tell him. They went crazy and killed themselves. But that won't happen to you."

"What! How do you know?" Faraday felt the blood draining from his head.

"Because you haven't displayed any of the symptoms!" Ahn answered.

"What symptoms?"

"Suicide attempts!"

Faraday's shoulders sank and he felt the color flush entirely from his face. *Something isn't adding up.* Anxieties built and his thoughts careened to dangerous places. He mentally checked out and visited the beach in his mind and calmed himself. *But I have to play along for now.* He straightened in his chair, sniffed, and nodded approval for the meeting to continue.

Jordan once again motioned to the helmet at the center of the table. Faraday sighed, still partially focused on the mental image of his sleeping son.

What the hell have I gotten myself into?

Chapter 26

Crash had only a moment to himself before a beat cop came running to check what the commotion was about. The officer took a look at Crash, a look at the open pocketknife, a look at the severed head, and then *zap*, nailed Crash with his Taser. Crash slumped to the ground, writhed, and managed to scream out a few blurbs before being thrown into the back of a squad car.

The headline broke immediately on news outlets worldwide.

Breaking News—Popular television host James "Crash" Jefferson was apprehended moments ago outside a public restroom in New York City. Bystanders reported Jefferson was wielding a knife and had evidence on his person that he had just committed a violent crime. Witnesses also claimed that the TV personality was detained with nonlethal force by local law enforcement, but not before launching into an obscenity-laden tirade against "alien oppression."

• • •

For most people, the news was another bizarre news bite in an already bizarre world. For Frank Faraday, it was a sign of something far more malignant.

The scientist sat in silence in the conference room chair. On his head rested the headwear he'd been told to put on, making him look not unlike an old lady in bifocals sitting under a hair dryer in a salon. Faraday quickly learned that the "hair dryer" had three functions. It helped him to focus, it could project his different thought-streams to the holographic displays above the table, and it had a built in massager, making the device rather pleasant for the most part. He'd only been trying out the helmet for a couple of minutes when he caught wind of the breaking story in New York.

"I think something just happened that you need to know about," he said aloud while he projected news of the celebrity arrest into the room. Jordan stroked his cheekbone as he scanned the floating headlines.

"It could be something, but it sounds more like a druggie on a bad trip."

"There's more," continued Faraday while he filtered the information and enjoyed a low-pressure scalp rub. "According to his last public update, Crash Jefferson was in the Amazon rainforest filming his television show as recently as yesterday, and although there is plenty of public knowledge of social media regarding Jefferson traveling to South America, there hasn't been a peep about him or any of his crew returning."

Jordan squinted. "What about a private jet? Could he have made it back on that, and gone on some sort of bender that resulted in this mess?"

Faraday's eyes glazed as he searched every database he could. "Given his financial status, the man wasn't wealthy enough to foot the bill for a private jet— Hold on. Video's being uploaded by a bystander right now. Got it. I see him."

"Well put it on the holo!" demanded Jordan.

Faraday closed his eyes for a moment, and blurry video projected above the table. The scientist's fingers painted the air around him as he pointed out his observations. Commander Ahn and Jordan watched while Frank described the images that floated between them.

"Notice he's standing outside a public restroom, but dressed in clothing appropriate for heavy trekking. That shredded fabric hanging from his hand is his shirt."

The image grew as Faraday zoomed in on the shirt and what it carried.

"The fabric is wrapped around the head of Will Armly, his producer."

Commander Ahn drew her hand to her mouth at the grotesque sight. She almost turned away before Faraday switched the view to Crash's midsection.

"Jefferson has a piece of fern wrapped around his belt loop that—it's grainy, but—searching—it could be a fern that is only found in South America."

Frank Faraday opened his eyes and pulled up his goggles to look at Jordan as the hologram showed Crash getting Tased and buckling to the ground.

"I might be wrong here," Faraday continued as the video looped back to the beginning, "but as crazy as it sounds, I think this guy just came out of the jungle."

"Straight from the jungle to New York City."

"Yes."

"Transfer booth?" Commander Ahn directed to Jordan. The man shot her a stern glance before looking back to Faraday.

"This is why you're here, Dr. Faraday. This could give us something," he said before turning back to Commander Ahn. "Send a team there immediately. Tell them to use *special* tactics if necessary. Our time is running out."

• • •

Sentlent Bool stared at the slimy mess in front of him. *What a catastrophe.* The only thing left behind from the escaped human was a smashed data device. Surrounding it were a few dozen dismembered tentacles, blubbery chunks of flesh, and the occasional eye.

Sentlent Bool received a request to report immediately to the Grammeral's chamber, and quickly punched in the code in the anywherevator. He stepped out into near darkness and stubbed his human toe on something and stifled a surprise yelp. Grammeral Zeezak spoke.

"Use your eyes."

"I don't see anything, my Lord."

"Use your real eyes, Sentlent."

The lesser octopus flushed pink with embarrassment. He had been in human form so long he had all but forgotten that his true eyes could see a much wider spectrum. The officer dropped the top of his fleshsuit, exposing his natural head. Everything became as sharp as a fifth-dimension holo. Grammeral Zeezak was staring out of his window, out into deep, black space. Out toward home.

Sentlent Bool took note that although the Grammeral told him to switch back to natural form, the Grammeral himself had not.

Grammeral Zeezak took a deep breath inside of his fleshsuit. "Report, Sentlent."

"We were unprepared, my Lord."

Grammeral Zeezak remained motionless. "Did you find out anything at all?"

"No, my Lord. We did not. The human was well trained, even using the head of one of his own as a weapon."

Grammeral Zeezak stroked his false chin. "The humans aren't known for that."

"No, my Lord, they aren't."

"Perhaps we don't know as much about them as we think."

Sentlent Bool didn't reply, unsure how to respond.

"Where did the transfer booth take the earthling?" the Grammeral continued.

"To a long-unused portal in their new city of York. We had created it when the Vyperian council was considering launching the invasion via transfer booths before inefficiency ruled it out."

"Ah, yes," replied Grammeral Zeezak.

For a long moment there was silence. Grammeral Zeezak took one last look out into space, and then turned and marched past his commander and to the chamber door.

"Sentlent, prepare the transmission channel to override all of Earth's digital and analog broadcasts. We need to act now, before the human endangers our plans. We might be able to buy the time we need to implement directives zero-two and zero-three before retaliation can be assembled. I do hope that directive zero-one has had enough time to gestate in the minds of the Earth females."

Sentlent Bool allowed himself to stand in awe of his Grammeral for but a moment, then put in the call to engineering to set up the planet-wide transmission for immediate implementation. He pulled the top of his fleshsuit back over his head.

It begins now.

CHAPTER 27

The pretty young brunette finished singing her song without ever getting a note right. Nobody clapped, but she had a look on her face that suggested everyone should have.

The three judges stared blankly for a moment.

"That was terrible," said the black dude.

"Simply awful," said the pouty woman.

"What made you think you had a chance here tonight?" said the snarky record producer.

The woman started crying. "All my life, my friends told me I was, like, the best singer they've ever heard."

"You really believe that?" said the black dude.

"You people don't know what you're talking about!" the pretty brunette screamed back.

The woman stomped and stormed off the small stage, knocking over a potted plant on her way out the door. The record producer opened his mouth to talk, and anyone watching knew he was about to launch into one of his trademarked tirades. And then the screens of every television set in the world flickered. Popular shows, local news, and terrible cable access alike all cut to the same transmission.

Grammeral Zeezak's head, shiny and hairless, peered into the homes of every television in the world. The small, strange, smooth man stared calmly for a good ten seconds, and then said the most significant words humankind had ever heard.

"Ladies and gentlemen of Earth. I am Grammeral Q'Shin Zeezak, commander of a vessel that has traveled through space to bring you a message of peace."

Grammeral Zeezak picked up a piece of material and wrapped it loosely around his neck. One of his early teams from the new city of York had made notes about earthlings' love for wrapping their necks with soft fabrics, and Grammeral Zeezak thought it might be a fitting addition for his announcement. No Vyperian had ever followed up to see if winter scarves were as popular elsewhere on the planet, since the idea of pockets of culture within the same species was a long-foreign idea to the race. No matter. Grammeral Zeezak looked elegant nonetheless with his swaddled neck.

"I, and my crew, have come here to learn from you, and to share with you. We have technologies that could benefit your species mightily, and we are hoping you have somethings to share with us as well." *Some things. Not somethings. Snerch!*

The display zoomed to a close-up of his head.

"As you can see from my features, our species are not terribly different from each other, and I hope we can learn much from one another about our origins and our journeys. I bring you this message today to hopefully assuage any ill will, and to give you advance notice that we will be arriving tomorrow in a shuttle from our main vessel. We will be landing in your new city of York during its local morning time. We hope you will welcome us with open arms. Blessings."

• • •

Jennica! sat on the floor of her hotel room in front of the television, mouth open and a shattered glass at her feet. Her prince had come. Thoughts raced. *Am I ready for this? Is this my destiny? Does love exist in space? What does* assuage *mean?* But deep down in her heart, gut instinct offered to Jennica! the comfort that she was about to embark on a romantic adventure that would guide her to a raw, pure love the likes of which she had never experienced.

The pop star traced her fingers across the television screen, although Grammeral Zeezak's handsome bald face had been replaced with George Costanza's squinty bald face. But the memory remained, and the fantasy was about to become reality. Jennica! knew it.

• • •

Rebecca and Mike Horton sat in shock on the same sofa, but with a buffer of a few inches. The space between them betrayed the caution she had for her husband. Rebecca looked to the face of the man she had known for so long. A sigh escaped her lips. Words followed.

"I'm sorry."

The two had been fighting tears all evening while Mike Horton did his best to act normal and Rebecca Horton did her best to try to understand him. Lizzie had been picked up by Grandma, and was told that Dad had become sick and needed Mom to take care of him. And so husband and wife spent more time together that afternoon than they had in years. When the broadcast of the space visitor happened, not only had the message changed the course of human history, it had jury-rigged Rebecca and Horton back together again, albeit with the weakest of links.

Horton forced himself to look directly into his wife's eyes. *I have to tell her.* He took a shallow breath.

"There's more. I need to tell you the whole truth this time. I can't leave anything out."

Rebecca Horton took her husband's hand and waited patiently.

"The—I," Horton fumbled for the right words. "I never wanted to hurt you, I just didn't know how to tell you." His body tensed and he bit his lip. His body trembled as he began to tell his wife the whole story of his infidelities with other men, of his own selfish desire to use his family as a public face for a life he was ashamed of. And through it all, his wife moved closer, not farther, and surprised him entirely when she replied to his confessions with a simple, "I've known for years."

Horton sat in stunned silence for a moment. "Why didn't you ever—why didn't you confront me?"

Rebecca looked her husband in the eyes. "I don't know. Maybe I should have. Maybe because I lived more for your career than I did for us. Or myself. I don't know. Maybe for Lizzie." Rebecca dropped her eyes to the floor as a single tear rolled down her cheek and dropped onto her blouse. She let go of his hand. Senator Mike Horton felt his wife's touch slip away and he broke down in tears.

Senator Horton. It's almost time.

The voice was a thunder in his head as it spoke. Swept up in the emotions, the struggling man had all but forgotten it for a moment. His shoulders knotted up, and his wife knew.

"You heard it, didn't you? The voice. Just now."

"Yes."

"What did it say?"

"It said it's almost time."

CHAPTER 28

Every major city in every connected country on Earth was bubbling over with near panic. Riots broke out. Already unstable regions were quickly tipping out of control. Conflicts ignited in Liberia, Egypt, North Korea, South Africa, Venezuela, Ukraine, Turkey, and Indonesia. And Canada. It seemed they had just been holding it in all these years.

Within minutes of the spaceman's message, society began to edge toward chaos. In Manhattan, the streets were filled with two groups of people: those trying to get out of Manhattan, and those trying to keep them in. Messages broadcast on loudspeakers, begging residents to remain calm and stay indoors. But those who were more inclined to stay calm and remain indoors were already remaining calm and staying indoors, and the troublemakers out on the streets weren't about to miss out on the action.

All the commotion in New York was making it quite difficult for the black town car to navigate toward the 13th Precinct. Thankfully for the four men inside, the streets had become less crowded as the night wore on and many of the rowdier citizens grew weary of freaking out and went to bed to refresh themselves for a new day of freaking out.

The town car stopped and idled outside the police station. Three of the men got out and walked up the stairs and into the old brick building. The station was a madhouse. Police officers were scrambling about everywhere, swat team members were assembling and suiting up, and people in custody were fearfully screaming about things that just a day earlier would have been chalked up to delusional nonsense. It seemed as if the population of the entire city had been turned into alien-conspiracy-touting paranoid schizophrenics in an instant.

A female officer at the front desk called out to the three men in suits as they crossed the lobby. "Can I help you gentlemen?"

The suited man in front spoke. "My name is Davis, we are with—" Before he could continue, two officers screamed "Move!" as they dragged a clawing, bleeding man across the floor between the suited visitors.

"I'm sorry, sir," the officer said as her eyes followed the chaos around the room, "but we're in an emergency lockdown right now, and I'm going to need you to move to the side and wait until someone can help you."

Davis calmly surveyed the disorganized madness and then pressed a button on his lapel. The officer shrieked and grabbed her head a split second before everyone else in the room followed suit, and joined her in their drop to the ground.

The three suited men walked uncontested through the security checkpoint and stepped around the writhing people. Davis walked to the security door and put a small device onto the lock. It clicked open, and the three men walked in.

The hallways were filled with more people frantically wriggling like salmon on the deck of an Alaskan trawler. Davis kneeled down next to an older woman in a suit expensive enough to announce that she wasn't just another detective. He touched her on the neck. She stopped clutching her ears.

"What—what happened?"

Davis looked into the woman's eyes for a moment. "Where is James Jefferson?"

"What?"

Davis touched her neck again and she curled back up in agony. "Six!" was all she could scream through her clenched teeth.

The three men walked to the elevator, chose the floor they needed, and rode up. The elevator doors opened to another scene of incapacitated humans, and the men walked to block six. Davis looked through the tiny window of a cell and saw a man bucking around in the corner. He placed his electronic lockpick over the cell latch, and again it performed its unlocking duties effortlessly.

Davis walked over and touched Crash on the neck, and the rugged man stopped struggling. "The hell are you?" Crash managed to get out.

"We're from an agency called Level 7. More importantly, we believe you."

The men backed up slightly and Crash pulled himself onto his bunk. "There's some shit going down," he said between gulps of air.

"The world is about to change, Mr. Jefferson," said Davis. "We'd like to know where you've been for the past twenty-four hours."

"So would I."

"We need your help."

Crash, bracing himself upright, stared up at the men. "Why should I trust you?"

"The beings landing here tomorrow aren't here to be your

friends," Davis replied nonchalantly.

"*My* friends? What do you mean, what about you—"

"We have air clearance," one of the other men interrupted. "The helicopter is landing on the roof in five minutes."

Chapter 29

The creature hadn't been sure of what it had sensed. Hadn't been confident in what it had felt. It had been so long since it had communicated with a receptive being, it couldn't help but second-guess the possibilities. But the leviathan had to make a choice. Had to decide to either fall back into deep hibernation to conserve energy, or take the risk of burning through the last of its fat reserves for the slight chance that what it had sensed hadn't just been a fluke. *What is the point*, it thought, *of dying slowly, if I now have hope to remain alive?*

And so the creature remained awake.

The spike returned. The slight tickle of the brain. The warm feeling behind the eyes. More and more, the creature felt the sensations, and it knew the beings were drawing nearer. *They are coming close enough to be useful.*

In its excitement, the creature burped out a small bubble of oxygen through the breathing pipe jammed into its airway.

They should have destroyed me when they had the chance.

CHAPTER 30

Crash took in the people around the table where he was seated. There was an important-looking older military-type guy, a woman who reminded Crash of a journalist he once hooked up with in Vietnam while recovering from bird flu, and some guy wearing a silly-looking bicycle-helmet thingy with wires hanging out of it.

Helmet guy flipped his goggles up and the woman spoke.

"Mr. Jefferson—"

"Call me Crash. Everyone calls me Crash."

"Crash. My name is Commander Ahn."

"Ahn. Like 'on' your feet."

"Uh. Yes. Like that. Sitting at the front of the room is Jordan. Across from you is Dr. Faraday."

Commander Ahn and Jordan filled Crash in on the details they had shared with Faraday, and Crash filled them in on what he felt like sharing with them, which was pretty much everything except the parts where he did things that didn't hold true to his well-groomed image, like punching himself out while trying to take revenge on a defenseless animal.

"And in the blink of an eye you were first in an empty room, and then in a different room with those strange creatures," Ahn said.

"Yeah, and I felt them trying to rape my brain. I felt violated."

"They can't actually read human minds, they can only communicate telepathically, and only if they've previously implanted you with a chip," Ahn responded as professionally as possible.

Faraday stifled a whine, then leaked it anyway before saying, "Hey, how come you didn't tell *me* that?"

"I did," replied Commander Ahn. "I told you when you first got here, 'At least we didn't put a chip in your head.'"

"I thought you were joking!"

"We gave you tiny robots that ate your brain and turned you into a computer. Why would you think I was joking?"

Jordan sighed in resignation. "Enough. Here's what I can tell both of you right now. I'm telling you, Dr. Faraday, because you now need to know. And I'm telling you, Mr. Jefferson, because I like your show."

"Thank you," replied Crash, beaming.

"You're welcome."

Faraday winced, miffed that Crash was receiving the star treatment, especially after the scientist had been belittled during his own first meeting in the conference room.

"I like your show," Jordan said again.

"Yeah, uh. Thanks," said Crash, not quite sure why it had been brought up again.

"I *likelikelikelikelikelike* your show," Jordan stuttered robotically.

Crash looked over at Commander Ahn, but she had just as much confusion on her own face. He met eyes with the scientist, and Faraday shrugged.

"These beings have already been here in small numbers," Jordan abruptly continued, back on track.

What the fuck? Crash thought.

But Jordan carried on as if nothing had happened. "We think they established multiple hidden bases around the world decades ago, for the purpose of studying us. They've obviously been experimenting here, as Mr. Jefferson has witnessed in the Amazon base with the giant rat."

"Capybara," replied Crash, thoughts still lingering on the strange verbal breakdown he just witnessed.

"Yes. As I was saying, things would have been much different had we known about this base even a week ago, but now we have neither the time nor the resources to investigate it further."

Faraday chimed in, deciding to move past Jordan's strange lapse. "Even so, there is some good information here. These 'transfer booths' you're talking about are fascinating. Instant teleportation, but it seems only within their own network. They can't just go wherever they'd like. Only from one booth to another."

"Precisely," replied Jordan. "Very advanced, but still quite limited."

"Still. Incredible nonetheless."

Crash massaged the bruised flesh on his hand caused by having the head-carrying satchel wound so tightly around his palm. "What do they want with us?"

"We think they need water," Jordan continued. "They are

very dependent on water, even more so than humans. We don't know if it's because their home world is out of it, or if intergalactic travel has dried them out. But we think they want water. Lots of it."

Glances bounced around the room, ricocheting from one face to the next.

"And we also know one more big piece of information about them. They want Earth's women."

There was a moment of silence.

"How do you know that?" Crash prodded.

Commander Ahn jumped in. "Dr. Faraday found a secret message embedded in a viral video that has spread around the planet. The message persuades on a very deep psychological level, but long story short, it basically programs Earth's women to lust after alien octopuses."

"Holy *shit*. That's exactly what I beat the hell out of!" rumbled Crash. "Those passive-aggressive motherfuckers. They know they can't compete for our women, so they're druggin' 'em. They're brainwashin' 'em!" Crash pounded his fist into his palm in anger. "I'll be goddammed if some space octopus lays a hand on any beautiful Earth women."

Chapter 31

Faraday was finding it progressively difficult to stay focused on action outside of his head. By the time the facts ran dry and Crash's stories became a braggart's tale, Faraday found himself more interested in the puzzle that nagged at the back of his mind.

"We work for no government, but are involved with them all," was what he was told when he first met with Level 7 so many years earlier.

Faraday had become quite good at filtering the noise in his head, and very good indeed at cross-referencing and digging deep into search results within his own mind. *So why haven't I come across a single clue about this operation? Why is Jordan a complete blank? Am I behind a firewall? What don't they want me to know?*

Furthermore, he couldn't even find any crazy conspiracy information about Level 7. No message boards, no paranoid blog posts, no mentions of anything out of the ordinary that even resembled "Level 7 organization." Area 51: twenty-eight-point-six-million results. Groom Lake, three hundred and fifty thousand results. Level 7, nothing.

He tried to start fresh in his thinking about his current situation. The windowless building he was in, as far as he could remember from the location, was registered to a local credit union, and there were no accessible records that led him anywhere. *Whoever these people are, they really are top secret, and it bothers me that this is so hard. But, shouldn't it be? If they're top secret, shouldn't they be hard to figure out?*

"What's the latest?" said Jordan.

Yanked out of his thoughts, Faraday blinked twice and stared blankly across the table.

"Well?"

"Scanning now," he said.

Faraday scoured live feeds from across the globe for anything that would provide him and Level 7 with instant updates, but most of the media that caught his mind's eye was from routine press conferences from various world leaders. The one he'd just found was of great interest; the US President was finishing up his first public address on the situation.

"—and although this is an unprecedented event in our country's history, as well as in the course of our species as a whole, we will remain calm, and we will act as a beacon of light, showing the visitors the best example possible of who we really are as a united, human race. Thank you. There will be no questions."

And then he felt it. A trend hit Faraday's mind, and he knew it was time for action. A light buzz started to build, and within a few seconds he was filtering through reported sightings of a saucer-shaped UFO cruising along the eastern seaboard. Blurry camera phone pictures started popping up, taken by the kinds of people that usually chopped their photographed friends' arms off with poor picture-framing skills.

Before long, however, a high-quality picture crystalized, and then another. *It's definitely saucer-shaped.* Then a shaky video appeared, and in the period of the minute Faraday had seen the newest information that anyone else on Earth had seen he thought, *I have the consciousness of God*. Although he was pretty sure God didn't have to wear a contraption on his head that looked like a hair dryer from an *I Love Lucy* episode. He flicked the switch to turn on the scalp massager as he prepared to broadcast his thoughts to the room. *Ahhh. Quite the invention*. But then he frowned. *I wonder if I'll ever invent things for Trevor again*.

Since being given the live feed of Trevor's playroom, Faraday hadn't drifted from it for more than a few minutes at a time. His mind could only handle about a dozen streams of information at once, but this was usually one of them. When there wasn't breaking news of a saucer landing, at least.

Faraday's entire chair at the conference room table had been replaced with the hair dryer's new extension, giving him a more complex rig that had extra padding and braces to keep him still and supported. As the members of Level 7 looked on, he pulled the goggles down from the half dome and plugged the wires into jacks in the armrests. With a quick burst of preemptive static, his thoughts were projected into the hologram floating above the table. Images, videos, tweets, and status updates regarding the saucer all poured out of his head just as they happened in cyberspace.

The saucer only took a few minutes to fly from Atlanta, where it had first been sighted, to New York City. The three around the conference table watched with unblinking eyes as live news streams and eyewitness updates flashed into existence in front of them. Faraday was becoming particularly adept at developing a rhythm of filtration; information that was bunk or less important only flickered through, while more meaningful content became larger and moved toward the center of the projection as it became more relevant.

Commander Ahn cast a smile at the super-brained scientist. "I knew you would get it. No one else could do it. No one else could develop a working way to filter the bad from the good. I knew you'd be the one."

But Faraday didn't hear her. She was filtered out, just like the other unimportant messages. The room buzzed while different angles of the saucer appeared, until almost every stream in the projection looked the same as it all converged into one event—the saucer stopped its travels across the sky and settled above Central Park.

Gawkers and loonies below the arriving craft screamed and yelled and whooped and hollered while they scattered out like ants from a nest doused with kerosene. The saucer waited graciously until everyone had safely moved far enough away, and then it landed.

Several news outlets had assumed correctly that the spacemen would land in Central Park, since it was the only open area large enough in the city of concrete. Those news stations broadcast the arrival to the rest of the world, and billions of people watched as the perfectly round craft hovered a moment and then landed right in the middle of Manhattan Island.

All eyes were on the disc, and the eyes in the Level 7 conference room were no exception. Broadcasters provided endless commentary on what was happening, what could happen, and what had happened, and all the stations had their own panel of experts that tried to provide insight into the situation, from what to do if the visitors were hostile to what to do if one showed up on your doorstep and needed to borrow a cup of ammonium nitrate.

The world watched in anticipation, wondering what would happen next. Well, most of the world. But not Crash, because he was locked up in a cell. Again.

They told him they had a luxury suite for him, and that there would be a giant breakfast of eggs and sausage. And he was starving and he loved eggs and sausage, so of course he went. In fact, it even smelled like eggs and sausage when he was being led by the suit guy down the hall past all the people doing oddly normal things for a top-secret base.

Crash turned the corner, felt a shove on his back, got pushed into a dark room, and once again found himself imprisoned, and once again for reasons unknown.

"Okay, what the *fuck*?"

CHAPTER 32

Thousands of people had rushed to Central Park once they heard that the saucer had landed there. Thousands of people from all walks of life, rich people seeking answers, poor people seeking answers, regular people seeking kicks, wizened people knowing their world had just changed forever, idiotic people attracted to the shininess of it all.

And Jennica!

Dressed down in a hoodie and sweats with giant bug-eye glasses covering half her face, hardly any of her skin showed. She knew all too well the perils of being recognized in public when she didn't want to be.

Jennica! had snuck her way from the hotel to the park, all the while trying to elicit some sort of response from her prince. She tried focusing really hard on a mental image of him, but that didn't work. She tried screaming thoughts at him, but that didn't work either. *Maybe if I try super hard.* She scrunched up her nose, opened her mouth, and screamed silently to the one that had called to her and promised a life where she could finally feel like she belonged, but again, nothing.

The streets were teeming, as they had been since the world found out it had neighbors, but it wasn't nearly as dangerous outside as Jennica! thought it might be. And in all the confusion, nobody paid much attention to the small superstar in sweats who was jogging her way toward the park. When she galloped against traffic across 5th Avenue, her heart raced. She could feel her destiny awaiting just ahead in time and space. Her pace quickened while she crossed Central Park and came to the clearing and then there it was, on the other side of a mass of people. And he knew, and finally answered her call.

You're here.

Yes!

I will come for you shortly. Wait for me.

Jennica! stifled a squeal.

• • •

Grammeral Zeezak stood solemnly in his cabin, packed into his human fleshsuit, knowing that billions of humans watched the saucer either via live broadcast or in person, wondering what unfathomable possibilities could be occurring inside the craft. He looked at himself in a reflecting glass and attempted a smile. It ended up looking like a man holding back a fart at his girlfriend's parents' dinner table.

"Smiling is a nightmare," he said.

His trusted Sentlent Bool was at his side, where they both preferred him to be.

"It is hard for me as well, my Lord."

"How do those snerched humans do it?"

"I don't know, my Lord."

"There must be a trigger. When we were discussing my favorite meats as we entered this galaxy, a strange feeling came over me and I felt the lips of my mouth stretch tightly. Do you think that was the beginnings of a smile, Sentlent?"

"Perhaps, my Lord."

Grammeral Zeezak continued his smiling practice in the reflecting glass. Sentlent Bool tried his smile out as well and failed terribly, his human lips looking like a quivering animal in the throes of death.

"Is it truly necessary for us to perfect this, my Lord?"

Grammeral Zeezak didn't answer for a moment. Then he looked away from the reflecting glass and toward his Sentlent.

"We have research. Multitudes of research. The smile is the most disarming psychological weapon humans have. We could march out right now and promise the secrets of the universe with a frown, and those snerched humans would open fire on us with their defense forces. But I could walk out and violate one of their world leaders at the foot of our ship, and as long as I was smiling, nothing bad would happen to us. It's all in the research."

"That sounds very illogical, my Lord."

"Doesn't it, though."

The two "men" continued their smiling practice inside the saucer while the people of Earth continued to wait in anticipation.

• • •

Social networking sites were flooded with millions of pictures, videos, and updates about the saucer. Twitter couldn't stay up, and Facebook's server farm was running so hot the air conditioner almost burned out to keep things cool. Even Faraday noticed a slight fever as he tried to keep up with the overload of information.

The warmth flushed to hot, hot heat, and he began to

sweat. Within a few seconds, his eyes rolled back into his head and he convulsed violently while thousands of live streams flew across the digital hologram.

"What's going on? Unplug him! *Now!*" Jordan yelled to Commander Ahn.

But before she could reach over and pull the plug on Faraday's hair dryer, his convulsions stopped and the holo focused.

"*Look,*" said Ahn.

Faraday's eyes rolled back down, and he cast his gaze upon what his mind was projecting; people were yelling and running amok in Central Park, and then all at once, they stopped.

The saucer was moving.

• • •

Since the spaceship landed, a few dumb people had actually dared to touch it. There was no protective shield around the vessel, and seemingly no immediate consequence to those who wanted a dangerously close look. It took a human with a lot of guts and no brains to be the first to break the police lines. He ran like a maniac the twenty meters from the barricade to the saucer, slapped it loud enough to make a noise that was audible on his friend's camera, then ran back to the safety of the masses.

Once the first person broke the barricade of fear, others followed. Soon, the police and National Guard had their hands full with people tempting fate for a photo op. #UFOSELFIE became the most viewed trend in the history of online media, followed by #UFOduckface and #saucerslut. For a few hours, the world had taken the most significant event in modern history and made it as superficial as a Kardashian sighting.

And then the saucer opened.

It started with a dot that appeared on the bottom bulge of the hull, and then the dot turned into a line, and the line traced a rectangle about three meters tall by two meters wide in a few seconds' time. When the rectangle was complete, the panel popped out and descended into a ramp to the ground.

And the whole world watched.

It was forever. It was seconds. The crowd stepped back. Armed officers stood tense, but without specific aim. Movement flickered just inside the new opening. Metal glinted. And then *they* marched down. Eight-foot-tall robots, with legs and arms of thick hoses, and cylindrical bodies like massive vacuum canisters, marched two at a time down the platform. Twelve lurched out and formed a corridor three meters wide on the ground in front of the saucer.

And the whole world watched.

The robots looked nothing like the humanoid that had televised himself the night before. The gathered people grew antsy. Triggers were massaged.

Strange and simple, with clunky bodies and big glowing red dots in the centers of their torsos, the odd look of the robots added to the fear factor, and the size they presented was threatening.

Before anything could accidentally get harmed one way or another, however, humanoids did exit the saucer and walk down through the giant robot aisle. There were three of them, and they were tiny next to the robots.

They looked bigger on television, thought Faraday in a way that wasn't projected to the others while he watched live from his hair dryer chair.

The three walked in a V formation. Hairless heads, bronze skin, and frilly purple jumpsuits on bodies five feet tall, the aliens walked out past the robot lines. The spaceman in front spoke with a big, crooked smile.

"Hello."

"Stern rules!" yelled someone from the back. The shout was followed by the sounds of tackling.

"I am Grammeral Q'Shin Zeezak, leader of this expedition to your planet. To my left is Sentlent Bool, my second-in-command, and to my right, Kreev. These machines that surround us are the volkites. Please do not fear them. They are only here to protect us."

As if on cue, a strung-out-looking hipster with a raggedy beard threw a beer bottle at one of the volkites. Before the bottle could make contact, the volkite swept its metal claw of a hand through the air and shattered the bottle to pieces. The world gasped all at once as a collective thought of *Holy shit some asshole just caused Armageddon* crossed everyone's minds. But the visitors were understanding.

"As you can see, the volkites are programmed to do no harm, but are highly effective at defensive maneuvers. We too, have ... overly excited individuals ... in our population."

The world exhaled together.

"We are called Vyperians," Grammeral Zeezak continued. "We have traveled halfway across this shared galaxy in an effort to meet with you, the humans. We hope we can learn much from you, and you from us. We have been watching you from afar for some time, and this meeting is the culmination of all our efforts throughout history to travel here. Let us work together for the common goals of peace and our undoubtedly similar quests for truth and knowledge!" The Central Park crowd cheered. A drunk man threw up on the side of the saucer.

"For now, all we request is an assembly with your world's leader. We shall await that meeting from inside our vessel. Thank you."

The Vyperians retreated into the saucer and were followed by half of the volkites. The anxious crowd stared in a combination of awe, fear, and need for sensory fulfillment, and a few people attempted to breach the police line to get closer to the remaining volkites and the saucer. One small thing in hooded sweats tried to push through the blockade, but was stopped by a large NYPD officer before she could break free.

"Whoa, whoa. Sorry, young lady, but you can't go any farther."

She pulled off her glasses and looked up at the officer with the kind of doe eyes that whispered innocence and naiveté in the headlights of her own destruction. "Please, I have to get on that thing."

The officer chuckled as he held her back. "You need to head back home and sober up, young lady." He stared for a moment. "Wait, I know you."

As Jennica! realized she had been made, she wrenched free from the officer's grasp and bolted back into the safety of the thick crowd.

"Wait!" the officer yelled. "You shouldn't be here by yourself. It's too danger—" But his words were drowned out by the screams of the mob.

CHAPTER 33

Time to leave, Senator. Bring the box.

Mike Horton dropped his spoon and applesauce splattered across the coffee table. He looked away from the television and toward his wife.

"They just gave word. I think I have to go to New York."

No, Senator. You have to go to Disneyland.

• • •

Faraday had settled somewhat from the information overload and was now steadily monitoring the alien visitors. The saucer was still in Central Park, and nothing of significance had developed since the visitor's announcement.

Meanwhile, world leaders were at each other's throats trying to determine which of them would be the first ambassador to reach out to the Vyperians. The alien in charge hadn't specified anything other than "your world's leader," and that vague statement was causing an uproar at the United Nations.

The United States Government argued it should undoubtedly be their president who met the aliens first, since the landing was on US soil, but there was a kink in that the US President was currently in London. He was being rushed to his plane, but it would still be hours before Air Force One could make it back stateside, and that left the door open for countless other nations to make a convincing argument.

Tempers were flaring, especially amongst countries with no chance. Equatorial Guinea and Uganda were being specifically nasty to each other, while France was all but demanding the opportunity to represent. China and Russia made convincing arguments about being on the upswing of the new industrial and technological revolutions, but the United States won out, and it was agreed that the US President would be the face of world peace for the world that didn't have the slightest clue about world peace. A messenger party was sent to the saucer to inform the Vyperians that the advocate for Earth would be arriving in the afternoon.

• • •

Faraday flipped his goggles up and the holo vanished from the center of the room. "I need a break."

"A break? From what?" replied Jordan. "You've just been sitting there."

Faraday sighed. "I've got to do something else. I've been plugged into this thing for a long time. I need a break. My brain needs a break."

Jordan snarled his response. "Fine. But if the world goes to shit while you're on a break, I'll personally kick your ass. Commander, please escort Dr. Faraday to the lab. Show him one of the toys you're working on."

Faraday unplugged and got up out of his hair dryer. He followed Ahn out of the conference room and was struck by an odd thought. *I haven't seen Jordan outside of this space.* He rubbed the part of his head where the helmet usually rested.

Then again, this is the war room. This is where he'll probably eat and sleep. He tried to talk himself out of his paranoia. The anxiety was straining his ability to focus and keep out unwanted streams. *But something is definitely off about this whole thing.* He let his eye line casually cross past the people in the hallways. *They're doing ... nothing. As if they're robots programmed to do the mundane.*

He thought of the conference room again. *Jordan never moved from the head of the table. He never even walked around. He's been in the same place since I first got here....* Faraday felt a chill.

Commander Ahn had sensed something was wrong, and was stopped outside the lab door and staring at him. Being deep inside his own head, he hadn't noticed.

"Is there a problem, Frank?"

He blinked. "No, no. It's just, I'm still getting used to this damn new skill of mine."

"Oh?"

"While we were walking over here, I somehow got stuck on nudibranchs, er, sea slugs, and I know more about them now than I think I could ever give a damn about." He gulped. *I wish I were a better liar.*

Ahn smiled slightly. "That brain of yours certainly is a marvel, isn't it?"

She dropped her shoulders slightly and pressed the button on the door, and it slid open. Faraday breathed in relief and looked across the lab. Everyone was in the same position, doing the same things they'd been doing the day before. More chills crept in, and his heart weighed heavy as he thought of his son. He checked back in to the live stream and saw that Trevor still played that damned game, and was all smiley and happy and ... not right. Trevor was never that happy. *Something is very wrong.* He started to panic. He could feel his heart palpitate, and the skin on his body became hypersensitive as adrenaline pumped.

"I'd like to show you something," said Commander Ahn.

His throat was completely dry, but he squeezed out a "Sure." They walked past the eerily unchanged lab workers and to a table. A gun rested on it. An exceedingly large gun. Faraday gulped dryly and forced spit onto his tongue to unstick it from the roof of his mouth. "Commander Ahn, where, uh, what happened to Crash?"

Ahn picked up the gun and pointed it at him.

"Time for your next lesson, Doctor."

Chapter 34

Faraday stood at the end of the giant gun barrel. Commander Ahn waved it back and forth.

"Care to make a hyper-educated guess as to what this is, Doctor?"

In his panic, he found it hard to focus, but he tightened up his thoughts and found a breadcrumb to follow. "If I'm just making an educated guess, I'd say it's some sort of nonlethal subsonic device that works on a lot of people at once. Renders them immobile for a time."

"Not just people." The words and the way she said them brought a slight sense of peace to him.

Ahn put the gun back down on the table.

"So what does it do?"

"You'll know soon enough. Let's get to work."

Faraday stopped in his tracks. *It's now or never.* "No. I want to know what's going on. Everything. Maybe you don't think I need to know, but I—"

He dropped to his knees. He had to. Pain ricocheted back and forth between his temples and he gripped his ears. The agony lasted only a few seconds, but it was the worst few seconds of physical misery he had ever felt. A dozen root canals at once. And he understood immediately what the pain meant. *Playtime is over, and they have complete control.*

Commander Ahn's expression hadn't changed. "Come,

Doctor. We have work to do. I need that reprogrammed immediately." She was pointing at what looked like a phone booth in
the far corner of the lab.

Faraday rose slowly to his feet, barely noticing that no one
else around him in the lab had bothered to react to what had
happened.

"I ... I want to see my son."

"I'm afraid that's not possible."

"Please. What do I—" The brain pain hit him again.

"I'm sorry, Frank, but you should have stopped asking
questions a while ago."

"I'm a fucking scientist, what did you expect?" he screamed
through gritted teeth.

He got another zap in the head.

$$\bullet \ \bullet \ \bullet$$

*What the hell have I done in my life to deserve this? I enter-
tain people for a living. Shit, I've never done anything that
bad. I mean, it's not like I've killed anyone. Well, not on purpose, anyway. Sure, I made mistakes. But that's just being
human. Except now it's not just about being human. Now I'm
in the middle of some fight against aliens and I keep getting
stuck in metal cages. And I lost my best friend's head.*

Where the hell is Will's head, anyway? Crash winced at
the thought. He remembered dropping it after being tasered by
the NYPD, but his memories were blurry after that. Scattered.
*Too much craziness going on. Like the tapir expedition during
the Burmese military conflicts.* He could only hope Will's head
had been given a proper burial.

Except aliens just fucking landed and who has time to bury a head somewhere? It's probably rotting in the Dumpster behind the police station.

Crash chewed on his fingers in a mindless anger. He sat up from his cot and looked around his cell. Not that there was anything to look at. *Wait, there is.* A plate of food sat near the door. He'd only really eaten once since the jungle. He scrambled over to it and grabbed the tray. It looked like leftovers of what he'd eaten earlier, before becoming a prisoner for the third time in a week, but that was more than good enough.

He wolfed down the food and savored every last morsel, sliding his fingers into the corners of the metal tray and licking them clean. He blinked twice and clutched his stomach. And then he started vomiting blood.

I've vomited blood before. Bring it.

Chunky, bloody tissue erupted from his mouth and Crash felt as if his whole body was being torn apart. He collapsed into a heap and watched through dying eyes as his own flesh fell from bone like the meat from prizewinning ribs in the mouth of a glutton, and his arms and legs dissolved into pools of gelatin.

Holy fuck. Please God, please let this just be a bad trip. Oh God, were Crash Jefferson's final thoughts as his body bubbled down into a thick, fleshy pudding.

Chapter 35

Jennica! wanted so badly to see her love, wanted so badly to see him up close with her own eyes. Touch him with her hands. Taste him with her lips. Feel his suckery tentacles on her thighs.

Huh. That's a weird thought.

It *was* a weird thought. But not unwelcome to the young woman. She didn't quite understand the depths of her attraction other than that it was *destiny*, but Jennica! had a hunger that outweighed any logic that might have been holding her back, although those big robot men scared her, and she was leery of getting caught by someone in the crowd. All it would take was one person to recognize her, and she'd have to bolt back to the safety of her hotel room. So the pop star left the mass of frenzied people in wait for something to happen and went for a walk in a quieter area of the park.

Jennica! soon found it was all quiet. There wasn't a damn thing happening anywhere else in Central Park. She walked alone in the late morning by herself. She came to a bench, the sight of which left her insides tickled with a fuzzy feeling. The pop princess sat down and reminisced way, way back, and remembered sitting in that exact place the first time her family came to New York, long before she was famous. She closed her eyes and soaked in the warmth of familiarity and the coziness of safety, and pulled the hood back from her head. No one was nearby, and if someone did stumble across her, she didn't care at that moment.

She stretched her legs out and smiled, her eyes still closed. It was the most comfortable she'd felt in this much of a public space in years.

"I did it just for you, you know."

Jennica! leaped up off the bench and almost twisted her knee in surprise. She looked to her left where the voice had come from.

He is here. My Prince is here.

"Oh, my God!" Jennica! squealed. He was everything she had imagined, although fairly short. In fact, he was barely as tall as she was. But everything else was there, as she'd seen—a beautiful bald head, bronzed skin, and a wonderfully crooked smile that only grew bigger as she ran the ten feet to him and jumped into his arms.

"I've waited for this day my entire life," she sobbed.

"I've crossed the galaxy for you," he whispered back monotonously through the locks of her golden hair while she nuzzled his neck.

Jennica! tried to talk, but her words got caught somewhere between her larynx and lips.

You don't have to speak. I can feel your love.

She smiled and kissed her prince softly on his lips, and then his cheek, and then back to his lips again.

I have so much to tell you, he thought-spoke to her.

All I care about is that you're here with me right now, she thought-replied.

Yes, of course my love. But I also have so many things that you've never seen before. Things that will change your life forever.

Cool. Can we just, like, make out for a while?

Errr. If you wish it.

The short, bald, bronze man and the superstar embraced and kissed passionately in the middle of the city that never stopped but kinda had, and just for them in that moment. But while Jennica! was melting into the embrace of her fantasy man from space, her fantasy man from space was thinking of bigger things. Although the Earth girl's mouth was very soft and strangely addictive.

Maybe just a little bit more Earth kissing. There aren't any other humans around—

Jennica! ensnared Grammeral Zeezak's tongue with her own and showed him what an Earth girl was capable of.

Perhaps directive zero-two doesn't need to begin just yet.

She rolled the tip of her tongue gently around the inside of his human mouth.

Yes, more kissing it shall be.

Then Jennica! did a thing with her hands where she somehow managed to scratch his back with her nails and rub it with her palms all in one movement. Q'Shin Zeezak was hooked.

What an unexpected delight.

• • •

Crash woke up and that surprised him, considering his last memories were of his own body dissolving. He sat up and saw that he was still in the latest jail cell.

"Goddammit!"

He walked over to the door and raised up his fists and, not

giving a damn if he broke bones in the process, he slammed into the metal door as hard as he could in frustration. And stood in shock as the door recoiled off its hinges and flew ten feet back.

What the hell?

He walked slowly out. The Asian woman he'd seen earlier was waiting outside, and smiling at him.

"What the hell is going on?" he demanded.

"The short answer is, you now have the strength of a hundred men."

"Excuse me?"

Crash held his hands out. They did look slightly meatier. He had marks on the bottoms of his fists where he made contact with the metal door, and felt a dull yet powerful soreness in the bones of his hands. He watched as the red marks blended back into the pinkish color of his flesh. And then the pain just slipped off, like old skin from a shedding snake. Hands still out, he looked back up at the Asian woman.

"I'm invincible?"

"Not quite. As long as you don't accrue fatal damage, you can regenerate. But you're just as susceptible to a shot to the brain or a fall from twenty stories as anyone else. However, as long your injury doesn't kill you, it will in fact heal almost instantly."

Crash licked his lips. "Anything else I can do?"

"That about sums it up, but I'm sure you have many questions about the nanotechnology that—"

"Nope, get the fuck out of my way, I'm out of here."

He made it halfway to the door before he was nailed between the ears by a sharp pain that dropped him to the ground.

"I'm afraid it doesn't work that way, Mr. Jefferson. You promised your help, and we need it. Your cooperation from here on out is much appreciated."

Crash whimpered on the floor, but Commander Ahn showed no sympathy for the three-time Emmy winner.

• • •

They took a break from their passionate kissing just long enough to rest their tongues. Jennica! sat on the park bench in the midst of the stillness, nestled in the arms of her lover.

"How did you sneak out?" she cooed.

"The back door."

Her eyes lit up. "That's so *cooooool!*"

The woman traced her small fingers around her lover's wide-open mouth.

He thought about how empty-minded she was. Although ... *Her physical beauty is striking.*

It was all a strange, new experience for Grammeral Q'Shin Zeezak. Peering down the slightly unzipped hoodie of the Earth female beside him, the octopus could feel a tingling. His logical brain couldn't understand it, but his Vyperian body felt warm inside the human fleshsuit. Like a warm, delicious lava. And nothing could have prepared him for how soft the female human felt in his arms.

She looked up at him with her big, brown eyes. "Are you looking down my top?"

"What? No." Grammeral Zeezak's tentacle tips shriveled inside the human sack they were crammed in while the alien experienced another new feeling, one of sexual embarrassment. *Why am I feeling this shame? I am the Second Tentacle of the Emperor! World leaders bow before me!*

"You totally are! You're looking at my tits!"

Zeezak felt his face flush and his genitals tingle underneath the fleshsuit. *What is happening to me? How can one human female hold so much power over my actions?*

"It's okay!" Jennica! giggled. She looked around to see if anyone was near, and then pulled the zipper down until her silky bra was exposed. Grammeral Zeezak's human jaw dropped so low that his fleshsuit almost slipped off his face.

Sweet nectar of marment. This is truly one of the miracles of the universe. It is perhaps greater than even the undead ice dragon on Narduuk or the singing comet of System X.

He dove into her open top and slobbered his way across the peaks of her mountains. *Emperor be blessed! This is truly a day of days!*

Jennica! moaned and her eyes rolled back into her head as the bald spaceman's tongue and wet nose tickled across her upper chest. He unzipped her hoodie all the way and roamed across her exposed stomach. She moaned louder, and Zeezak rolled one of his legs over hers. They held tighter and kissed harder, his hands exploring her body and her body enjoying the touch. Frenzy overtook him, and his fleshsuit bulged, showing a hint of his true shape. Tentacles snuck out the back of the humanoid bag and roamed over Jennica!'s body, cradling it in a net of slimy desire. Blinded by programmed lust, the pop star melted into the wild sensation.

Jennica! heard a pop, opened her eyes, and saw her alien lover for the first time in his true form as he shook off the wrinkled fleshsuit. Her breathing slowed and her lips trembled. Grammeral Zeezak retained his composure just enough to realize that directive zero-one—the persuasion of Earth's women to Vyperian attraction—was now being fully tested. But Jennica! stood firm, and a smile escaped her lips. The Earth woman before him lusted not just after his human form, but his true form as well.

Directive zero-one is a success.

Pulling his princess closer, Zeezak used two of his free tentacles to gather leaves and form a coupling nest next to the bench while his beak lightly pinched his lover's tender skin. Jennica! was in heaven, enraptured by subconscious desires. Zeezak used his body's slime as a lubricant, sliding suckers across the arms and neck of his lover, and then dripped the excess onto the bed of leaves to hold it together for the dry-land mating process.

I think this is how they do it.

The alien caught Jennica! casting a wary glance at the gooey mound of dead foliage.

Snerch! Perhaps I should have done more research.

Zeezak was snapped back into the present as Jennica! massaged his fourth tentacle, and the warmth inside of him rose to an undeniable boil.

Ah! I can wait no longer. The slime leaf pile will have to do.

He stared deeply into her eyes with his perfectly round orbs and prepared to throw his Earth female into the leaves. The moment was perfect. *At last, I shall have my Earth princess.*

RETURN TO SAUCER IMMEDIATELY.

No! Not now!

Grammeral Zeezak's wide eyes widened more as the telepathic message of alarm echoed inside his mind. He pulled his body back into the fleshsuit with surprising quickness, bouncing back into human form. The movement startled Jennica!, and she reached out to grasp the repacked human body of her new lover.

"What's wrong?" she cried out. Zeezak gently deflected the singer's embrace and rose from the bench.

"I ... must return to my ship."

"What? Why? *Now*?"

"I will come back for you."

"When!"

"Tonight. I promise. I will find you."

Before Jennica! could argue, Zeezak bolted into the awkward sprint of a man trying to remember how to run.

Jennica! wiped her tearing eyes on the sleeve of her hoodie, and zipped it back up as she watched her dream lover run off, abandoning her when she needed him most like so many others had. But he wasn't running toward his ship. He was running away from it.

• • •

Jennica! watched her beautiful spaceman run until he was out of her sight, and then she plopped back down on the park bench. Her soul ached already, and her prince had only been gone for a minute. She pulled up her hood and yanked her sleeves down. There was still a thin spread of slime across the body parts where Grammeral Zeezak had massaged her with his appendages. It didn't seem nearly as attractive to Jennica!

as it had when he was touching her. And it smelled like oil and cleaning supplies.

Wham. A terrible pain pierced Jennica!'s skull, and the physical shock of it made her fall off the bench as she clawed at her head. She screamed in her mind for her prince to return, but there was no response. A blur of men in suits slap-wrapped plastic strips around her wrists and ankles, and they snapped shut like manacles. The brain pain left as quickly as it had come when a gag was stuffed into her mouth. The men hoisted her up, and one of them slung her over his shoulder as the man in front said, "If you're trying to communicate with the alien, don't bother. We're blocking your signal."

Blocking my signal? thought Jennica! *I thought we were communicating with love!* And then she started to cry as someone slid a blindfold on.

• • •

Jennica! awoke in what looked to her like a playroom. There were toys scattered around, and a couple of big beanbag chairs and a large flat screen on the wall. A kid was playing video games on it.

"Hey, kid."

"Hi," the boy replied without ever looking away from the game.

Jennica! sat up freely. Her restraints had been removed. She got up and walked over to the boy and sat down on the edge of a beanbag. "What's your name?"

"Trevor," he said, still without looking away.

"How long have you been here?"

"I dunno."

This kid sure likes his game. "Do you know how long I've been here?"

No answer.

"Hey, did you hear me?"

"Sorry, it's a really good game. I dunno ... I guess I fell asleep and you were here when I woke up." The boy couldn't pull himself away from the game enough to talk without pausing.

"Oh." Jennica! started watching the action on the screen. "Where am I?" she asked, but Trevor didn't answer, and Jennica! stopped caring after a moment.

"This game looks really good."

"Grab a controller."

She did, and she was hooked. She fired at a building with a giant cannon, and it exploded all across the screen and out into the room in 3-D.

"*Oh, my God.* That was *so* cool." Ten minutes in, and she had already forgotten about her prince, her fame, and her horrible childhood as the subliminally enhanced game lured her in. Jennica! had found her drug of choice.

CHAPTER 36

Grammeral Zeezak wished two things as he ran. He wished he could use his tentacles to run faster, and he wished he could have made it to at least what earthlings called third base with Jennica! before being beckoned to return to the saucer.

However, there were bigger things to worry about, such as why his telepathy wasn't working. Vyperian telepathy worked on line of sight unless one had an implant, which then allowed communication across a planet and even out into shallow space. As an officer, Grammeral Zeezak *did* have an implant, yet he heard no chatter and received no response when he tried to psychically inquire why he had received the urgent request to return.

Cut off from communication, the little man-alien had to return to the saucer, but the only way back was the same way he had emerged: from the decrepit transfer booth in the small park blocks away.

Zeezak had considered making an urgent attempt to return via the front ramp. *No,* he'd thought, *that would only raise dangerous questions.* As long as the people of Earth assumed the other-worlders were all on the ship, conditions would be stable for the time being. Humans couldn't find out that the Vyperians had the capability to roam the city as they pleased.

Zeezak jogged awkwardly yet unbothered across Manhattan, which lacked its usual midday buzz with most everyone focused on the spaceship. It took him no more than a few minutes to run to the public men's room that housed the old transfer booth. The bald man pushed open the rusty door and entered the dank bathroom to find the stall with the secret panel to the transfer booth occupied.

Great novae of Rigel. This is no time to wait for a human to complete his primeval task. Perhaps I should strangle him until his head pops. Zeezak dropped a tentacle from his fleshsuit. *No, that will only leave a mess and bring unwanted attention to this place.* His tentacle withdrew. He tapped on the stall door with a human hand.

"Excuse me," spoke Zeezak in his stilted Earth English.

"What," came the agitated reply from the other side of the stall door.

"Will you be much longer?"

"Fuck off."

Grammeral Zeezak was not used to being talked to with the tone of disrespect he detected in the human's voice. His true face flushed red with rage. Still, he kept himself in check. *I must maintain composure.* He called over the top of the stall again, "Apologies, but I must use this facility."

There was a pause before the man responded, "Use the other stall, weirdo."

"I require this one."

Through the door, Zeezak could hear frustration in the man's actions as he shuffled his feet and huffed.

"I take my first dump in a public bathroom in a year," croaked the man in the stall, "and I get a whack job outside trying to get into the dirty-ass shitter I'd pay good money to not have to be on right now. Well, you know what? Fuck you. I ate some bad Chinese and my shit is runny and it splattered all over the bottom of the seat, and I'm not going to clean it for you when I'm done, which I'm not even *close* to being, so you can just eat a sack of dicks be—"

Two tentacles blasted simultaneously over and under the stall door and wrapped around the shitting man like pythons on a goat, and before the man knew what had hit him, the tentacles squeezed his torso and pushed up so hard that his head popped swiftly off his body like the cork from a champagne bottle. Blood spewed everywhere.

Fool of a human. Now I have to get rid of this mess. Zeezak snaked the head in one tentacle, the body in another, and used a third to swipe in the invisicode on the wall behind the toilet. The panel slid open into a small room with a transfer booth hidden inside. Zeezak slithered in with the accumulated body parts and entered the transfer booth code for the ship, and instantly transported.

• • •

As soon as the brain pain ebbed from being zapped, Crash pulled himself up from the ground. He saw the scientist standing next to the Asian woman. Crash couldn't remember if the guy had been there since the TV host had forced his way out of the cell, or if the guy had walked in while Crash was writhing around on the ground. He didn't really care. He was about to ask a question when a flash of intense light leaked from the cracks of the weird phone booth in front of him, and the front of it slid open in a puff of burning ozone.

• • •

Grammeral Zeezak peered out of the transfer booth. In front of the alien stood, not his Sentlent Bool and a Vyperian welcoming party, but the besnerched human that had teleported to his ship from the jungle and cut down half a dozen of his warriors.

"What is this?" Zeezak clicked in surprise. Preparing for battle, he dropped the remnants of his bathroom victim and dropped his fleshsuit as well.

• • •

The sight of the transitioning octopus took both Faraday and Crash aback, but Commander Ahn remained calm as she gave a command. "Knock him out, Mr. Jefferson. Aim for the temples."

Crash had no problem with the order. In a blink, he cocked his fist back and walloped a single throw into the blob, effectively knocking it unconscious and leaving it quivering on the floor. Blood poured out of the decapitated body of the human that Zeezak had pulled through the teleportation, leaving the room a mess of flesh, blood, and slime.

"They really do look like octopuses," Faraday said, seeing the Vyperian in its true form for the first time.

"Yes," answered Commander Ahn.

"You've known for longer than you let on. Before Crash ever mentioned seeing them," Faraday pressed.

Ahn stared blankly before answering as men in suits entered the lab to clean up the mess on the floor. "We've been familiar with the Vyperians for a long time now."

Crash looked quizzically over at Faraday as Ahn continued. "As a matter of fact, the real reason they're here is because of us."

The two men shared another glance, and Crash moved aggressively toward the woman.

"What do you mean by that? What do you mean, because of 'you'?" Crash pushed, and pushed too far as the piercing brain pain sliced through both his and Faraday's heads.

"Goddammit Crash, you had to take it too far!" screamed Faraday as he clutched his head.

"*Aaaaarrrgggghhhh* hey fuck you, bud, you wanna know as much as I do. *Aahhhhhh.*"

The two men dropped to the ground, knees splashing in the headless human's blood. Davis and his men in suits stopped their cleanup to grab the two writhing men and one unconscious alien, and carried them out as Commander Ahn finally exhaled.

• • •

The two men and one space octopus sat in three corners of the cell. Both of the men stared at the octopus, which was still knocked out. Grammeral Zeezak's sleeping body oozed slime onto the cell floor. He smelled like silicone and fish. In his natural state, he looked like a five-foot-long piece of bait, with only a belt around his waist that had a few knobs on it.

Crash stood up and walked over, pinching his nose as he went in for a closer look. He twiddled a knob on the alien's belt, and a tentacle fell off the body as if severed with a hot blade.

"What the hell did you do?" Faraday yelled out.

"I don't know! I just turned a knob and his damn ... thing ... fell off!"

"Well stop it!"

Crash sat back down in his corner, looked at the ground. "You know, they did something to me. They put something in my food that made me strong. Real strong."

"Nanotechnology."

"What?"

"Tiny robots that broke you down to a molecular level and then reconstructed your body with modified DNA. I'll wager you can regenerate too?"

Crash looked up. "Yeah. They do it to you?"

"Sort of. They only did it to my brain. Basically, I have advanced cognitive ability coupled with access to the entire database of humankind's knowledge."

"Jesus," replied Crash as he crinkled his nose. The smell of the slime trickle from the severed tentacle had made its way over to them.

"God, that's awful," said Faraday as he tried to waft the smell back from whence it came.

The tentacle began twitching on its own, coiling and uncoiling on the cell's floor. Crash watched anxiously. The being slightly reminded him of the giant Pacific octopuses he had worked with at the Monterey Aquarium, but the beyond-human intelligence of the creature added a level of creepiness to the wriggling tentacle that left a bad feeling in his stomach. "Doc, what do you think is really going on here?"

Faraday motioned slightly to the ceiling, as if to say that Level 7 was listening.

"I don't give a damn! They can listen all they want. I mean, hell, if they're so advanced they're probably watching holograms of us right now in ten different bases across the globe, right? Probably monitoring our thoughts, too, those cocksuckers."

Faraday chuckled for the first time in days at Crash's blunt, simple, and probably correct reasoning. "Yeah, probably."

"And you thought you were the smart one."

"Hey! It's not always so easy. I have to filter through multiple streams and train my focus to—"

"Doc, I don't give a shit. Tell me what you think is happening."

Dr. Faraday looked over at the octoblob. "I don't know if we can trust anything that Level 7 has said at this point."

"Well I know this guy isn't a friend," Crash replied while motioning to the deflated octopus in the corner. "His buddies tried to kill me without warning when I beamed aboard their ship."

"Perhaps they were just trying to defend it because they thought *you* were invading."

Crash shrugged, took a breath, waved the smelly air back toward the octopus, and resigned from the conversation.

"We don't know jack shit about what's going on right now, do we," Crash said.

"Not a damn thing."

Chapter 37

Commander Ahn sat alone in the conference room. She remembered when she had first been propositioned by the men in suits. How they had approached her at her graduation from West Point. How she had first turned them down when they offered her wealth, but how she gave in when they reconfigured their proposition with promises of power and of legacy. They told her she would change things. That she would be a part of the most important strategic defensive operation in Earth's history. They told her she could either watch from the sidelines or design and execute a master plan for the forces of good, but no matter what, war would be coming.

Rachel Ahn was supposed to be commander of a top-secret government intelligence agency. She ended up an errand girl for something she didn't understand. By the time she began to figure out what was happening, the military prodigy was trapped. Her life had been sucked from her; her soul was little more than a flicker. Once an ambitious young cadet on the path to a career filled with adventure and meaning, Rachel Ahn was now a candle about to burn out in a room no one knew about.

The viewing screen crackled to life. As usual, it revealed nothing, although Ahn was certain she could be seen.

"Commander," rumbled a grating voice from the blackness.

"Yes, Marnshoth."

"I see my creations are adapting to their new abilities. They will suit my purposes well."

"Yes, Marnshoth," Ahn replied robotically, lifelessly. "When will they be leaving?"

"Prepare them now."

• • •

Grammeral Zeezak was awake, in his octopus form, and examining his severed tentacle.

"Who turned my knobs?" he demanded in passable English.

"Uhhh, that was him," answered Faraday in a stumble of words that had to be pushed out of his agape mouth while he stared at the blobby sight in front of him.

Crash smirked. "Yeah, it was me. I'd cut them all off if I could." He made a slashing motion toward the octopus.

Grammeral Zeezak wobbled to an upright position in his corner. "You could have indeed. Why didn't you?"

"Because we're not killers like you," said Faraday.

Crash steeled his jaw. He actually just hadn't thought of it. "You know what, I'll finish you off right now."

He stood and balled his fists and started walking across the cell and then *bam*, there it was, the sonic weapon bouncing between his temples again. Faraday also got the brain pain, and again the two men rolled around on the ground like babies.

"Goddammit, Crash! I'm tired of this shit!" Faraday screamed.

The pain stopped quickly, but the men were slow to get up.

"Sorry, Doc," Crash gasped.

The door to the cell opened; the men in suits stood outside and at the ready.

"Out," ordered Commander Ahn from beyond the door.

Crash and Faraday did their best to stumble out, and the octopus followed suit, scuttling upright and carrying his loose tentacle.

"You do anything that I don't order you to do, I drop you with the brain pain, got it?" warned Commander Ahn. She looked at the alien. "Now, Grammeral, I know you're a fighter to the end and you're right now thinking about what move you're going to make, but I assure you, you'll want to comply."

Zeezak hesitated and flexed his wormy limbs. "And why is that, human?"

"Because we have your mate."

Zeezak tensed. "Liar!"

"Isn't that right, Frank?" Commander Ahn continued.

Faraday had wondered who the new girl was that had just joined his boy. "Blond, short, gray sweats. She's safe. She's ... playing video games with my son—" His enhanced mind flickered, and his expression changed to one of surprise. "Your mate is Jennica!?" he exclaimed in disbelief.

"The pop star?" Crash added with a snort.

"Yes," replied Zeezak sternly.

"The shitty pop singer from *this* planet?" continued Crash, voice dripping with confused amusement.

"Yes."

Crash stared at Grammeral Zeezak, who had turned a fleshy red in the universal sign of embarrassment. It was all too much for him.

"So you're, like, this octopus from another planet, and you've flown across the galaxy, and you're in love with a pretty Earth girl who sings terrible music. And you've known her for what, like a day?"

Grammeral Zeezak's octopus face looked melty and sad. Crash yanked on his own hair in frustration. "Well that's it. I officially don't know what the fuck is happening anymore."

"I don't care about her," responded the alien in a terribly inexperienced attempt at feigning indifference.

Commander Ahn didn't bite. "Of course you do. You came here for her."

"We came here for resources!"

"You came here for resources. And to mate. And you found *her*."

Grammeral Zeezak's tubular body deflated. He felt more powerless than he had ever felt in his life cycle. Here he was, the Emperor's Second Tentacle, an incompetent mess because of his feelings for an Earth female he had only just met. He lowered his gaze in defeat and lightly snapped his beak.

"I, also, do not know what is happening anymore," the octopus said with resignation as he submitted without a fight to Commander Ahn and her dozen men in suits.

• • •

The caravan marched to the transfer booth.

"In," ordered Commander Ahn. The booth was barely big enough to fit the three captives.

Crash grimaced as he rubbed up against the slimy space octopus, and wished he could beat the shit out of it. Then

Commander Ahn wedged in and added to the misery. The woman all but needed the octopus's slime to slip her body into the transfer booth. Crash smirked, actively observing the spectacle of everyone trying to fit in.

"You know, for a top-secret organization that has all this futuristic technology, you guys really suck at a lot," said the TV host.

"It'll make sense in a moment," said Ahn as everyone grunted with discomfort while she maneuvered her arm through the tightly packed bodies to the operation controls.

"Why, you gonna tell us your master plan before you kill us?" Crash followed up.

Ahn hit the transfer button, and the four left the base and the men in suits behind with a flash of light and a blast of ozonated air.

And materialized in Grammeral Zeezak's saucer in Central Park.

"No. I'm going to tell you the master plan because I'm on your side," she said in Crash's ear just loud enough for him alone to hear it.

CHAPTER 38

The two men, woman, and blubbery space octopus squeezed out of the transfer booth. Crash recognized the familiar room as the location of his previous massacre. The mess had been cleaned up, and there was a fresh slew of space octopuses disguised as ugly little shaved men for him to butcher. They stood prepared. Grammeral Zeezak spoke natively with one of them before anything could happen. It sounded to Crash like two cats trying to cough up fish bones.

"You're on Earth, motherfucker. Speak English," said Crash.

"They want to eat you. Cut you into little pieces first for easy chewing," replied Zeezak. The hocking and wheezing continued between the Vyperians.

"Did you tell them I'm much stronger than last time?"

"I told them my princess is being held captive."

"Oh." Crash winced, ego bruised from not being the topic of conversation.

"About that," said Ahn. But Zeezak wasn't ready to talk yet. At least not to them.

"One moment," said the Vyperian leader before returning to his native tongue. An octopus handed Zeezak an injecting device and a writhing, circular blob that looked like a diseased jellyfish. Grammeral Zeezak slurped down the jellyfish, plunged the injector into his stump, and pulled the trigger.

Within seconds, his stump grew back into a full-size tentacle while Faraday watched with curiosity. Crash was not impressed.

"Big fucking deal. I can do that too."

Zeezak, refreshed, faced Commander Ahn. "You have my accord that no harm shall be done to you while you are on my ship. We each have something that the other needs."

Ahn nodded.

The Vyperians surrounded Crash and Faraday and splintered them from the other two in the group. Zeezak dropped the tips of two tentacles in a finite motion. "I, of course, was talking to the female. You two will be disposed of."

Tiny weapons that looked like bubble guns were raised toward the two men, and Faraday sighed his seventy-fifth sigh of exasperation of the week. Crash tensed, not planning on going down without a fight.

Tentacles on triggers with barely a microsecond to spare, Commander Ahn yelled, "Stop!" at the top of her lungs.

"They will *not* be harmed. They will be treated with the same respect as I am. They have something I need as well."

Grammeral Zeezak clicked a command in Vyperian. The weapons were lowered. "Very well. I would offer you nourishment and relaxation in our guest quarters, but we have little time. However, we shall talk in a more suitable environment than a transfer booth room."

The Vyperians, weapons lowered but still drawn, encircled the humans and motioned out the door with a wobble. The three earthlings followed Grammeral Zeezak to the anywherevator. Only one of the aliens followed them in, and the five slid across the ship to the atrium.

. . .

Commander Ahn marveled at the atrium. Faraday marveled at the atrium. Crash marveled at the atrium, but tried not to show it. The round room couldn't have been more than fifteen meters in diameter, but it felt ten times larger. The ceiling wasn't so much a ceiling as it was a moving, breathing, living sky with its own weather. Flowing through the room was a stream filled with a light orange liquid. In the liquid were glowing, flashing creatures that moved too fast to make out their shapes. Filling out the room around the stream were giant plants, leafy and purple.

"Is this what your home world looks like?" asked Ahn, eyes not sure what to settle on.

"Our home world is mostly water," replied Grammeral Zeezak.

The other Vyperian that had followed them into the atrium continued Zeezak's thought. "We have the means to create whatever environment we like on a small scale."

Crash raised his eyebrow. "Yeah, we can do that too. It's called a garden."

"I don't—" the smaller Vyperian started to reply.

He was cut off by Grammeral Zeezak. "Crass Earth humor, Sentlent Bool."

Commander Ahn shot Crash a *stop trying to get us vaporized* look as Zeezak turned the conversation to more important matters.

"Commander, you transported us away from your armed entourage and possibly saved my life. Why?"

Crash eyeballed Ahn, wondering the same thing.

"It's simple, really. We have used our own transfer booths since we acquired the technology from your race years ago. The base we just came from was, as a matter of fact, thousands of miles from where we are now."

Crash blinked his eyes. "What? Where the hell were we?"

"In the Australian outback, outside of Coober Pedy."

"What!" Crash looked at Faraday, who answered from a similar state of shock. "I ... had no idea."

Commander Ahn carried on.

"As you are aware, Grammeral, a transfer booth can only be used if one has the direct coordinates of a receiving booth. We had coordinates for all our own locations, but none of yours. That was, of course, until Dr. Faraday was able to lock in on the booth that Mr. Jefferson teleported to in the public bathroom, when he created a public stir."

Faraday noticed both of the Vyperians were turning a slight tint of blue and although he didn't know what exactly it meant, he guessed it wasn't a positive emotion. Grammeral Zeezak snapped his beak.

"And you intercepted me and received the coordinates to my saucer's transfer booth, and then you used that information to get yourself and these other humans onto my ship."

"Yes," said Ahn. The two space octopuses flashed even bluer.

"Why?"

"Because I've been sent here to trade for something from it."

Grammeral Zeezak and his Sentlent Bool both snapped their beaks rapidly, and ripples of bright red color spread across their hides. With little warning, Vyperian warriors sprang from hiding places in the orange stream and flew through the air, landing in a full circle around the three humans. Grammeral Zeezak held up a tentacle to hold off any further aggression, but the Vyperians new to the party were clearly ready to attack as they wobbled aggressively on their tentacle tips.

"And what, human, would you happen to need from my ship? More important to you right at this instant, why should this conversation continue any further?"

"Might I remind you, Grammeral, that I have your mate?"

Zeezak flicked the tip of his tentacle a touch, and the threatening Vyperians scuttled back a half meter.

"Perhaps a more delicate approach is appropriate," said the alien leader. He clicked and wheezed with Sentlent Bool for a moment.

Lost in the alien-ness of it all, Faraday felt dumber than he had felt in some time. Crash tensed like a puma, waiting for an excuse to tear everything to pieces, and Ahn stood her ground, ice in her veins.

The Vyperians nudged closer.

"The Earth human is important to me," Zeezak said. "But not as important as the mission we have come here to complete. That is why I have decided that you are no longer of use to us. And as much as the potential loss of my Earth female torments me in ways I do not logically understand, the will of the Vyperian collective is more powerful than that hurt could ever be."

Commander Ahn broke out her secret weapon. "Marnshoth."

Sentlent Bool screeched in surprise. Grammeral Zeezak's round eyes widened to the point where they looked about to fall out of his bulbous head, and he snapped, "How do you know that name! How do you know the name of Marnshoth?"

Commander Ahn cocked her head. "You should probably pay close attention if you want any chance of making it out of this alive."

• • •

Grammeral Zeezak, Sentlent Bool, Commander Ahn, Dr. Faraday, and James "Crash" Jefferson sat on the saucer's bridge in the midst of dozens of other Vyperians, all of which toiled away at their unified task of running the ship. Surrounded by so much exotic and incredible technology, Faraday made mental notes of everything that caught his gaze. He catalogued as much as he could, from the circularly organic way the ship and its parts were designed to the way the Vyperians themselves acted. He was especially fascinated by the smooth metal that had no sharp edges and was always comfortably warm and soft to the touch.

Faraday was also put aside by how quiet everything was. There were no mechanical noises, no sounds of movement (except from the humans), and no idle chatter between Vyperians. *What I wouldn't give to see just how everything fits together.*

He was on the verge of asking a string of serious technological questions, but Crash got his piece out first.

"You guys really like things smooth."

"Yes, we do."

"And quiet."

"Yes."

"Huh."

"Well, I can't really add anything to that," said Faraday with a touch of anger. But the words were taken more as resignation than sarcasm, and Commander Ahn barreled into her own story before the scientist could have his queries heard.

CHAPTER 39

"The situation was strange from the beginning with Level 7. At first, I assumed that was simply because of the sensitive nature of the work. I'd been recruited to formulate strategies and command personnel, but all I did was read books on military history. I never went back to the lab I'd been shown during the recruitment phase, where I assumed I'd be working. It was a mentally exhausting process—"

"As it is for us right now. What of Marnshoth?" Zeezak interjected.

She took a hesitant breath. "I report to her every day. She made it clear from the beginning that she was my superior, but I've never met her, never seen her. I came to realize she has no connection to any military. She never responded to *sir* or *ma'am*, only Marnshoth. I started to get worried, confused ... lonely. I decided I wanted out, so I told her as much. And that was when she threatened my parents."

Ahn refused to cry, but light tears still slid down her face.

"I was briefed that invading forces were coming from the other side of the galaxy, and it was time to prepare. I'd been handpicked for this mission, and if I wanted to see my parents again, I didn't have a choice. They—she knew everything about them. Where they lived, where they worked, everything. She showed me pictures taken of them. So there I was, trying to comprehend the notion of an alien invasion, worried about my family's safety in the middle of a cold, barren ..."

Ahn's words trailed off and more tears fell. The Vyperians stared blankly, but Faraday offered a comforting touch to her hand, and she grasped his fingers and picked up her story again, directing her words mostly to the humans' familiar faces.

"I was kept far away, but from what I've gathered, Marnshoth is somewhere on the West Coast. Near Los Angeles, I think. My parents are from Koreatown, and I got the impression she isn't far from their home, transfer booth or not. Not that I could protect them anyway. I was under constant surveillance. The men in suits came with me when I left the base, and that wasn't often."

"Who are they?" asked Faraday as gently as he could.

Ahn glanced at him through moist eyes. "I don't know. I don't know. But I'll tell you this. I think they are the only real people inside that base."

It took a moment for this to sink in. Crash broke the silence. "What do you mean, 'only real people'?"

"Exactly the way it sounds. I think the rest are just holograms, or robots. Maybe both."

"They are her puppets," said Bool dismissively. "She has no courage to act on her own."

Faraday's mouth opened slightly and he blinked a dozen times in a moment. "Holy shit." *It all makes sense now,* the scientist thought. *Why the interactions were so awkward, even for me. Jordan's weird breakdowns, the emotionless 'workers,' the lack of response while I was vomiting blood.*

Ahn pushed on, driven to finish her story. "I was told there was a plan for you, Dr. Faraday. That you had been handpicked at an early age for your mental capacity."

"And what about me?" said Crash. "Was I handpicked too?"

"No, you just kind of dropped into our laps. Marnshoth needed a strong person as well, but those we can find anywhere."

Crash turned red with anger. "What the hell. Do you know many times I've cheated death?"

Faraday, still holding Ahn's hand, put his free hand on Crash's shoulder, partly for comfort, partly for restraint.

"I've won three fucking Emmys!"

"Calm down, Crash," said Faraday soothingly. Crash steamed as Vyperians—already nervous from the talk of Marnshoth—took defensive postures. The adventurer noted this and cooled himself, but still stared down Commander Ahn.

"Why?"

"Why?"

"Why give him a brain and me the strength? Especially when you kept us locked up in a cell when you could've been forcing us to do work when you needed us the most."

Ahn nodded, acquiescing to Crash's desire for an answer. "Well, you weren't actually designed to be used for any of this. I was just ordered to keep you busy while you were still on Earth."

Faraday's eyebrow went up. "Still on Earth?"

"I might be wrong, but I believe Marnshoth created you to be her companions while she traveled back to her home planet. You, Dr. Faraday, as an interactive encyclopedia of Earth's history. And you, Crash, as ... well, as some muscle to help around the home."

Crash's face had been returning to its natural color. It flushed to red again. "What the fuck."

He shrugged Faraday's hand off his shoulder, but the scientist didn't notice. He had other things on his mind.

"What do you mean, back to her home planet?"

Sentlent Bool stared at Grammeral Zeezak for a moment. "Tell the earthlings," Zeezak said.

As the Sentlent began his account in imperfect English, Faraday made mental records, cataloguing the story and adjusting it accordingly to counter any Vyperian bias. In the midst of probable exaggeration, alien concepts, and propaganda, the scientist listened in dumbfounded amazement.

I really hope I live to share this.

Chapter 40

DR. FRANK FARADAY
MEMORY FILE 01178
SENNATIAN HISTORY
SCRUBBED FOR BIASES

Life had been peaceful on Sennat for eons. A small planet of mostly water, it had been occupied by many races of intelligent beings for millions of years. As time trudged forward, two species established themselves as dominant—the octopus-like Vyperians, and the whale-like Farceen.

The Vyperians had established their dominance with technological advancements and sheer numbers. The Farceen were far fewer in numbers and operated as a hive mind, linked psychically, and received all its directives from one source. Every goal, every plan, every objective was set by the one at the top of the hierarchy, and the others worked toward the goal for the benefit of the entire race.

When the Vyperians grew in numbers, their consumption of resources grew as well. Their populations swelling, Vyperian masses clogged the Sennat seas, crowding out many of the other less-evolved species. At first, the Farceen didn't raise concern. But the Farceen were enormous creatures. Although small in number, one Farceen had the mass of thousands, sometimes tens of thousands of Vyperians. Creatures large enough to consume massive amounts of food.

Conflicts broke out over food supplies, particularly a species of krill known for its intense flavor. Vyperians would smear a taste of it on a kelp leaf. Farceen would open their mouths and devour an entire school at a time. But in the course of the ever-expanding Vyperian population wants and needs, the krill was depleted and eradicated forever from Sennat. The Vyperians subsisted on a wide range of foods and for them, the lack of krill was just a luxury that would have to be replaced by something else. For the Farceen, it posed a far bigger problem.

The Farceen hive mind put its best effort to finding a positive solution, but while the krill had only been a delicacy for the Vyperians, it contained the complete nutritional balance the Farceen required. Other fish and plants could fill a belly with empty calories, but the Farceen species saw itself become sickly and weak in the span of one generation. And then they started to die.

It was only by a chance act of desperation that a solution was found. At least, that was the Vyperian guess, because the Farceen hive mind never spoke of the origin of its big secret to outsiders.

The secret that Vyperians were delicious *and* nutritious.

Some said it was a young rogue whale not completely absorbed into the hive yet. Others said it was a last-ditch effort by the leader of the hive herself, for the survival of the species. No one really knew when or how a Vyperian first ended up in a farceen's mouth, or how it was discovered that the Vyperians made a better meal than cohabitant. Some speculated that because the Vyperians ate so much of the krill before driving it to extinction, their bodies changed because of it, and if that hadn't happened, they never would have been nutritious to the Farceen in the first place. The whole race might have made themselves irresistibly tasty.

The harsh truth was, there wasn't any other food available that could nourish the Farceen. Worldwide war broke out. Hundreds of thousands of octopuses armed with harpoons and torpedoes and riding in powered submersibles versus hundreds of giant intelligent whales armed with brute strength and big appetites collided in a watery war zone. Occasionally a Farceen would just eat its way through a front line. Vyperians would sacrifice themselves, rigging their bodies with explosives and then allowing themselves to be eaten and then *boom*. No more whale.

Intel started to accumulate in the Vyperian ranks. The Vyperians had always known that the Farceen were controlled by a single being, and the decision was made that the best chance at ending the war would be to capture and kill the Farceen leader.

Locations and patterns of movement were studied, and much like all the fingertips on a human hand lead back to the palm, the Farceen underlings pointed back to the leader. A queen. The queen was ultimately pinpointed and found in a volcanic lagoon in the warm shallow waters of Garveel.

The Farceen queen was protected by her strongest fighters, but they were no match for the numbers of the octopus army. Led by Grammeral Q'Shin Zeezak on direct command from the Vyperian Emperor, the lagoon was stormed and the Grammeral confronted the queen of the Farceen: Marnshoth.

Grammeral Zeezak stood on the bridge of his ship. The Vyperians had long since evolved lungs and could breathe in air or water, but most hadn't traveled "pure" (the term for traveling freely outside of a ship or armed convoy) in some time, for fear of being eaten. As large as Grammeral Zeezak's ship was, it still didn't match the size of the Farceen. Its arsenal, however, more than made up for the imbalances. The Vyperians had little desire to drive Marnshoth and the Farceen into complete extinction. It was simply collateral damage that so much blood had been shed, of creatures unfortunate enough to be caught up in the fight for survival.

"Marnshoth," announced Grammeral Zeezak through his ship's out-speaker. "You have lost, and are ordered to surrender."

Marnshoth knew there was no point fighting on. Her species had been cut down to a quarter of its size, and for a species that didn't breed more than once every hundred standard years, it would take thousands of years for the Farceen to grow back to a healthy number.

But the Farceen didn't have thousands of years. The Farceen didn't have another day. Their time had come. Marnshoth surrendered. As her will gave, the remote appendages under her control stopped fighting. Stopped doing anything. The remaining whales floated around the oceans, confused and without direction.

Fueled by rumors that if Marnshoth were killed, another appendage would take over as queen, or that Marnshoth might change her mind and reorganize the rest of the Farceen to inflict whatever damage she might will, the Vyperian council decided to exile the fallen queen. Marnshoth was loaded into a gigantic freighter-turned-prison-cell and launched into space, condemned to drift across the universe over the remainder of her long lifespan.

END MEMORY FILE

"And that is where the Vyperian history of Marnshoth ended. Until now," finished Sentlent Bool.

Faraday shook his head slowly, Commander Ahn took a deep breath, and Crash bit his lip and then spoke.

"So ... just so I have this all straight," Crash looked back and forth between the Vyperians and Commander Ahn, "you put a giant whale into a giant aquarium and launched it into space. And then that thing crash-landed on Earth years ago—maybe near Los Angeles—and the whale figured out a way to force humans to help it become powerful enough to lure a fleet of you guys here to steal your spaceship. Oh, while fucking with our DNA with tiny robots so we can be its toys while we jet across the universe so it can get revenge on you for killing off most of its friends and family."

Grammeral Zeezak thought for a moment. "Yes."

"Well what the fuck."

CHAPTER 41

The thousands of people surrounding the saucer in Central Park were starting to get restless. Nothing had happened for hours. More and more "are you fucking kidding me, why would you do that?" incidents were occurring. Bottles had been thrown at the saucer, TV crews got a little too close with their cameras, and the volkites were being taunted endlessly in the style of, "Fuck you, robot!"

So when the volkites abruptly came to life and started moving, there would have been a lot of "I told your dumb ass you shouldn't have insulted it" chatter going around, had there not been a lot of pant-wetting going around. The National Guard and police who'd been spending all their combined power trying to keep people back were instead trying to keep people from trampling each other as they ran far away.

The humans were in such a panic, it took most citizens a while to realize that the six volkites had only walked far enough away from the saucer to clear space for takeoff.

"Where the hell is it going?"

"Why did they leave their robots behind?"

"Throw another bottle at them!"

Whifffffff. The saucer spun, flew straight up with nary a noise, and when it reached a few thousand meters of altitude, slung itself due west.

The volkites remained, silent and motionless.

Chapter 42

The panic in New York had not yet spread to the West Coast. SoCal residents were far too wrapped up in their own lives to worry about some spaceship that had landed in Manhattan. At first, it had been cool to mention off the cuff that one had a friend who talked with the aliens in person, but before long that story grew stale and things soon got to the point where it wasn't cool to talk about it at all.

"Man, what the hell is gonna happen with that, do you think it's an invasion, or that they wanna help us with global warming or something?"

"Yeah."

"Yeah what?"

"I have to get to a party in West Hollywood."

And so it was business as usual in Southern California as the saucer swooped in and then stopped on a dime above Dodger Stadium on the hill overlooking downtown LA.

The three humans inside the saucer had no idea that they'd just flown cross-country, and that it had happened before the aliens finished talking about Marnshoth, the great war, and their home planet.

Ahn looked in silence toward her fellow earthlings. She wanted to apologize. Wanted to tell Faraday and Crash that she was sorry she made them take the pills, sorry she had Trevor abducted. That she was sorry for the pain she had caused. Ahn knew she was just a pawn. Still, she wished she could do *something* positive. But caught between two warring alien species, she no longer knew the right thing to do. She had led Crash and Faraday out of the frying pan and into the fire, and for the first time, an unsettling possibility sprang to life in her mind.

What if there are no good sides in this war and we're screwed no matter what?

The earthlings had settled into a sort of galactic sofa, which was the only thing they felt comfortable sitting in on the Vyperian ship's bridge. The sofa was more reminiscent of a ten-foot log of firm jelly, but it conformed to their bodies as they sank in, and was ultimately quite relaxing. Although it smelled like the sea. Crash particularly didn't like the scent.

"So does your whole planet smell like red tide?" he asked Grammeral Zeezak.

"We have arrived."

"Huh?"

Zeezak signaled for the remotescope to activate, and the screen across the front of the bridge flickered on to show the ship floating slightly higher than LA's downtown skyline.

"Why did you take us here?" asked Ahn, snapped out of her train of defeated thought.

"You said you believe Marnshoth is here. We agree. Which also means my princess is here."

"Probably," said Ahn.

"Good," responded the alien leader. "You will proceed as normal with your previously arranged plans to deliver Marnshoth's playthings."

Crash and Faraday both grimaced at the slight. Ahn's revelation of their being "enhanced" just to be slaves to a traveling alien stung fresh in both their memories. Grammeral Zeezak paid them no attention and continued.

"Once inside, you will retrieve my mate, and make sure she is returned safely to me. Of course, you may free this earthling's child as well," Zeezak gestured to Faraday. "One can only imagine the horrors Marnshoth might inflict upon the young human."

At that mention Faraday panicked, and checked into Trevor's feed and saw his son still just engrossed in his game. He took a deep breath. *The empty beaches of Costa Rica.* His mind settled. *The first time I used that trick seems such a long time ago.*

Crash chuckled and stood from the sofa. Vyperians moved toward him, weapons out, and Grammeral Zeezak cocked his blubbery head to the side.

Faraday said, "Crash, what the hell are you—"

"Don't worry, Doc, Rach, Zeezog—"

"*Grammeral Zeezak,*" corrected Sentlent Bool.

"Whatever. I'm not gonna do anything crazy. Plus, I'm guessing there's some sort of insurance that our slimy friends here have, just to make sure we take this unwanted mission seriously. Am I right?"

"Of course you are, earthling Jefferson," stated Zeezak.

Crash smirked. He might have been at the mercy of his captors, but he wanted to at least try to look like he had *some* authority, even while surrounded by armed space octopuses in the thick of enemy territory. "So what are you going to do if we *don't* make it back with your girlfriend?"

Sentlent Bool clicked an undecipherable phrase to Zeezak,

who then replied to Crash in English.

"We will unleash a scourge of monsters on your planet that will annihilate your civilization."

Crash scratched his nose. "I ... hmm. Wasn't excepting that." The adventurer took a quick inventory of his surroundings. "And if I destroy you and everything else in this room before you have the chance?"

Vyperian weapons again steadied on the humans as Crash's body noticeably tensed. A vein popped on his forehead. His knuckles crackled like a pinecone on a fire as he balled his fists.

"You could surely do that," said Zeezak. "I'm aware of your strength and prowess. Of course, if anything were to happen to us, the orders are to launch the directives from the armory on the other side of this vessel, so you would be single-handedly responsible for destroying your planet."

Crash took a breath. "And they have the orders to do that over there, huh."

"They do now," said Zeezak with the Vyperian equivalent of an eye twinkle and confident smile.

"Okay. So let's say we do this mission. What's in it for us?"

Zeezak clicked his beak. It sounded like a mocking cackle. "You have quite an arrogance about you, earthling. Do not forget, your counterpart's child is being held also, so there is *that* incentive for you three to follow through. Let me be precise," he thundered as he lifted four tentacles in a grandiose manner, stretching them wide from his body. "We can either kill you all right now and rain destruction on your planet, or you can free my mate, the other male can see his offspring again, and perhaps you might all live to see what might come next for your planet. If you don't return, I'll wipe entire cities off this besner-ched rock until you do."

Zeezak pointed an open-faced tentacle toward Faraday. "Consult the intelligent one. He will tell you. There are no other options."

Faraday nodded slowly but without hesitation, and Crash knew they were at the mercy of the Vyperians. He gave no fur-ther argument. The alien leader dropped his tentacles and con-tinued, his tone casual.

"We have no transfer booths in this part of your world and we can't directly send you to one of Marnshoth's, so we will dump you out of the airlock before a crowd of your stupid earthling peers arrives to throw rocks at us. Now, if you will, follow Sentlent Bool."

Without any other reasonable option and at the armed suggestion of a few dozen Vyperian warriors, Crash, Faraday, and Ahn exited the bridge for the anywherevator. Just before the door slid closed, Zeezak left them with a parting comment.

"If Marnshoth knows or deduces what has happened be-tween us, tell her the truth."

"The truth?" asked Ahn.

"The truth."

The door closed, and they were off to the airlock.

• • •

The three humans walked out onto the rim of the saucer and found themselves hovering about two meters above the Dodger Stadium parking lot. The sound of sirens carried up the hill from every direction, louder by the second.

"We need to get the hell out of here or we're not accomplishing anything," said Crash.

The three sat on the edge of the saucer and hopped down onto the asphalt. The first police car came into view at the far end of the parking lot and roared toward them.

"We're in some serious shit here, let's go!" yelled Ahn as she popped up from a rough landing. The three bolted to the grassy slope at the edge of the parking lot.

"I still feel like I'm in less danger than a Giants fan," Crash joked.

No one laughed.

"'Cause Giants fans get stabbed here a lot."

Only the sound of footfalls and approaching sirens.

"I guess you guys aren't baseball fans."

"Or," gasped Ahn while they cleared the ridge and ran down the slope for cover, "we're too busy running from aliens and the police while trying to save the damn planet."

"Whatever," Crash hissed effortlessly with his enhanced lungs. "No time's a bad time for a Giants joke."

Stumbling through brush and litter, Faraday, Crash, and Ahn ran as fast as they could. After about a minute of tripping over themselves, they hit the bottom of the hill and darted into a residential area. *Damn nice to be in friendly territory again,* thought Faraday, but that was all he had time to think while the three ran around a corner and the two physically normal humans doubled over, huffing for air. Crash kept running for a second before he realized his rebuilt body wasn't the least bit exhausted. He stopped, turned, and came back.

"Sorry guys, I forgot how powerful I am."

The other two were too tired to answer immediately, so

Crash continued. "We need a plan. Where's this damn ship at?"

Ahn shook her head while finishing catching up with her breathing.

"No? No what?"

"I don't know where her ship is."

"What do you mean? Haven't you been there?"

"Only from the inside. I always transferred out to a remote location when I left. I just know it's 'somewhere' near Los Angeles."

Faraday finally caught his breath enough to stand up straight again. "I'm monitoring emergency channels right now. No one saw us leave the saucer. We're in the clear."

"Well that's good," said Crash. "Now we just need to find a hidden alien spaceship with a whale in it, rescue a pop star, sneak out before we become intergalactic pets, bring the shitty singer back to this spaceship here, find a way to not get vaporized, and then save the planet. 'Cause you know these bastards are gonna blow shit up anyway once they get what they want. I mean, what's the point, right? Maybe we should just get the hell out of the city and chill out in the mountains."

Ahn looked at the ground. Faraday looked at Crash. "My son's there too."

Crash frowned. "Sorry. I forgot that part."

Faraday shook his head.

"Hiding in the mountains was just, you know, a suggestion," said Crash, foot still in mouth.

Faraday walked past him without looking at him and Ahn followed suit.

"Look, I just spaced on that part, okay. You guys might not know this about me, but I don't run from trouble. I'm not just a

TV hero."

The two kept walking, but Ahn yelled back over her shoulder, "Well then, what are you waiting for, Mister 'Not Just a TV Hero'?"

Crash frowned again and ran to catch up.

• • •

The three stopped at a Subway for a quick meal. All of them mentioned feeling guilty about putting off the saving of Earth for a bite to eat, but they had spent far too much time lately in weird places that sorely lacked human food. Plus, Buffalo Chicken was the six-dollar sub of the month.

Although he had a new shirt, Crash was still wearing the shorts he'd worn during the Amazon excursion, blood, filth, and all. "All" also included his emergency money belt which hadn't been found by the police during the chaos. The TV host bought the subs, Faraday complained about hating olives 'cause they dropped one in his sandwich accidentally, and then the three started formulating a plan.

"I honestly don't know where to start," said Ahn at the hi-top table the three sat around.

"I do," replied Faraday. "I'm running a scan of recent anomalies. There was an earthquake so localized, it only affected Disneyland."

Ahn's eyes widened. "I think that's it."

"Why?" asked Crash while wiping sauce from his lips.

Faraday continued Ahn's thoughts. "Because there are only two places something that big could remain undiscovered for so long. Underwater, or underground. Rachel, do you have any idea how Marnshoth created multiple bases? You know, being a giant whale locked in a ship and all."

"All I know is that there are some other people working for her."

"The guys in suits," said Crash.

"Yeah. But I don't know much about them, or where they came from. I was under the impression when I was first recruited that they were going to work for me, but the suits always did their own thing."

Crash looked over at the next table. A Hispanic family was listening intently to their conversation.

"Are you afraid of the saucer people?" a young boy asked them. His mother chastised him and guided the boy to the other side of their table. "*Lo siento,* sorry, sorry," she muttered at Crash.

Faraday pulled his partners back into the conversation. "That earthquake was unnatural, to say the least. It registered a massive hit on USGS radar, but it wasn't even felt outside of Anaheim. It was as if something big was moving around directly underneath Disneyland."

"The freighter," said Ahn. "It might be too damaged to fly in its current condition, but Marnshoth is preparing. She's getting ready to get out of here."

The Mexican boy watched on from behind his mother's body while she ate her meal and spoke with her husband and pretended like her youngest son wasn't staring at the strangers talking about sneaking into a space whale's buried prison aquarium.

Crash shook his head. "I don't get it. Now that these other guys know that Marnshoth is here and lured them to Earth, wouldn't they be really suspicious? I mean, why come all the way out to Los Angeles? Just for the singer that this Gram-meral guy has known for a couple of days? I mean, don't get me wrong, I'd bone her. But no girl is worth potentially having your whole crew get killed for. Right?"

"I don't know what's going on with that," said Ahn. "But I do know we should head to Anaheim. Disneyland is our best bet. Besides," she continued while looking at the Mexican boy. "We need to get Frank his son back."

• • •

Faraday and Ahn quietly followed Crash down the long, bleak hallway. Glancing around nervously, he came to a nondescript entry. With one final cautious look, he reached down for the handle, inserted a key, and opened the door.

"Welcome to my place."

The three of them walked into Crash's fifteenth-floor condo.

"Make yourselves at home."

Ahn, running on fumes, plopped down onto the couch. "Let's take care of what we need and be out of here in ten minutes."

Crash went for the shower. "It's probably going to be more like fifteen. I need to wash all this blood off."

Faraday frowned and held his stomach. "Uh, let's maybe count on twenty."

Crash gave him a look as he closed his bathroom door. "There's a guest bathroom down the hall. Light a goddamn match when you're finished."

Faraday trotted to the other bathroom. Ahn leaned back on the couch and thought about her parents, wondered if they were still in danger. Head rested on the luxurious cushions, she thought for two seconds about borrowing Crash's phone to call her mom and dad before passing out in exhaustion.

CHAPTER 43

Grammeral Zeezak stood in the command room, his mind on Jennica! He had been relentlessly trying to communicate with the woman, even with the knowledge his attempts would all be blocked by Marnshoth. But his cravings defied logic. *That fertile young Earth woman has cast a spell on me.*

The alien's concentration was broken as a parade of Vyperians swished in from the other side of the room. Each octopus carried a different creature. Sentlent Bool scuttled past them all and joined the Grammeral. The first Vyperian squiggled up to the commanding octopuses with a small cage cradled in its tentacles. He held it up for examination. Inside was a cricket.

"What do you think of this Earth beast, my Lord?"

Zeezak stroked the ring around his beak and leaned in for a closer look. "It appears awful enough. Is it an aggressive creature?"

"No, but it makes a horrendous noise when it rubs its leg on its—"

"A horrendous noise that we, no doubt, would hear also," Sentlent Bool interjected. "Next."

Another Vyperian approached with a parrot perched firmly on a stick. "This creature has a beak that could do terrible damage, my Lord!" The parrot abruptly screeched, causing many of the Vyperians in the room to wobble erratically in surprise. Before Sentlent Bool could utter a response, Zeezak whipped out his ray gun and vaporized the bird, exploding it into a puff of burnt feathers.

"No."

The next Vyperian presented another creature in a cage. "This, my Lord, is what the humans call a 'cobra.' A specimen this size has enough venom to kill two hundred of their species. It is so widely feared across this planet that it strikes terror into earthlings that will never even see one in a lifetime."

"Does it make any awful noises?"

"No, my Lord, it is nearly silent."

The cobra reared up inside the cage and spread its hood while locking gazes with the alien leader. With two tentacles, Zeezak swooped the clear cage away from the lesser Vyperian and brought it up to his eyes. The cobra remained still for just another moment, and then it struck, struck, struck again, leaving smears of venom all across the inside of the cage where its fangs had hit.

Grammeral Zeezak's beak ring flickered purple.

"This," he said softly. "We shall start with this."

• • •

Crash pounded on the door to the guest bathroom. "Jesus Doc, what are you doing in there?"

"Sorry, I got lost in my head," shot Faraday through the bathroom door. "It's distracting sometimes. Sorry."

Faraday finished up and walked out to join Crash and Commander Ahn at the kitchen bar. For the first time, Crash realized how rough everyone looked. Except for himself, though, since he had just showered. Also, his nose was looking quite exceptional as he caught his reflection in the toaster.

"Shouldn't we get going?" asked Faraday while he re-tucked his shirt.

Crash pulled out a bottle of whisky. "Yeah, but when's the last time you had a drink?"

"I don't drink anymore."

Crash motioned to Ahn.

"I don't either," she echoed.

Crash poured a triple shot of the mash and held it up. "Well fuck you both then. To saving the world." He bumped the shot into the other two's hands and threw it back. "Let's go save a pop star."

Ahn hesitated. "What are we going to do once I get you two in there and we grab everyone? Go back to the Vyperians? They'll never let us leave."

"If we don't at least go that far, they'll destroy Earth," said Crash.

"They're going to destroy it whether we bring them the girl or not," Faraday added hastily.

Crash poured another double. "Well shit, I don't know. We need a plan. Come on, Doc. You're the genius here, with added genius on top."

Faraday shrugged. "Since we're in LA, I assume you have a car?"

Crash grinned. "Oh yeah, I have a car." He opened a drawer, pulled out a keychain, and slid it across the counter.

• • •

The Ferrari 458 burned down Wilshire toward the freeway with Faraday in the driver's seat. "Dammit Crash, what the hell were you doing drinking so much?" he growled. And to Ahn, "And why didn't *you* stop him?"

Ahn was on Crash's lap, and Crash was doing his best to remain conscious with all the alcohol flowing through his body.

"I wasn't paying attention!" Ahn said. "How much did he drink?"

"I don't know. Too much."

Crash lurched his head up. "Ay. *Hey.* Don't worry. I can feel the little robots, *uhh* ... I can feel them fixing me right now. I'm only gonna be drunk for like another five, *uhh* ... five minutes."

"Great. You sober up *after* we had to bust our asses dragging you into this tiny damn car," Ahn mumbled while she struggled to find a comfortable position in the Ferrari's two-seat cockpit. Faraday tried to remain focused while he scanned traffic conditions with his mind and piloted the car through the streets of Los Angeles.

Hang tight, Trevor. I'm coming for you.

• • •

News of the saucer's arrival in Los Angeles had spread by the time the Ferrari whipped into Orange County. Faraday pulled into a supermarket parking lot to figure out the next step. The lot was swarming with frantic people coming to shop for emergency supplies, but there was one free space near the back and he pulled in.

Ahn didn't wait for Crash to open the door before jumping

off his lap and over the side. The 458's top was down, and that was all the invitation she needed to bail as soon as they stopped.

"You know," Crash said while they gathered themselves and stretched their legs in the parking lot, "you could've just taken the Range Rover and we wouldn't have had this problem."

"Range Rover?" Ahn snarled at him. "Why the hell did we take this tiny thing? Why didn't you tell us?"

"I was drunk and the key's on the keychain, what's there to tell?"

Faraday turned the Ferrari off and pulled the key out. Sure enough, there were keys to a Range Rover as well. "I guess I didn't see those."

"And this is what that brain of yours gets us?" Ahn snapped while she massaged her stiff legs, and then to Crash, "if you hadn't gotten drunk—"

"That's enough. We need a plan here," Faraday interjected to derail the bickering.

Crash and Ahn glared at each other.

"I agree with the doc," said Crash. "And the first thing we need are code names."

Ahn shook her head. "Christ, you're stupid."

"Okay, you know what? You need to seriously shut up," Crash retorted.

Faraday squeezed out of the car and physically and verbally stepped in between the others. "We do not need to be doing this right now."

"You're right," agreed Crash, "and I'm just saying we don't know what we're up against, and we need to be as discreet as possible, so let's just make up some code names real quick and we can go from there."

Faraday looked over at Ahn, who sat on the hood of the car watching scores of people rush into and out of the supermarket.

"Fine," she relented.

"Great," said Crash. "Now the way I've always done it, you take the first initial of your middle name and you swap it for the first letter of your favorite superhero. I'll start. My middle name is Jonathan, and my favorite superhero is Batman, so my codename is Jatman."

Ahn grimaced. "This is stupid. I'm supposed to call you Jatman now?"

"Only when we're in enemy territory."

Faraday offered up his codename in another attempt to make peace between the two. "I guess that would make me A-ulk? Aulk? It's Alan and Hulk. That's not even phonetically possible. You're right, this is stupid."

"Dammit Doc, just use your first name then."

"Fulk? Come on."

"Hey, it works. Now what about you Ahn."

Ahn glared some more. "I don't have a middle name."

"Use your first name, like the doc here."

"I don't like superheroes."

"Fine, I'll pick a name for you. Ratwoman."

"Really? Ratwoman? Really?"

Crash ignored her objections, ready to move on. "Now that we have step one down, let's get rolling and figure out how we're going to pull this off while avoiding the thousand or so ways we could get killed."

CHAPTER 44

The white van sped back toward Los Angeles with Ratwoman at the wheel. Jatman, Fulk, Jennica!, and Trevor were all riding in the back. Everyone was giddy and hugging and laughing at the ease of the mission's success. Dr. Faraday hugged his son as tears of joy streamed down his face.

Crash eyed Jennica! as the pop star sat quietly on the opposite side of the cargo area.

"You're prettier in person, you know," he throatily exclaimed.

"Thanks," she said without smiling.

He ran his hand through his hair, and then traced his finger down his forehead and across the side of his perfect nose. "Do you know who I am?" he asked.

"Of course. Actually, I—well, never mind."

"What?"

"Well," purred Jennica!, "I've always wondered what it would be like to suck your dick."

"What? I mean, there's a kid in here. Like three feet away from us. He's staring at us right now."

"I'll hide what we're doing under my hair."

"Okay, *let's do it.*"

The sexy young singer bent over, flopped her hair into Crash's lap, and then her fingers became tentacles tipped with razor blades that shredded Crash's pants right from his body.

She dove onto his crotch like a hungry lion on a dying gazelle's flank, and screamed like a banshee as she attacked his package furiously. And then Crash woke up.

Goddammit. That was about to get good.

Crash tried to sit up. He was in chains.

• • •

A team of men in suits had been waiting for Commander Ahn and her "prisoners" by the time they got within a kilometer of the rubble that had been Disneyland. Any scheme or plan the three had was thrown out the window when Davis greeted them by saying, "We've been monitoring everything Dr. Faraday has seen or heard. Marnshoth is waiting."

The reception team was dozens strong, and they were all armed with big guns. Crash knew he could take more than a few out, but he also knew they'd all get cut down in the process. Jatman, Fulk, and Ratwoman had no choice but to surrender.

They were led through the half-destroyed but still touristy wreckage and into a staircase that went down, down, down to an elevator, which took them even farther down and into a room that was familiarly metallic to the three. And then they were gassed.

Chapter 45

Senator Horton's secured aircraft landed at John Wayne Airport in Orange County. The tarmac looked disquietingly creepy, his plane the only craft moving. There was a car waiting.

"Where to, sir?" asked the driver.

"Disneyland."

"Sir, an earthquake—"

"I know. Just drive."

• • •

The traffic was a nightmare, but the senator couldn't determine if it was because of the saucer or simply because that was how it always was. *Probably a combination of both.* He thought of the love he had for his wife. Not as a lover, but as a person. How Rebecca had such strength, and how their daughter had glimmers of that same toughness. Horton felt shame and guilt bubble up from the well of secrets within him, stress preventing his ability to repress those feelings like he normally could. Flooded with emotion, he wondered why he was thousands of miles away from home, about to do something undoubtedly dangerous, for reasons he wasn't given. And he wondered why it was he who was chosen.

The town car pulled up to the Disneyland parking lot, and

Horton thanked the driver and sent him on his way after a bit of convincing that he would be okay. He surveyed the rubble in front of him.

God, what a mess.

Much was destroyed, but the big parking structures were mostly undamaged. They were also eerily empty. *Big, modern tombs,* he thought. An uncomfortably familiar tickle licked at his eardrum.

Walk to the center of the parking lot ahead of you.

The voice. The voice that tormented him and controlled him and threatened him.

He hesitated and was teased with a moment of intense pain, and then he broke. He didn't care anymore. He did as he was told and walked to the center of the parking lot.

Place the box on the ground.

He did.

Open it.

Horton took a deep breath. Was this a bomb to destroy California? Knock it clean into the ocean? Hell, this could be a bomb to destroy the entire planet. *Maybe Disneyland is just a symbolic place to detonate, so they can show us the futile pursuits of our greed-fueled mindless escapism? Maybe all I'm dealing with are intergalactic terrorists.*

He frowned and wiped sweat from his forehead with the back of his hand.

Open the box, Senator.

The brain pain crept into Horton's head, but before it grew unbearable, he knelt and opened the box. A rhythmic thumping pounded through the empty parking lot as the box pumped noise like a thunderous subwoofer.

Horton felt a stirring in his loins. A sexual pressure, deep and in desperate need of being fulfilled, built inside him. He couldn't remember ever feeling so much desire.

"What is going on here?" he asked gruffly to no one.

The box continued its pulsations, and Horton started to shake with sexual need as the voice spoke again.

There is a button in the box. Push it and then move as far away as you can.

Horton fought off the intense desire to stick his hands down his pants and instead stuck his hand into the box and pushed the only button inside. Immediately, he was surrounded by hundreds, thousands, tens of thousands of beautiful women.

"What the hell."

• • •

Ahn woke up strapped to the same kind of gurney she had strapped Faraday onto just two days earlier. The room she was in was dark. Marnshoth's voice spoke through speakers in the walls.

"You did well, Commander."

She didn't answer.

"You brought me my creations, and you brought the Vyperian saucer within striking distance. Soon, I'll have my second meeting with Q'Shin Zeezak. I suspect this rendezvous will deliver somewhat different results than the last time he and I met."

Marnshoth paused, but Ahn kept quiet.

"The saucer is just a local ship. The mother ship, a Vyperian battle cruiser, will soon be here as well. It has been waiting on the far side of Earth's moon. When it arrives, arrangements for my journey home shall almost be complete."

Every time Marnshoth paused, the last few words of her sentence would continue on as an echo in the chamber.

"Are my parents safe?" Ahn finally asked.

"Yes. You have my word."

"I'm in restraints. What good does your word do me?"

"You *are* in restraints, so what good would lying do?"

Ahn exhaled slightly. "I've done what I was supposed to do. You have Jefferson and the scientist. You've got what you need: muscles and a brain. Let me go. Please."

"I'm sorry, Commander. I can't do that. I need you."

"For what? What else could I possibly do?"

"The Vyperians follow a standard procedure for conquering new planets. When they launch their next directives, I will need all the help I can get. So too, will your planet. As such, earthlings Jefferson and Faraday aren't the only ones I evolved."

Ahn stopped breathing momentarily as the words sank in.

What's going to happen to me?

CHAPTER 46

On the far side of the moon, in a ship the shape of a skyscraper, fifty thousand horny octopuses had been waiting with lingering shreds of patience. An excited Vyperian in the communications room activated a comm and spoke in its native tongue.

"Bridge, this is communications."

"Go for bridge."

"Scanning has just picked up a message beacon from Earth."

"Coordinates?"

"Local name is Anaheim, California. United States."

"What is the message?"

"'Come immediately. Earth females are aroused and waiting for us.'"

There was a moment of silence. Second Sentlent Sarlz's voice crackled through the comm. "Do we have contact with the saucer?"

"No sir, still clouded by interference."

There was no response from Second Sentlent Sarlz on the bridge.

"Orders, sir?"

The acting Sentlent forced himself to think logically, but his hormones were getting the best of him. With no prior experience for being able to ignore the powerful drive of his newfound lust, the octopus couldn't stop himself from giving in to a closer look. He gave his command.

"Set a course for Earth's upper atmosphere. We need a visual."

His men silently rejoiced. They had flown across space for this mission. This moment. This chance to get laid.

• • •

The battle cruiser aligned itself with Earth's orbit six hundred kilometers above Southern California. Second Sentlent Sarlz, acting in Grammeral Zeezak's absence, ordered a closer look at the saucer as it hovered above the hills of Los Angeles.

"How long since we've had contact?" Sarlz questioned.

"It's been almost ten Earth hours now, sir."

Hmm. "Any signs of damage or distress to it?"

The Vyperian at the scanner swiped in some commands. "No sir, all signs read normal. We just don't have any open lines of communication."

Second Sentlent Sarlz scuttled stiffly across the tips of his tentacles toward the remotescope. "Visual on the message beacon."

The view on the giant remotescope switched from an overhead view of the saucer to an overhead view of a parking lot with a mass of wriggling dots peppering it.

"Enhance."

The dots grew bigger.

"Enhance."

And bigger.

"Sweet Nectar of Marment."

Displayed on the massive screen at the front of the bridge

were thousands of beautiful Earth women, all giggling and happy and scantily clad. Every Vyperian on the bridge stopped what he was doing and stared.

"Sir," said the ensign. "What ... what are they doing?"

The girls shimmied and wiggled and blew kisses and hit beach balls into the air.

"They're waiting for us."

There was another long moment of silence as the Vyperians bubbled with primal urges. The sounds of beaks clicking and skin oozing slime filled the bridge with unearthly noises.

"We must go to them!" screeched one of the ensigns.

Yelps of agreement echoed throughout.

"Silence!" Sarlz bellowed. "We wait for communication from the saucer first."

The screams of excitement turned to whispers of boos and hisses.

"Quiet! We wait!"

CHAPTER 47

"You realize Commander, it's been a horrific time for me here on your planet."

Ahn was in no mood to talk while strapped on a gurney at the mercy of a giant space whale.

"Do you know how long I've been on Earth?"

Ahn didn't play along.

"Two hundred and four of your Earth years, I've been trapped in this ship, buried in dirt. Somehow, fate allowed me to crash-land on your planet, right here, and somehow again I didn't expire, even as the crashing freighter dragged across your plains so heartily, it buried me deep into the soil. I must thank the Vyperians, at the least, for their solid construction of interplanetary crafts.

"Most of those two hundred and four years I've been alone, wondering when my life support systems would fail. Wondering where exactly it was that I had landed. When your species discovered radio-wave communication, I was able to listen in and calculate where I ended up. As years went by, my hopelessness turned to apathy. And still I lived, until the apathy turned to emptiness. But the emptiness left me with a spark of hope. And so, by the time your species learned to communicate with wireless visuals, I had begun to develop a plan.

"I found a way to communicate with a few of your people, and used them to do my work above the surface. My first contacts all tried to betray me and give me up to their superiors, however. A funny thing, by the way, your Earth superiors. Many of them hold no real power over you, yet you would do anything for them.

"To think, most of your race can be swayed by entertainment and empty promises. Tell me, Commander, is this what your species is going to be known for in the history of the universe: a being so simpleminded, it can be controlled by the illusion of free will dressed up in a shiny presentation?"

Commander Ahn decided it was time to speak. "You know what? I don't care. I don't care about how ignorant you think we are, or how stupid you've decided our species is, or how worthless our contributions will be in the grand scheme. I just want to be happy with my family. So if you're planning to destroy us and the planet and the Vyperians, so be it. You really don't need to explain to me why you think we deserve to be condemned to death."

Ahn heard a heaving that she could have sworn was a laugh.

"My dear, sweet human. I don't want to destroy you, or your family, or *anything* on your planet. The Vyperians might, but I can't speak for them. No, no, no.... I'm lonely. I'm sick. Most of who I am was eradicated by the creatures on their way here right now. If I had any reason to kill anything, it would be them. And I plan on doing that. But really, Commander, I only want one thing. To return home. Now I do need to build some strength, and I do need help to repair this besnerched freighter and turn it back into a space-worthy vessel. But I assure you, it will come with as minimal damage as possible to your planet."

Ahn felt a lump in her throat. *Still.* "That's a lot of nice talk from a being that threatened my family, and is imprisoning me and a kid and who knows who else who's tied up, locked up, and 'evolved' to meet your needs."

Ahn's arms fell out of the restraints as an unseen force loosened the straps. She sat up and massaged her wrists as Marnshoth's voice continued.

"Commander, imagine for a moment to have been imprisoned in darkness on a world where no one can know, help, or understand you without 'persuasion.' I no longer have the time or energy to ask for help. All I can do is hope I don't get killed by your ignorant species in the process. It's survival of the fittest, and I think I've been pretty fucking gentle all things considered."

CHAPTER 48

Seven minutes had passed on the battle cruiser. Second Sentlent Sarlz raised a tentacle, rubbed it on the circle around his beak. "Still no word?"

"Still no word, sir."

The restlessness on the bridge became overwhelming.

"Enhance visual."

The remotescope swelled again with the overhead view of the Earth women, still bouncing around. Still being gloriously arousing. Second Sentlent Sarlz could take it no more.

"Snerch it. Go to Beta alert. Set landing coordinates for that open space directly next to those females!"

"Yes, sir!"

A whirlwind of tentacles punched buttons, slid across touchscreens, and swiped at levers. Second Sentlent Sarlz stood firm at the foot of the remotescope.

"Rejoice, Vyperians! We have traveled long and far for this day! Soon, we shall reap the rewards of our toils!"

The sounds of excited hissing and clicking coursed throughout the spaceship.

"Prepare for landing. Endless pleasures await us!"

• • •

The saucer was floating a hundred feet above the south parking lot of Dodger Stadium, and just as in New York, a massive crowd had gathered in a short amount of time. There would be no public appearances from the Vyperians this go-round, however. The time had come to launch directive zero-two.

With the saucer's sudden cross-country trip, the people of Earth had become less trusting that goodwill was afoot. Sentlent Bool could feel tension growing on the saucer as well. Plans had not gone as expected. Everything had changed with the startling revelation of Marnshoth's Earth presence.

Still, the Vyperians were a proud race, and a race of accomplishment. They had come for resources and women, and it was resources and women they would reap. Marnshoth might have sent a chill across the tubes of some, but Sentlent Bool knew his Grammeral well, and knew him to be of sound decision-making. They had come too far and too long to turn tentacle and scramble, and if the Vyperians could wipe out Marnshoth once and for all, the sweet nectar of victory would be that much sweeter. *Yes, victory will be coming soon,* Sentlent Bool thought as he stood at his post on the bridge.

"Sir, you need to see this," said an ensign, breaking the second-in-command's train of thought.

• • •

Grammeral Zeezak had sought a moment of quiet in his cabin when the call from Sentlent Bool came through from the bridge.

"My Lord, we have an emergency. The battle cruiser is approaching."

"What?"

• • •

The door to the anywherevator slid open, and Grammeral Zeezak exited and slid across the bridge in a hustle.

"Scanners up!"

The giant screen displayed a hologram of the battle cruiser blasting down from Earth's orbit.

"What the skwerm are they doing?"

"We don't know, my Lord."

"Communications are still down?"

"Yes, my Lord."

All eyes were on the visual as the hologram quickly descended. But not toward them.

"They aren't coming to us. What are their exact coordinates?"

Tap-tap, swipe-*tap* on computers. "The Disney land, my Lord."

The Disney land. "Is there time to intercept?"

"No, my Lord."

"Give me a visual of the Disney land!"

Tap-tap-tap swipe.

"Well?"

Tap-tap-tap poke. "It seems as if the atmosphere is too thick with pollutants, and we would have to ascend."

An orange, hazy view of south Los Angeles appeared on the screen. The faint outline of a tall, metallic object burned through the smog as the kilometer-high battle cruiser landed fifty kilometers southeast of Dodger Stadium.

Grammeral Zeezak stroked his ring. What could possibly be going on? *The humans couldn't have contacted the battle cruiser. It* must *be a trap by Marnshoth. But what could she be planning? She can't have enough resources at her disposal to pose a realistic threat. But if she could possibly take down the battle cruiser—*

"Sentlent Bool."

"Yes, my Lord."

"Until we know more, we must keep the saucer at a safe distance. Assemble a team. Take the bubblejets to the Disney land. Make contact with the battle cruiser. Find out what is happening over there. Go."

"Yes, my Lord."

Sentlent Bool hurriedly put the call out on his comm while he slipsucked to the anywherevator. By the time he had reached the bubblejet launch room, his team of six Vyperians and two volkites were waiting.

• • •

Like their name suggested, the bubblejets looked like bubbles with jets on them. Teardrop shaped, with the bubble part at the front and the organically smooth jet tapering off at the rear, the bubblejets had the ability to become completely transparent in the sphere portion, leaving the occupant a clear view of all forward and peripheral surroundings. Even the control screens were transparent. The only components that couldn't achieve translucence were the control rods, the seat, and the smooth jet that protruded from the back. There was room inside for up to three Vyperians, or one Vyperian and a volkite.

The saucer's side opened seamlessly, and humans watching below screamed "Look!" as three of the Volkswagen Beetlesized bubbles shot out with a strange sound not unlike a child blowing bubbles in a bathtub.

"Is it laying eggs?" one person asked.

The bubbles flew due southeast.

• • •

Like many of the ships the Vyperians had originally designed, bubblejets were created for fast travel in deep, high-pressure water, and once initial research came in from the advance team on Earth, it was found that the machines would work just fine in Earth's atmosphere with a few modifications, although there hadn't been time to increase the top speed and so the peculiar ships burped through the Los Angeles sky at a not-so-scorching 112 kilometers per hour.

Sentlent Bool sat with his pilot and another Vyperian and relayed on the comm to his team and the saucer, "Arrival time, six minutes."

"Be safe, Sentlent Bool," he heard back from his Grammeral.

"Yes, my Lord."

"But not so safe that you don't figure out what's going on."

"Of course, my Lord."

CHAPTER 49

Shit, these chains are strong. Crash had been pulling on the manacles in the dark for what seemed like hours, but probably was less than one. He decided to yell out, as he was prone to do.

"Hey. *Hey.* Let me out of these goddamn chains!"

A single light turned on above him, blinding him momentarily as his eyes adjusted.

"You have been told my plans for you, yes?"

The voice startled Crash as he shook the cobwebs out of his head. "What? What plans?"

"Don't play dumb, earthling Jefferson."

Crash wasn't exactly *playing* dumb.

"You were created to help me return to my home planet. I have made you stronger than a hundred humans, and you will live longer in health than any human has in history. Do you understand what I have given you?"

"Maybe I would if I wasn't locked up all the damn time. I haven't even had a chance to *do* anything yet."

"I was in pressing need of a strong and determined human. I couldn't know exactly when the Vyperians would be arriving, so I had to make a hasty decision when chance dropped you into my possession."

"Listen, if you think I'm gonna go willingly with you to some underwater planet to be your slave, you're out of your mind," Crash said. "You knew the kind of person you'd need for whatever it is you need, and that means you know that I'm a stubborn motherfucker, and I'll fight you with everything I've got until I die."

Crash was straining against his chains, talking up toward the ceiling as if he thought his captor was above him in a strategically superior place.

"Earthling Jefferson, I think you've misunderstood."

"Have I?"

"I do not require you to leave your planet. I only need your help here. And once you are finished, you will be free to do as you please with your life."

Crash thought a moment. "I think you're full of shit."

"What could I possibly gain by lying to you, earthling Jefferson? I have you in restraints, and I can drop you to your knees with a simple command any time I choose. I want to go home, and I'm not in the position to be able to ask for help diplomatically. I've told Commander Ahn the same thing."

Crash relaxed his muscles against the chains. "And the doc?"

But Marnshoth didn't answer that question.

• • •

The battle cruiser's landing legs extended like a tripod as it settled the final few hundred meters to the parking lot adjacent to the mass of wild, partying women. Mike Horton was half-running, half-looking behind him to see what was going to happen next. The farther he ran from the middle of the parking lot, the more the lustful pressure in his groin subsided.

News channels worldwide, already providing saucer coverage around the clock, started picking up on the story of the new, larger ship. News choppers were being diverted to Anaheim, and attention that had been given to the sedentary volkites in New York was now shifting to the skyscraper of a spaceship that was landing near the saucer in California. The whole world watched and waited for whatever was going to happen next.

• • •

As the bubblejets crossed from LA County into Orange County, Sentlent Bool could clearly see the battle cruiser in the cleaner air. And he could also see what was next to it: tens of thousands of seemingly excited people.

"Pilot Scarv, enhance those humans."

The screen at the front of the bubblejet zoomed in.

"Four hundred percent, Pilot."

All women. All beautiful women. Sentlent Bool felt a tingling.

• • •

The pull was too strong. The longer the Vyperians were on Earth, the harder it became to resist the temptations of its women. Grammeral Zeezak had been smart to keep his crew separated from the Earth females for as long as he had. The same urges that pushed the Vyperians to cross the galaxy needed to be kept in check until the time was right. And Sentlent Bool knew why as he looked upon the luscious bodies of

Earth women as they gyrated and bounced and waited for their space Romeos.

"It's the promised land," screeched Pilot Scarv while he tried to remain focused enough to handle the bubblejet's controls.

Yes, thought Sentlent Bool. *But ... something isn't right.*

Few Vyperians had had any experience with any earthlings, let alone Earth's human females. But Sentlent Bool had been immersed in Earth female research from the beginning of the Vyperian talks of conquest. He knew how they moved, how they acted. They had patterns to them. And something about the way these beings moved triggered something instinctually in the Sentlent.

"It's a trap."

Pilot Scarv didn't answer, just kept flying toward the writhing beauties. "We'll be there in less than a minute, Sent—"

"No, Pilot. Halt progress immediately!"

Pilot Scarv ignored him. "This is it, Sentlent! This is what we've been waiting for!"

Bool snaked a tentacle around the pilot's tubular body, but out of the corner of his eye, saw the tentacles of the third Vyperian stab toward his own body, and he couldn't react in time.

"Regineer Zel, what are you doing!"

Regineer Zel was a brute of an octopus, having earned his scars on the front lines of the war with Marnshoth. Driven by blind lust, he managed to easily pin Sentlent Bool to the inside of the bubble so Pilot Scarv could continue flying.

"I'm sorry, sir, but you won't stop us now," the Regineer stated through the huffs of physical struggle. "We've been waiting years for this. I can't let you get in the way."

"Regineer Zel, Pilot Scarv—look at what you're doing. Listen to yourselves! You're not thinking *clearly*, you're not—"

One of Zel's giant fat tentacles slapped down onto Sentlent Bool's face so hard, it knocked him out cold.

"Thank you, sir," yelled Pilot Scarv.

"We don't need to hear that right now," said Zel. He opened his comm so only the bubblejets could hear it. "This is Regineer Zel speaking on order of Sentlent Bool. Earth's women await us. Continue as planned."

Zel could hear a moment of excited snapping and hissing before he shut off the comm. "Time to go get some pussy."

Chapter 50

The battle cruiser stood a kilometer high and looked like a skyscraper would if it needed to cut through an atmosphere. Shiny and metallic and relatively thin, it still barely fit in the flat parking lot. When the blast door opened, it opened on a landscaped tree and crushed it. With none of the caution they should have used, a stream of Vyperians exited the craft, charging toward the swarm of sexy women who awaited them.

All fighting to be first, the Vyperians tripped over themselves to get to their prizes. Like a blood clot, the Vyperians first out of the blast door had caused a bottleneck from a chain reaction of tripping up. Still the octopuses pushed forward impatiently. And so the whole group moved together as a slowly stumbling blob the half kilometer to the ladies in waiting. Alien passions burned hotter and hotter, and the first Vyperians to reach the women didn't tarry in their seductions. Tentacles groped out, and uncommon lust overtook the mass while it morphed into a blubbery mess of sexual frenzy.

• • •

The bubblejets had landed just behind the battle cruiser, and out slinked the five conscious Vyperians, their two volkite protectors thudding in tow. Consumed with sexual fire, none had bothered to ask or even notice why Sentlent Bool was not with Pilot Scarv and Regineer Zel. There was only one goal now.

• • •

The Vyperian warriors from the battle cruiser were smashing into each other, trying to push to the front of the line where all the action was. Having no concept of foreplay, the octopuses that had reached their women first went straight for the kill— by whipping their tentacles right up between the legs of their chosen ladies.

Only to find their tentacles whip right through thin air.

What is this! one octopus thought.

As soon as the whiff happened with the first, it spread to the rest via their line-of-sight telepathy. Not long after the first figured out it was a trap, the rest knew as well. But by then it was too late. The crawl from the ship had been too long, and more than half of the Vyperians had left the safety of the battle cruiser for the potential taste of Earth's women. And even in the knowledge that the women weren't real, they still found themselves pulled deeper and deeper into the field of holographic temptation. Something primal had awakened within the Vyperians, and it was not something easily put back to sleep.

Regineer Zel, finally understanding the gravity of the situation, fought his own desire to push deeper and thought-projected a command to all Vyperians in sight.

We must turn back! There is nothing but disaster to be had here! We must retreat to the ship!

His entreaty fell upon deaf frontal lobes. The Vyperians were not ready to give up just yet. The lure was too powerful. The thirty thousand aliens that had made it out of the big ship were close enough to be dangerously hooked, even in the face of a now-obvious trap.

And then the trap sprang.

The same small DO NOT OPEN UNTIL box that had launched the holograms and thumped the rhythm of the sex drum emitted a pulse that stunned the Vyperians' neurons and disabled all electronics for kilometers around.

. . .

Senator Mike Horton watched from the top of a collapsed parking garage as dozens of men in suits sprang from hiding places and spaced themselves around the countless stunned and quivering Vyperians. The men were lugging tubes that looked like bazookas attached to vacuum hoses. In sync, the suited men aimed and fired into the air over the immobile creatures. Packets exploded, and a fine white powder settled slowly down upon the Vyperians. As it dusted the octopuses, Horton could hear from his shelter the horrified clicking of thousands of beaks.

What is going on here?

Before he could take cover, a breeze kicked up and blew some dust his way. Panic stirred inside him.

Horton braced himself for a violent reaction, but the reaction didn't come. The powder was fine enough to make its way onto his lips and into his mouth.

Salt!

Scrambling back up to peek over the ledge, Horton saw the Vyperians' bodies shrivel as the highly concentrated salt dried out their membranes. The Vyperians were being jerkied alive.

• • •

Sentlent Bool regained consciousness, gathered his senses, and looked outside the bubblejet's window just in time to see the tail end of the massacre.

Oh, no. He tried to activate the comm, but it didn't respond. He soon found the bubblejet's systems were all entirely shut down. The octopus watched from a distance, helpless, while thousands of tentacles flailed in tragic thrashing while being salted to death. The sickening realization came: only the safety of the bubblejet had protected him from the same fate.

CHAPTER 51

Sunlight blinded Faraday as he was escorted from the staircase into the open air of a rubble-strewn parking lot. *No, not rubble.* Bodies. Thousands of bodies, all gelled together in a pudding of suckers and crusted slime. *With those damned suited men spraying some sort of dust onto the pile.* Faraday sucked in as much information about his surroundings as possible and calculated that the Vyperians were, in fact, being salted. But he had his own problems to deal with.

Marnshoth had gassed his fellow humans, then separated them, and that was the last Faraday had heard about anyone else, except that they were alive. At least, according to the alien whale that was holding them all hostage. He'd been kept in seclusion for only a moment, and then was given a speech through speakers in the wall by Marnshoth about how he was the only one on Earth who could help get her back home. Faraday countered by saying it wasn't as if he had a choice. He had been stalked, lied to, and then had his son kidnapped. And then Marnshoth surprised him. She let him see his son.

The door slid open and there had been Trevor, still playing the game Faraday had watched him play in his mind's eye whenever he had access. And right next to him was a perky, pretty young thing that could only be Jennica! Trevor's eyes seemed glued to the screen as he heard the door slide open, but Marnshoth cut the power from the screen and almost immediately, he fell back into reality. He looked to the doorway and his eyes glowed and his feet and knees pushed his body up from the floor.

"Dad!"

Trevor dropped his controller and ran to his father while Jennica! watched with a big smile on her face. Father and son embraced, and Faraday scooped up his son to hug him at eye level.

"Oh, Trev, I've missed you so much. I'm so sorry."

"I missed you too, Dad. It's okay, though. I'm good."

Trevor pointed to Jennica! "We're good."

Faraday hugged Trevor tight one more time and set him back onto his feet. "Are you sure? You haven't been hurt? You look skinny, are they feeding you?"

"Dad! It's okay. Really. There's this great game and—"

"Yeah, but are you eating anything?"

"Yeah, plenty of food, Dad."

Faraday walked over to the dark screen that had placated his son and the girl for so long. He looked at Jennica! "And you? You're okay, too?"

She giggled. "Yeah, I'm okay."

Jennica!'s eyes became shiny and sad. "A little lonely."

Grammeral Zeezak's brainwashing was still in effect, even from afar. Trevor tugged on her hand. "It's okay, my dad's gonna get us out. Right, Dad?"

Faraday hadn't thought about that. But a video stream in his head answered for him. A flurry of abstract color and the rumble of a disembodied voice that could only be Marnshoth.

You must leave them here for now.

No! he thought back.

They are unharmed, and will remain that way. You must help me finish my preparations.

I won't leave my son again!

Trevor could see the intensity on Faraday's face. "Dad? What's wrong?"

"Nothing. I ... I'm just thinking about what to do next."

Even if I let you all go free right now, they will be safer here. Search your mind and you'll know it to be true.

Faraday looked down at his son and held back tears. "I have to leave for a bit, but I'll promise I'll be back as soon as possible."

Trevor couldn't grasp his father's words, but Jennica! seemed to understand. While the boy asked his father whys and what-ifs, Jennica! took one hand and Faraday took the other, and they led Trevor back to the game that would blind him to his sadness.

They will be safer underground, earthling Faraday. Terrible danger is coming.

CHAPTER 52

Through his remotescope, Grammeral Zeezak watched the live Earth media coverage of what was happening fifty kilometers south. A traffic helicopter had just arrived on the scene, and although a force field had prevented it from flying too close, its cameras picked up enough of the gruesome sight to cause every Vyperian watching from aboard the saucer to screech in shock and rage. It was nothing less than a massacre. Thousands of bodies lay salted and crinkled in a killing field. There wasn't a live Vyperian in sight.

Communications to the battle cruiser were still jammed, and there was no response from any of the bubblejets. Grammeral Q'Shin Zeezak, the Emperor's Second Tentacle, methodically stroked his beak in frustration. *What a grave mistake we have made in the name of carnal pleasures. What a foolish undertaking we have committed ourselves to.* The alien leader's tentacles coiled and uncoiled slowly and rhythmically. *We have done this to ourselves. But we will not have come here for no gain.* He turned to face his bridge crew.

"War Wager Kreev!"

"Yes, my Lord!"

Zeezak snapped his beak so hard that he chipped the end. The effect brought chills to every Vyperian before him.

"Launch Directive Two."

• • •

Outside a coffee shop, a group of struggling Los Angeles actors enjoyed lattes and some of the most delicious hazelnut chocolate cake that could be found anywhere in town. The weather was warm and sunny, yet the three young people all wore scarves, and they sipped their drinks and nibbled their cakes and chatted.

"I don't understand how you keep getting auditions."

"You have to be memorable, bro. Look, the easiest way is to have a weird name. I learned that from a girl when I first moved out here. Her name was Stephanie, but the casting director misheard her one day and thought her name was Stevi, and she actually got a callback. So she kept using that name and they kept bringing her in for parts. That's how it works. You gotta stick out. Be unique. So I did the same thing."

"So you don't go by Todd anymore?"

"Fuck no. I go by Abraham."

"But your last name is Lincoln."

"Exactly."

"Don't they, like, think it's weird that they're auditioning someone named Abraham Lincoln?"

"Every damn time. And they never fuckin' forget, either. And I use it at bars, too. As soon as I tell girls my name is Abraham Lincoln, they're hooked. Shit, it happened last weekend. I was into this girl and told her my name, and when she asked if I was related to the prez, I told her no but we both agreed on one thing: some things were meant to be free. Then I yanked her top down. We fucked all night."

"Sick, bro. I gotta try that name changing— *Oh my God,*

what the hell is that?"

A giant cobra crashed through the intersection, destroying the cafe and turning everyone on the patio to streaks of pulpy red and splinters of chalky bone.

With a body a thousand feet long and fifty feet wide, the snake annihilated everything in its path with the sheer weight of its bulk.

Just around the corner, a white rental car came barreling down the boulevard.

"Turn right here, Larry. This is Melrose. *This* is the place. Larry, turn right here!"

"Yeah, okay."

"Here, Larry!"

"*Okay.* Christ."

"I don't want to miss it! Wait, this isn't Melrose Place, this is something else. Pull over so I can read the book. *Oh, my God!*"

The giant cobra tore through the rental car at fifty miles an hour, smearing the vacationing couple from Macon, Georgia across the asphalt.

The cobra tore through every thing and every person without bias. Trust-fund hipsters with expensive cameras and cheap glasses. Doughy tourists learning that Hollywood is a shithole. Sincere artists trying to make a living. Celebrities trying really hard to look like they didn't want to look like they wanted to be noticed. Single mothers taking a quick lunch break with their kids. Mexican vendors grilling bacon-wrapped hotdogs. All were destroyed by the cobra.

• • •

"I thought it would be biting more," proclaimed Grammeral Zeezak as he watched the carnage from the remotescope. "But I suppose crushing is fine too."

"My Lord," beckoned a Vyperian officer on deck. "The humans below are beginning to suspect that we aren't their friends."

The view on the remotescope changed to an angle looking down from the saucer onto the Dodger Stadium parking lot. Police officers had weapons drawn, and someone was shouting something from a megaphone.

"Let them use their cones. They'll soon know the power of the Vyperians."

The remotescope switched back to Los Angeles. The cobra was still tearing through the city, but then it took a turn toward the hills and slithered up a canyon, away from the more populated areas.

"Where is it going?"

The behemoth slipped up into the hill and with a flick of its tail, disappeared out of sight.

"Where'd my serpent go?" Grammeral Zeezak demanded.

"Out of visual range. Scanning now, my Lord."

With a few swipes of the monitor, War Wager Kreev had an answer.

"My Lord, it has slithered into the mountains and is coiled up in an unpopulated canyon."

"What! Why?"

War Wager Kreev scanned the details of the Earth creature research on his thin touch. "It seems that's what they do, my Lord. We weren't aware of that trait. Apparently Earth serpents shy away from both extreme heat and other animals, and we—"

"Enough!"

Grammeral Zeezak stroked his ring as it turned red with fury. The beast had looked so menacing. *How could something that looked so awful be so ... complacent?*

"Nectar of Marment. Grow me some other beast that would rather destroy a city than hide in the sand, or I will personally pull your tentacles off one by one."

The officer's second throat tightened. "Yes, my Lord."

Chapter 53

Seeing his son in the flesh gave Faraday hope that Marnshoth was being honest about not wanting to hurt anyone. And then came a quickening of sorts as the alien queen unlocked a firewall inside his mind.

Instantly, the scientist had access to the prison ship's vast records of Sennatian technology. Detailed notes about the ship Marnshoth was imprisoned on, and extensive notes about the Vyperians, all flooded into Faraday's mind. His super brain worked in overdrive to process the vast amount of new information as some of the established rules of physics themselves seemed to be challenged and bent. *The empty beaches of Costa Rica.* He took a breath and allowed the tsunami of data to wash over and through him. He calmed, and the final part of Marnshoth's plan was ready to be executed.

• • •

There was Faraday. There was Davis and another dozen armed and well-dressed men. And there was Crash. The destination was the battle cruiser. They marched cautiously but quickly.

"Good to see you again, Doc."

"You too."

"The whale treat you all right?"

"I got to see my son."

"Oh yeah? What about that hot singer?"

The men weaved and cleared around a tangle of exposed rebar jutting from the crumpled asphalt.

"Yeah, she's fine."

"She's really hot."

Faraday didn't answer. His attention was on the slightly opaque, dome-shaped force field that kept the scene of alien destruction separated from the rest of humanity. Military and police alike were surrounding Disneyland, formulating strategies and preparing for whatever it was they thought they might be able to do if they could get through. But whatever that strategy might be, the humans outside had no chance as long as the force field was up. Faraday took it all in while he triangulated the origin of the barrier.

The force field is coming from the Vyperian ship, not from us.

He shuddered. *'Us.' I grouped myself in with Marnshoth.*

He shrugged it off. As Crash and he ran up the extended gangplank toward the still-open blast doors of the battle cruiser, the men in suits unslung their gigantic rifles, in case any stray Vyperians hadn't been disabled by the neural blast.

The sounds of crinkling skin from the giant salt massacre below overpowered any other sounds inside the starship's entry airlock as the men first entered, but as they moved deeper into the bowels, the outside sounds faded and were replaced by dead silence from within. Every system and machine had been shut down by the box, and stunned Vyperians were everywhere: slumped across consoles, sunken into their ergonomic jelly seats, collapsed into formless, blobby piles in the walkways. No signs of movement anywhere. The men didn't lower their guard.

"We have eighteen minutes before the stun effect wears off," said Davis.

The men walked with purpose, led by Faraday's confident stride, which in itself was directed by his newly heightened knowledge of the Vyperian ship's schematics. There were no engineering surprises; Faraday knew exactly what would be around each corner and behind each door, save for the random fallen octopus. And he knew Marnshoth's end game. Both the battle cruiser and the prison freighter were powered from the same kind of energy source.

"Crash, when we get to the reactor core room, there's going to be something called a Beledet crystal. It's going to be heavy. That's why you're here."

Crash stepped over a wayward tentacle. "How big is it?"

"About the size of a grapefruit."

Crash huffed. "And that whale infected my body with little robots for that?"

"It's really dense."

"So?"

Under cover from his armed companions, Faraday pushed open a sliding door. "Density makes it heavy."

"How heavy?"

"About a thousand pounds."

Crash stopped. "Jesus. That might be too heavy, even for me."

"Let's hope not."

Davis tapped on Faraday's wrist with the barrel of his gun. "Sixteen minutes."

They marched on.

Chapter 54

The glowbats were burning red. Literally. As creatures slaved to the emotions of their master, the bats had the ability to fill a room with the entire spectrum of soft light options. But right then, they burned so red with rage that many of the glowbats were burning ulcers through their abdomens. Such was the fire of Grammeral Zeezak in his cabin, to whence he had retreated to soothe himself after the failure of the cobra.

War Wager Kreev stood before him.

"The new monster is ready, my Lord. Dosed with as much of the growth serum as it could handle."

The red light of the room accentuated the ridge of Grammeral Zeezak's beak ring.

"Unleash it," he snapped.

"Yes, my Lord."

Moments later, Zeezak watched attentively on his personal remotescope as a fluttering moth the size of a football stadium dropped into view over the museum district on Wilshire Boulevard in mid-Los Angeles. A few beats of its wings were enough to send tornado-strength gusts through the Westwood corridor, destroying a dozen residential towers in seconds. The glow of the room cooled quickly to a light blue while Zeezak looked on with Kreev.

"You see my Lord, although quite menacing in its appearance, the serpent was driven to seek refuge from the heat of

Earth's star, and thus made its way as quickly as possible to a place of cool shelter."

The moth on the screen flapped slowly and awkwardly around the Los Angeles skyline. It settled on a thirty-story glass skyscraper, and the giant insect's sheer weight immediately crushed the building to a pile of metal, concrete, and mirrored glass. Kreev continued.

"But this creature, my Lord, although only a few Earth centimeters long before the growth serum, is far more destructive. During the day, it simply floats about, landing on things. That in itself wreaks havoc. But at night, that is when the real devastation will occur."

Grammeral Zeezak watched the moth beat its wings twice, and destroy an art museum. "And why is that?"

"Because, my Lord, the thing it craves most of all is light. And all Earth buildings emit light in the darkness. It will flit around across the city and crush it, simply by doing what it would do innocently as a tiny creature."

Zeezak pulled himself into his fleshsuit, changing into human form, confusing War Wager Kreev for a moment. Zeezak smiled darkly.

"My apologies for presenting this disgusting body, War Wager Kreev, but I felt it was appropriate to respond to you with a projection only a human could create. They call it a 'smug.'"

War Wager Kreev hissed. "With all due respect, my Lord, it loosens my stool and insults the Emperor."

Zeezak pulled his fleshsuit down and returned to his true form. "I could not agree more," he said while the moth flapped its wings in Koreatown and destroyed a liquor store.

• • •

Faraday had Crash pry open a blast door, and the men walked into the chamber beyond—the Vyperian battle cruiser's reactor core room. And exactly as he saw in his mind, there was the docking cylinder for the Beledet crystal. Meticulously positioned inside it, in a thick, translucent metal harness was the crystal itself, pulsing deep blue light from its center.

"Crash, there's one thing I didn't mention about the crystal. It's radioactive and highly toxic to organic material."

Crash arched an eyebrow. "Oh? As in, it's going to kill me and this is a suicide mission?"

"Well, from what I can surmise about your regeneration abilities, you shouldn't be exposed long enough for it to kill you."

Crash's face held a combination of amusement, horror, and anger. "Doc, all I hear you saying is that I'm probably going to die."

"Ehh. Not probably. I *think* it's still less than fifty percent."

Crash eased up to the pillar with the Beledet crystal harnessed in the hollow middle. "What am I supposed to carry this thing in once I get it out?"

"Your hands. It would burn through anything else we'd have right now."

"Great. Anything else I need to know?"

"Nope."

"Six minutes. We need to go," Davis updated.

Crash eyeballed the suited men. "Wait a second. Why couldn't the whale just inject you guys for her bullshit plans?"

Faraday grimaced. He had been thinking the same thing. *But now isn't the time, Crash.*

Surprisingly, Davis answered. "Because our bodies aren't capable of the same protection against radioactive poisoning that your human bodies are, even with help," Davis replied.

Faraday and Crash made eye contact and thought the same thing. *What do you mean, our human bodies? What are—*

"Later!" Davis exclaimed, as if reading their minds.

"I ... but. Ugh, okay. Fine." Crash breathed deep and tensed his muscles for the herculean task in front of him. "Everyone get out of the chamber. Stay just close enough ahead so I can follow you around each turn once I pull this thing out. I don't want to get lost in this creepy metal tomb."

The room cleared and Crash pulled a stunned Vyperian off its oddly shaped chair. He tested the seat, found it sturdy and heavy, and then swung it with all his power.

The metal chair smashed into the harness holding the crystal, but nothing happened.

Hmmm. Crash gave it another swing. No effect. One more swing, and the chair disintegrated into a few large jagged pieces. The pillar remained unscathed. He heard Faraday yell from the next room. "Any luck?"

Crash didn't answer. He opened his palms and swung his arms like paddles at the pillar, connecting with it like a Shaolin monk lifting a burning urn with his forearms.

Crack.

He arched his back and spread his arms, and snapped them closed again. This time, he fractured the case surrounding the crystal. Something leaked, and the room smelled of ozone. Crash beat the pillar again, and again, and finally it shattered enough to allow the crystal to fall out onto the floor under its own weight. It landed with a flat thud, and rolled a couple of inches before stopping. Crash looked around for anything to help carry the crystal out. Nothing. Lights flickered and machines started buzzing.

"What's going on?" he yelled out of the room.

"The ship is powering back on. Hurry up. We can't get stuck in here when the defense systems come back online."

Crash looked down at the sleeping Vyperian from which he'd swiped the chair. *Good thing these guys aren't coming to yet.* He hunched over and picked up the crystal, which was still pulsing blue. *Shit. Doc wasn't kidding.* The rock weighed half a ton and it burned the skin of his hands into blisters almost immediately. He stood and cradled the crystal like a football and could feel his muscles ripping and repairing, his skin burning and healing as the nanobots did their jobs. Straightening his back as much as possible, he turned and dragged himself out of the room.

"Let's go!"

*

CHAPTER 55

Horton had seen enough. A towering spaceship. Thousands of octopuses clamoring for bikini-clad women who weren't really there. Rugged, well-dressed men with guns that shot—of all things—salt. But he couldn't leave the chaos. He stood a foot away from military officers, members of the press, local police, and frenzied civilians, yet the force field prevented him from touching or hearing them. An official-looking woman on the other side wrote simple questions and statements on her tablet and held it up to the "glass," but there wasn't anything Horton wanted to say. He just wanted out.

He sighed. "I just want to go home," he said aloud to himself.

As do I.

Horton was surprised to hear a response in his mind. The voice had been silent since he activated the box.

Where are you? the exhausted man thought back.

Buried beneath your feet.

Horton mulled the words over a moment before think-speaking again. "And where is your home?"

A long, long way from here.

Horton frowned and tapped on the force field, and it made a sound like a rubber band being strummed. "I did what I had to do. Why can't I go now?"

I'm not in control of the force field. It is an emergency

mechanism from the Vyperian ship. Wait and find a safe place to hide. No one under my control will harm you, but I cannot say the same for the Vyperians. And they will awaken shortly.

Horton wandered away from the edge of the force field, lost in his own head. He sat on a curb, facing away from the frantically waving people on the other side trying to get his attention.

"Why me? Why did you put me through all this?"

Why not you?

"All this misery I had to go through just to … push a goddamn button?"

You fit the needs I required. Nothing more or less than that.

"What did I do that millions of others couldn't?"

You have travel clearance. And you lust for males of your species.

Horton felt a lump in his throat. "How—"

The box had to be built with materials from far off, and then brought here safely, outside my usual network of transport. So I needed someone with access to private air travel, at a time when I knew air travel would be restricted for most of your species.

When he didn't reply, she continued, explaining that the box projected realistic representations of attractive human females, coupled with the subconscious lure of sexually rhythmic sounds. In close range of that technology, any male with interest in human females would be unable to resist their own urges.

Unless, of course, there was a deviation. A deviation such as yours.

So his "deviation" was one factor in the choice of him to do this. He gave a bitter chuckle, but she either didn't sense what it meant, or didn't hear it.

You felt the urge, but with that deviation, it did not overly tempt you. Otherwise you would have become overwhelmed by the temptation, and then either remained conspicuously in the area, or errantly triggered the stun bomb before the optimal time. That is also partly why I leveled this region when I did: to provide an area clear of any other humans who might spoil the trap.

Horton remained silent and traced his finger in the dirt. The chuckle might not have informed her, but silence, she seemed to understand.

Perhaps there is more to why I chose you. I relate to your isolation, your loneliness. You have been struggling in a world that might not accept you, entombed by the false life that surrounds you. As have I, but in far harsher conditions. And so I have planned, I have saved my energy for just this time, for this slim chance to return home, though most of what I know there has been destroyed. Your emptiness and your pain, though surely not pleasant or trivial, is ultimately incomparable, earthling Horton.

Tears welled in Mike Horton's eyes. Tears for himself, for Rebecca and Lizzie, and for whatever was speaking to him through his mind.

I'm sorry, he thought.

He looked over to the towering Vyperian ship, the top of which was visible over the parking garage he'd run behind for safety. Lights started flickering on and off as the power returned in phases. He turned to look at the people outside the force field, but they'd stopped trying to get his attention and were looking at the ship too.

"Are you still there?" he asked.

Yes.

"If you've been buried here this whole time, how did you pull this off?"

The Vyperians have been on your planet studying humans for most of the last Earth century. Imagine my surprise at their arrival. It was then that my plan started to take shape. The Vyperians have basic telepathic power, can communicate subconsciously, but can only do so by line of sight unless they use implants. I, however, can reach out across a planet. I managed to slowly, carefully, take control of the minds of the weakest in their early teams. I separated the corrupted Vyperians from the collective, and then used them to exponentially increase my work.

The lights on the ship were steadily blinking now. The power was almost completely restored. Horton sighed, his mind scrambled and exhausted. His lips were drying out from the lingering salt in the air. He licked them. Cast his gaze back toward the dying mass of octopuses.

"I don't understand why they would even put in all this crazy effort just for our women. I guess I'm not the best source for understanding that motivation, but it all seems a bit illogical."

Quite the opposite, earthling Horton. It's all entirely logical once you know the truth.

"What truth?"

But before he could press further, the conversation ended

when the sun was blacked out from the sky by the fluttering of humongous wings. A giant moth filled the horizon.

"What the holy hell?"

Seek heavy shelter, earthling Horton. Danger is coming.

Chapter 56

"My Lord, a bubblejet is approaching."

Grammeral Zeezak curled his tips. "Who is it?"

"We don't know. Its comm system is offline."

"Could it be Marnshoth's doings?"

War Wager Kreev thought about the possibility. "Perhaps."

"Is there any way of knowing before it flies closer?"

"No, my Lord."

"Very well. Let it approach, but track it with the death ray at all times. Keep Flentlod Vernv on the weapon controls. His trigger tentacles itch for destruction."

"Yes, my Lord."

The bubblejet made no unusual moves or threatening maneuvers. It docked to a welcome committee of armed-to-the-beak Vyperians, but as soon as the transparent dome of the bubble jet was visible, cautions dropped at the sight of the occupant inside.

• • •

Grammeral Zeezak sat at his command throne on the bridge as the door to the anywherevator slid open and Sentlent Bool entered with his escort. Bool sported a big, fat bruise across his face. Zeezak stifled the urge to exuberantly greet his old comrade.

"Welcome back, Sentlent. Report," the leader spoke in clicks and hisses.

"Female projections! A trap set by Marnshoth!"

"*Trap?*"

Sentlent Bool continued, and Grammeral Zeezak ruminated on the news for a moment. A trap of holograms? How could Marnshoth have known far enough in advance of the Vyperians' desire for Earth's females to construct such a device? *The only way—*

"War Wager Kreev," summoned Zeezak. "In the original data messages from our first research missions on Earth, from the missing scouting team presumed lost by accident ..." He trailed off.

"Yes, my Lord?"

But the Vyperian leader discovered the answer on his own. "Nectar of Marment. She used our own technology against us."

"I don't understand, my Lord."

"That besnerched creature triggered us with our own transmissions. She knew the crew would be briefed on the Earth mission with those data streams. We only programmed Earth's women to desire us because we were programmed to desire them *first*."

Speaking those words, Grammeral Zeezak's third stomach sank. "She set the bait, and we took it. Marnshoth has been in control from the beginning."

The alien leader sat back in his command throne as reality fully set in.

She changed the very destiny of our species just to suit her plans.

CHAPTER 57

It was a hell of a lot harder to get out of the battle cruiser than it was to get in, at least for Crash. The crystal's weight strained every muscle, bone, and joint in his advanced body. And without any protective shielding, the glowing power source leaked energy that burned through Crash's flesh. The nanobots struggled to keep Crash intact while they repaired tears, burns, and rips across his frame. And though they did their job well, he realized he was still falling apart faster than they could put him back together. And they did nothing for the pain.

"Couldn't they have put some morphine injectors in me?" he screamed through gritted teeth.

"*What?*" Faraday yelled back from a dozen meters ahead.

"Argh ... nothing!"

Crash stepped over a Vyperian as its tentacles began to move like eels snapping at passing minnows. *Crap. Hope these slimy bitches stay down long enough.* The stun effect was wearing off, and the humans were only halfway back to the blast door. It would be at least another five minutes before they were out of the ship.

Up ahead and in the lead, Faraday navigated across corridors and around the shut-down anywherevator conduits while the men in suits made sure Crash remained within eyeshot. With all the knowledge he possessed, Faraday still had no idea who the "men" were, or why they were helping Marnshoth. Or, for that matter, why they all wore expensive suits all the time. *If there were ever a bad time to wear a suit, it would be in a breach mission into an alien spacecraft.*

"So just who are you guys, anyway?" he asked in tones hushed partly due to caution, partly to exhaustion.

The men in suits ignored him as they moved forward into a massive hangar.

"Don't you have anything at all you can say to me?" Faraday pleaded, then turned back for a moment to make sure Crash was still close. Davis looked to the right side of the hangar as a fallen Vyperian first flexed its tentacles, and then rose to stand. All at once, Davis and his men quickly formed a protective circle around Faraday. The group moved ever closer to the exit. One by one, the Vyperians in the large room wriggled themselves upright.

Faraday exhaled slowly. "We don't have much time left, do we?"

This time Davis answered.

"We don't have any time left. *Jefferson, let's hustle!*"

• • •

Sluggish and falling behind, Crash heard the plea for quickness from about twenty meters ahead of him and hunkered down. Cradling the crystal between his hands and gut, he could feel the intense energy sloughing his skin off, could smell his flesh burning. It stank like the barbecue from hell.

Almost there. Almost there. C'mon.

Crash dragged his feet around the bend of the hallway as his knees bent under the weight. Something grabbed his ankle.

His upper body kept its momentum while his foot remained anchored, sending him spilling face-first into the alien ship's cool metal floor. The crystal spilled out of his clutches, rolled a meter, and hit the side wall with a thud.

What the hell? He twisted himself around to his back and saw the Vyperian that had tripped him. This one was bigger than the others he'd come across. This one wasn't some softy ship commander. It was a warrior. Thicker, fatter, covered in scars. It rose to its tips and scuttled hard and fast into Crash's personal space, and raised two tentacles like blunt, heavy weapons.

Good thing I've got my little friends to help me.

But the nanobots were almost entirely devoted to healing the massive damage the radioactive crystal had caused to Crash's system. A normal human would have burned to char within moments of being exposed, and although Crash was far from normal, he still had burns across half his body that would take the nanobots minutes to fix. Minutes that Crash didn't have.

Thwack. The two flattened, fat tentacles smacked down on Crash's chest with tremendous force, knocking the air out of his lungs with an "*Oooff.*"

"Crash, what's happening back there?" Faraday yelled from the hangar. "We've got to get out, *now!*"

But Crash had his hands full, and the warrior Vyperian had its tentacles full of Crash's face. Suckers ripped the skin off the man's cheekbones and upper chest.

"No!" Crash's sculpted nose and cheekbones crushed under the intense pressure.

"No *no no nooooo!*"

The Vyperian still had Crash by the ankles with two of its other tentacles, and whipped him up off the ground, holding him upside down. Standing on two tentacles, holding the human upside down with two tentacles, and ripping at the man's face with two tentacles, the Vyperian still had two free appendages, and it used them to beat at Crash's dangling body like a boxer on a speed bag. The octopus alternated between straight punches and open-tentacled side slaps, beating the TV host senseless and leaving the nanobots no time to do their repairs. Crash was losing the battle, and quickly.

About to lose consciousness, Crash saw through fading vision the Vyperian's skin bubbling, and then the octopus too became aware of its flesh frying. Frantic, it looked over to see the Beledet crystal a few meters away. The warrior Vyperian screeched and bolted out of the room, dragging the helpless Crash in tow.

• • •

There was cold silence on the saucer bridge after the devastating realization of Marnshoth's scheme against the Vyperians. Finally, the urgency of the situation sparked Sentlent Bool to continue the debriefing. He explained his failed attempts to abort the mission to the battle cruiser, the lust-driven mutiny that had occurred, and the despondence of waking up to a massacre of his fellow soldiers.

"As soon as the bubblejet's systems recovered from the blast, I took a low-flying route straight here, my Lord. There was nothing I could do for the others."

"You did the right thing, Sentlent. You would have been

salted just like the rest of our warriors, may they rest. Any idea of the status of the battle cruiser?"

"No, other than systems were slowly coming back online. I assume the stun effects of the blast should be wearing off as well. Beyond that, I do not know."

"And my princess?"

Bool's ring flashed indigo. "No word, my Lord."

Zeezak thought about his Earth mate suffering at the hands of Marnshoth, and tried to shake off the idea. Tried to ignore the anguish. *Our bond is not even real. Only a trap fabricated by my sworn enemy. We must remember what is important.* The alien leader thought of the thousands of Vyperians still on the battle cruiser, and the battle cruiser itself still being in the heart of danger. *If we don't get that ship safe from the clutches of Marnshoth, none of us is getting home.*

Frustrated, Zeezak looked to the remotescope as the giant moth continued to flutter down random destruction across Los Angeles. "Is there any way we can control that creature?"

War Wager Kreev gulped. "Well, my Lord, it is not the most intelligent being. It, uh, is just more of a total destruction—"

"Can we give it commands or not?"

The bridge fell silent. Grammeral Zeezak was not known for losing his temper.

"No, my Lord. It will not listen."

"Are there *any* Earth beasts that will obey my commands?"

"Not that I am aware of, my Lord. And we haven't had the time to engineer a manipulation implant for any specific—"

"Anything at all that won't just hide under a rock or flap around like an intoxicated velveen? Something we can trust to not destroy us along with the earthlings?"

War Wager Kreev looked around the room.

"What are you looking around for, Kreev? I am asking *you!*"

Kreev's ring turned blue with fear and embarrassment. "No, my Lord. The only intelligent species on Earth are the humans, and only barely."

Zeezak took a seat on his command throne and watched as the moth mindlessly flapped and landed on things and destroyed them without reason or purpose. *At least it is effective at destruction.* He dropped his gaze from the remotescope to the floor of the bridge and took a slow, deep breath. *This entire mission has been a disaster,* he thought with an uncharacteristic hint of defeat. He looked up again at the screen as Sentlent Bool approached the throne.

"My Lord."

Zeezak stared straight ahead at the remotescope and watched the giant moth flit around with deadly daintiness. It fluttered high, then a wind current dropped it onto a shopping mall, then a highway, then a grassy sports field. None of that mattered to him. Random chaos was fine, but what he needed was to regain control.

"My Lord," Bool said again.

"Yes, Sentlent." Zeezak looked to his Sentlent and saw the lesser's ring to be a curious mix of colors.

"I have an idea," said Bool.

CHAPTER 58

In the hangar, Faraday and the men in suits were surrounded by Vyperians. Big, nasty-looking Vyperians. Faraday calculated the odds of survival with his advanced mind. *Shit.*

"Crash!" Faraday yelled without taking his eyes from the gradually smothering circle of Vyperians.

There was no answer.

The Vyperian circle tightened around the human circle and tentacles readied for striking. The humans had their weapons, but more Vyperians poured into the big hangar as they one by one recovered from the stun attack. In seconds, the humans were outnumbered two to one, then three to one, then four to one. The Vyperians poised for an onslaught, and the circle of men in suits surrounding Dr. Faraday readied their assault rifles.

A horrific screeching tore through the open space as a massive Vyperian ran into and through the hangar. All attention shifted to the beast as it ran past, its skin smoldering and burnt and its rear tentacles dragging a human. Faraday blinked. "Crash?"

• • •

The ten-second reprieve from the beatings while the Vyperian dragged Crash away from the crystal was just enough for his little friends to reverse the trend of cell destruction and begin healing Crash's body faster than it could die. By the time he was pulled into the middle of the room by the burning octopus, he was strengthened enough to wrench himself free of the Vyperian, which at that point was far too concerned with its own burning flesh to worry about the human who'd just wriggled loose from its grip.

The octopuses and humans in the hangar watched Crash roll free and stand up. He patted himself and dusted off, wincing from the pain of the burns and beating. All eyes on the TV host, Crash nodded to Faraday past a crowded eye line of slimy protuberances.

"Hey Doc. Check *this* out," said Crash enthusiastically while he began to dance erratically by himself, as if he were drunk and alone on his birthday and not in the middle of an impending bloodbath.

"*Uhhhhhh* what? We ... kind of have our hands full, you know, at the moment."

"You weren't kidding when you said that crystal was heavy!" Crash continued as he stomped his feet and pumped his fists into the air. "I feel so light now. I just gotta shake *loose!*"

The Vyperians stared at Crash and wobbled in utter confusion. They had not been briefed on the human behavior on display in front of them. The only being more confused than the octopuses was Faraday, who watched the madness with an extremely puzzled look on his face.

What. The. Hell is he doing?

The answer struck Faraday as Crash's face began to visibly heal in the middle of a leg kick and arm windmill. *He's buying a few seconds to get stronger, that's what.*

"Wow, Crash. You've got some moves! Show us some foot-work!" Faraday called out, playing along. Crash pumped his legs harder, channeling his inner MC Hammer and trying to remember how the running man went.

The Vyperians had kept their distance, not sure what to make of this strange behavior in the midst of battle. But the element of surprise was quickly wearing off, and they began to once again close in.

Crash stopped dancing, threw his arms out, and screamed, "Wait!"

The Vyperians halted once more for just a moment.

Crash looked at the octopuses and then to Davis and thought, *This is as good as I'm gonna get.* He gave Davis a slight nod. Davis gave the subtlest of acknowledgements back, and Crash dropped flat to the floor.

All the guns fired at once.

The weapons tore through Vyperian flesh, severing tenta-cles and blasting holes. The men in suits had only enough time to fire off a few rounds each before the Vyperian circle col-lapsed on them, wrenching the weapons from their hands with hundreds of snaking tentacles. And then it was hand-to-hand from there on out, with Faraday trying to stay safe in the mid-dle.

Crash—still somewhere between normal human strength and indestructible super-weapon—ripped through the thick of the Vyperians, tearing limbs off and crushing tube-shaped bodies with his bare hands. Two tentacles swung at him from opposite sides, and he grabbed them both in midair and twisted them into a knot. Two more tentacles came at his ankles, trying to trip him, but he jumped and landed in a pushup position, pinning the tentacles to the floor. He pushed himself back up to his feet for leverage, and then yanked on the tentacles, bringing the attached bodies of the two striking Vyperians flying to him. He sidestepped at the last possible microsecond, allowing the two octopuses to smash into each other with such force that their sacs popped and ooze leaked out like goo from Junior Mints mashed between the fingers of a child.

Slime was *everywhere.*

At the center of the brawl, Faraday couldn't see past his protectors, but occasionally a tentacle would find its way in, and he'd do his best to avoid getting coiled up in it.

Tentacles jutted between the legs of the men in suits as they slashed away with combat knives, and the sounds of snapping beaks drew closer and closer. Through the cracks, Faraday saw the body of one of the men getting pulled apart, all limbs yanked and separated at once by a mass of wiry tentacles. As the man screamed one last time, Faraday looked away. But not before seeing an odd sight.

What the hell was that? But his view was obstructed again and he didn't have the presence of mind to analyze the situation further.

There were just too many Vyperians. Too many, and too strong. One by one, the men were picked off until only a few remained. *The odds are pretty damn different when you don't have a stun bomb,* Faraday thought as he desperately tried to avoid being grabbed by a wayward tentacle.

Only Davis and another man in a suit were left standing, sandwiching the scientist between them for safety, and beyond them, all he could see in his few feet of viewing range was tentacle and beak.

Faraday prepared himself for the worst, and even thought about burying himself in the fantasy of whatever video he could pull up in his mind. But he chose to watch his son instead. He saw Trevor, sitting still in front of that damn game, oblivious to all the problems around him. Trevor didn't know about the war raging. He didn't know the fate of the world was right now being fought for, didn't care that everything had changed forever, one way or another. Didn't even care about the pretty superstar playing the game next to him. Faraday wondered what would happen to his son once Marnshoth figured out her fancy, upgraded humans had failed to get her back to her home planet. She was powerless without outside help, and Trevor was locked in a room underground with a pop star and a stupid game that kept him complacent.

Until what? Until he runs out of water and food? Why would Marnshoth even care once her mission fails? She won't. She'll just let them die there. Frank's eyes teared up. *My son can't die like that.*

While the two other men fought frantically around him, he saw one of their rifles on the ground, half covered by the body of a dead Vyperian. He plunged his hands through the slippery pile of body parts, made a lunge for the gun, and wrenched it free. His brain told him what to do and how to best do it, and he flipped around on his back and shot upward into the impending doom. Blast after blast burned through Vyperian after Vyperian, giving the two men standing above him some brief cover as they fought on. But as each Vyperian was hit, it seemed as if two more took its place. They were awakening across the entire ship, and coming from every corner to help in the hangar.

And where the hell is Crash? Faraday felt a moment of anger, and then a moment of fear and sadness as his thoughts of Crash abandoning him melted into a more likely scenario: that Crash had been overpowered before he had a chance to get back to full strength. Still he blasted away.

And then the gun stopped firing. The power source was depleted. He looked around. Nothing but blood, slime, and flesh. And the only thing protecting the men now was the crater they were in, a crater created by a six-foot-high rim of dead bodies. On the top of the rim, a perimeter of Vyperians assembled. There were no guns left. Davis and the other man were drained, and could barely stand. The look of surrender was in their eyes.

Except there would be no surrender. The Vyperians had no need for prisoners. Their plans had been decimated, and there was no reason to do anything to their enemies except destroy them.

Faraday took one last look at his son in his mind, and then made his peace. *I'm sorry I've failed you, Trevor. I'm sorry things couldn't work out better with your mom and me. I'm sorry. I love you.* Trevor kept playing his game, but Faraday pretended he could hear his father's every word. *Maybe one day he'll know.*

He looked up. There had to be twenty massive Vyperian warriors standing above him and the other two men. They all raised their tentacles at once. The two men in suits slumped, and dropped themselves to sit next to Faraday. They were tired. They were ready to die.

The Vyperians clicked their beaks and their rings turned

bright red. And just as they were about to rain down pain and death upon the humans, a bone-jarring scream filled the chamber. But it was not a Vyperian scream; it was a human scream. And not a scream of pain, but of intimidation.

Faraday saw the Vyperians switch their gaze from the humans below them, but it was too late. A massive metal pole swung through the group with such force that it exploded the octopus bodies on impact. With a couple of passes, the entire group of Vyperians had been felled. So much slime poured down the sides of the crater, Faraday had to stand to his feet to keep from being submerged as it settled in the pit.

The men looked up cautiously. No more Vyperians came. Faraday struggled to get words out.

"Crash? ... Crash?"

The sounds of scrambling trickled over the top of the octopus body-crater, and Crash appeared, looking as virile and chiseled as ever. The three men peered up at him and Faraday grinned.

"Jesus, Crash, where the hell did you go?"

"I was hiding."

The smiling immediately stopped and jocularity turned to anger. "*What?*"

Davis took over. "While you were hiding, we were getting beaten to death."

Crash furled his brow with sincere concern. "I'm sorry. I had to. I was getting too badly hurt. I had to give myself time to regenerate. Otherwise we'd all be dead. You understand, right, Doc?"

"I suppose," Faraday said.

"Good, because we need to get the fuck out of here," Crash

said. "There are a few thousand more of these guys headed over here from the other side of the ship, and it's about to get ugly."

Crash pulled the three men out of the hole of flesh, and for the first time since the battle began, took note of the casualties. The entire room was filled with dead bodies. Hundreds of octopus bodies—some full and many in pieces—were quivering across the expanse of the hangar. *There isn't one spot of the floor still showing. It's all been covered by death.* Crash shook it off.

"You guys stay ahead of me, same as before. I still have to grab the crystal. But I'm strong enough now to not hold you back. Let's move!"

He stomped through the flesh to retrieve the crystal from the previous room, and the three other men climbed down from the mountain of bodies and continued toward the blast door. *Get me out of this place*, thought Faraday as he crinkled his nose from the rotten smell of slime and innards.

Chapter 59

Second Sentlent Sarlz was one of the lucky ones. On the bridge, far from the blast door, he hadn't been able to push through the bottleneck of horny invaders in time to make it out of the battle cruiser. Furious at first, now he understood that it was only dumb luck that kept him from being slaughtered with thousands of his underlings in the trap outside.

The acting lead officer on the mother ship wondered where the help was from the saucer. *Perhaps they have been attacked as well.* His beak ring flushed blue. *Perhaps this mission will turn into the ultimate failure for the Vyperian race.*

As the systems came back on line one after another, Second Sentlent Sarlz watched through the remotescope as a handful of earthlings dismantled an entire squadron of his best octopods. Watched as a human somehow managed to carry out a Beledet crystal *all by himself.* Watched as the human was intercepted by multiple squadrons of Vyperian warriors, and then watched in horror as the human all but single-handedly killed them off. Then the human rescued his peers, gathered up the crystal again, and left the ship. Second Sentlent Sarlz could have sent more squadrons, but for what? After that display, he knew he would be sending his warriors to their deaths. No, they would be more valuable to him and the Vyperian race as a whole if he held back for now.

We have to regroup. We have to make a plan. And I have to make contact with the Grammeral.

. . .

Once off the Vyperian battle cruiser, Faraday, Davis, and the other suit paced twenty meters ahead of Crash, back toward the hidden entrance to Marnshoth's buried ship. Crash was once again on the downward spiral of cell destruction, and the skin of his hands was frying off faster than it could be stabilized.

"Crash," Faraday yelled back, "you get ahead of us and get down there first. The faster we get that thing secure, the safer I'll feel."

Crash gritted his teeth and tightened his cradling grip on the crystal. While he dragged himself to the secret entrance to the elevator, he saw the ruins of what had been a caramel apple stand. He'd come to Disneyland so many times as a child, and that stand might have been the very one his parents had bought him apples from year after year. He momentarily felt sadder about its destruction than he did about the war he was caught in the middle of.

The suited men were barely able to stand as they waited outside for Crash to descend in the elevator. Faraday had missed most of the action, being at the bottom of the body-pile while the suits took most of the hits. He glanced at Davis; his fancy suit sleeves were sliced and shredded, and his dark gray pants were stained with Vyperian blood.

"Is there anything I can do to help?" Faraday asked. Davis shook his head no. The other man, quiet as ever, took a final look at Faraday and fell face-first onto the ground.

"Oh *shit*." Faraday kneeled down and rolled the man over

to turn him face up. Except there was no face. At least, not a human one. It was Vyperian. The man's body shimmered for a second, and then the fleshsuit gave way and out bulged the tubular, tentacled shape Faraday had grown to hate.

Davis sank to his knees. "Get me ... inside."

Faraday pulled Davis up and around his shoulder and half-carried half-dragged the disguised Vyperian inside the entrance to Marnshoth's threshold.

• • •

Crash reached the bottom of the elevator shaft and Marnshoth's voice was waiting for him. "Thank you for your help," it rumbled.

"Yeah, no problem. I'm burning alive. Where the fuck do I take this?"

"Apologies. Second door on the left. You'll see a chamber that looks very similar to the one you removed the crystal from on the Vyperian battle cruiser."

Crash walked a few dozen meters with the Beledet crystal still occupying his hands and still killing his body, and hit the panel with his hip to open the door. Sure enough, the room was almost identical to the one on the battle cruiser. The technology was older looking and seemed from a previous generation, but still familiar.

The pillar in the middle of the room had a crystal of its own in it, but the glow was barely noticeable. *This battery's burned out.* Crash walked over quickly, excited by the fact that he'd be done carrying a half-ton rock that was killing him. He dropped the fresh crystal.

"I had to crack open the pillar on the other ship," he said. "I assume there's an easier way to get it open?"

"Yes," the omniscient voice answered. "There is a blue button on the console behind it. Press it, and then twist to the left."

He did as he was told, and the shielding slid open.

Much easier.

He pulled out the old crystal, which was as heavy but not nearly as painful to hold, and dropped it on the floor. He popped the new one in, and then hit the blue button to lock the crystal securely into place. He immediately felt better, and could again feel the shift as the nanobots were able to repair him faster than he could break apart.

The rugged adventurer looked down at the old crystal. *It must be so dead that it can't burn me.* He picked it up. It burned his skin. *Okay, dead enough that it can't burn me unless I'm touching it.*

"What should I do with this old *Bele*-whatever?"

Marnshoth didn't answer.

"Hello? What do I do with this thing?"

"There is a containment box on the side wall near the door."

Crash saw it.

"Dispose of it there. Quickly. There is trouble on the surface."

Crash lugged the old crystal to the containment box. "What kind of trouble?"

"Big trouble."

CHAPTER 60

Ahn stood alert at the door sliding open and Faraday dragging in a staggering Vyperian, which in turn was dragging a fleshy sack with what looked to be shreds of a nice suit hanging from it. She gasped and jumped into a defensive stance.

"No, no. It's okay," growled Faraday while he dragged the Vyperian over and laid it down on the gurney that Ahn had until moments earlier been strapped down to. "He's on our side. Or Marnshoth's side. Which might also be our side. Shit, I don't even know who's on who's side, but he saved me."

Ahn moved in for a closer look. "What do you mean he's on our side?"

"This is the leader of Marnshoth's men."

Ahn was stunned. "The men in suits? This is Davis?"

"Yes."

"What happened to the others?"

"They died defending me."

"Where's Crash?"

"Right here," Crash answered as he entered the room.

• • •

Crash and Dr. Faraday filled Commander Ahn in on the battle cruiser, the power crystal, and the fact that the men she'd been working over, with, and for were not in fact men, but Vyperians. Crash gave an elaborate account of how he launched a one-man wrecking crew to save Faraday and Davis and get the crystal out, to which Ahn responded with an eye roll before steering the conversation back on track.

"Holograms and Vyperians. So no one working for Marnshoth in that lab was a human except for me?"

Crash had been prodding the Vyperian on the gurney with his finger, but stopped when he heard Commander Ahn's words. "Are you?"

Ahn gave Crash an angry look. "Of course I am, you asshole."

"Okay, *okay*. Fine," Crash relented.

"Jordan and the men in suits were Vyperians," came Marnshoth's voice through the walls, startling everyone.

"Jesus Christ," yelped Crash. "I always forget you're here."

Faraday pushed off the wall he had been leaning on. "How was this done?"

"Many beings from Sennat use telepathy, earthling Faraday, although my abilities are much stronger than most. When the early Vyperians arrived here, I made contact with those I sensed to have weak minds, and lured them away. The others thought they had died in an accident. In reality, they became my workers. My species relies on remote appendages, all controlled by a central mind. This was not much different.

"The first Vyperians became my extensions. My hands. Using their ability to camouflage themselves as humans with their fleshsuit technology, and then with an added layer of detailed projection, they became indistinguishable from your race from the outside, and therefore well suited for my needs. There are some things, however, for which Vyperian physiology is not appropriate. They were my original subjects for the first experiments with nanotechnology. Unfortunately, the results were ... poor."

As Marnshoth continued, the three humans watched the prone Vyperian like it was the visual aid in a show-and-tell.

"In addition, the more beings I directly control, the less attention I can give to the actions of each. That is why you might have experienced odd encounters: lack of emotion or responses, and even the occasional glitch as my control was stretched thin. Sometimes there was just too much going on at one time. I believe you can relate, earthling Faraday. As such, that is why I required additional help from all of you."

The three humans exchanged glances. Faraday looked back down at Davis, the last of Marnshoth's Vyperians.

"This one has served me well," Marnshoth spoke.

Boom.

The entire subterranean ship shook violently, knocking everyone to the ground. The humans struggled to return to their feet. Crash, recovering quicker than the rest, yelled out, "What the hell was that?"

Boom. Another massive hit, powerful enough to cause the ship to creak.

"Earthling Jefferson, there is a panel on the wall directly in front of you. Please open it and remove the contents."

Another boom, and the ship rocked, creaked, and settled slightly. Crash slid open the panel and found what Marnshoth was talking about: a small vial of dark purple fluid. It appeared to be burning, and a flame licked about the sides of the tube as Crash held it up.

"Drink that quickly, earthling Jefferson."

"What? It's on fire! It'll burn my insides up! I don't even know what it is!"

"It is a concentrated serum derived from a species of burning bush located on another planet far from here. The Vyperians use it in times of war. Your enhanced body will quickly handle the dangers of the liquid."

"I don't—"

Boom! This time, the ship shuddered longer and more heavily than before. The buried freighter was falling apart.

"Drink it, earthling Jefferson, or we will all die."

"What about Davis?" Crash asked, even though looking at the withered, destroyed body of the Vyperian at his feet was answer enough. The TV host looked around and into the eyes of Ahn and Faraday, searching for encouragement or suggestions of alternate possibilities. He found nothing but shrugs and silence.

"Well *shit*." Crash popped the lid off the vial and threw back the fluid. A stream of the purple liquid trickled down the side of his chin and erupted into flame just long enough to burn off the skin and epidermis even as streaks of metal crisscrossed Crash's wound and healed him in seconds.

"Now, earthling Jefferson, you must go to the surface. Bring Commander Ahn with you."

Crash and Ahn locked eyes. "Uh, okay. What am I supposed to, you know … do?" Crash asked as he grimaced from the pain inside.

"You will both know when you get there."

"Really? Are you sure? Because you've said that before and it hasn't always worked out so well—"

When the shockwave came this time, the damage was palpable. It wouldn't be long before the ship's hull would give out and bury them under millions of tons of dirt.

"Go!" Marnshoth called out.

Crash tensed his muscles, and with a skeptical glance at Faraday, Ahn grabbed him by the hand and ran with him to the hallway that led to the elevator.

CHAPTER 61

The hangar with the slain Vyperians had been sealed off in the battle cruiser. The systems had all booted back online. Thousands of warrior Vyperians had been killed, but Second Sentlent Sarlz's core crew was mostly intact: only warriors had had the time to leave the ship before the devious trap was sprung. Communications were still down, and Sarlz's resources were depleted. One of the Beledet crystals had been stolen by the humans, but there were spares.

Sarlz looked down from his command throne on the bridge, looked upon the beaks and rings of the octopuses sworn to follow him, and could see the loss in their big, round eyes. He felt it himself. The feelings of betrayal, of anger, of sadness. Even fear. They were lost. Grammeral Zeezak and Sentlent Bool hadn't been heard from since the madness began, their fates unknown.

A thunderous sound rumbled, and the entire ship shook and swayed. Red alert sounded automatically.

"Is it the moth? That damned beast!" yelled Sarlz.

"No sir, the moth is fifty kilometers to the north!" replied an officer.

"Remotescope to visual!"

The remotescope filled the front of the bridge, and spanning the entire screen was Sentlent Bool. All seven hundred feet of him.

• • •

Crash and Ahn stared at the giant Vyperian before them. Towering over everything but the massive needle of the battle cruiser, its tentacles could have easily reached a half kilometer if stretched out. It scuttled its way slowly yet effortlessly through the force field that bubbled over the area in which they were all contained.

"What the holy *shit*," Crash said. "How am I supposed to know what to do with that?"

Ahn leaned in to squeeze his shoulder for comfort, but missed and hit the middle of his back instead. She frowned. *I don't remember him being that tall.*

Then Crash got even taller, and burst out of his clothes.

And kept growing taller.

A whole lot taller.

"Holy shit. *Holy shit!*" Ahn yelled while Crash grew faster than she thought her words could travel. "Get away from here before you crush me!"

Crash seemed to hear her, and took a few giant steps away. His fully nude body kept growing and growing as the giant Vyperian scuttled closer.

This. Is. Insane, Ahn thought.

Crash grew so quickly he felt as if he was taking off in a fighter jet. As his view changed, his perspective changed, and soon he was looking at much of Southern California with a bird's eye view.

He expected to keep growing until he was the same height as the octopus, but as quickly as he started growing, he stopped—a few hundred feet short of the Vyperian's height.

But still. Four hundred feet was four hundred feet.

• • •

Horton *thought* he had seen it all. Thought there wasn't anything else that could surprise him. And then he saw the giant octopus from across the horizon, and watched it lumber straight toward him. Or rather, straight toward all the craziness he was in the middle of. And while the creature ambled so close that Horton was positive he was going to get crushed, he turned and ran, no longer feeling safe in the rubble of the parking garage where he'd been watching the action.

He swore to himself that he'd only been looking away for a few seconds, but when he turned back to the chaos, there was another giant being. A giant, naked man. Out of nowhere, a giant naked man had shown up and was standing across from the giant octopus. *To do what? Fight? What the hell is going—holy shit, look at the size of that dick.*

• • •

With the battle cruiser to his left, a giant octopus in front of him, and the ruins of Disneyland at his feet, Crash didn't know what the hell to do. Sentlent Bool, as luck would have it, solved the problem for him.

"You murdered my warriors," a voice boomed in cracked English.

Sentlent Bool whipped out a tentacle and caught Crash by the ankle, tripping him up and almost upending the rugged adventure host. Crash caught his balance with a hop-step and stared down the octopus.

"You were the one in the back when I first beamed onto your ship," Crash bellowed back.

Bool said nothing.

"Your big rodent killed my best friend. So I killed *it*. And I killed your 'warriors.' And I'm going to kill you, because I'm huge, and someone has to."

Bool snarled and launched his entire body—tentacle first—at Crash. Caught by surprise and still wobbly with his new size, Crash couldn't move out of the way in time, but was able to grab the ends of two tentacles and torque his own body, swinging the massive octopus's bulk around in a full one-eighty before letting go. The centrifugal motion slung Sentlent Bool violently through the air. Right into the battle cruiser.

The battle cruiser shook and swayed and almost toppled over, and Second Sentlent Sarlz and his crew on the bridge shrieked, and he knew he had to get the snerch out of there. "Enough of this Earth madness! Take us back to orbit!"

"Sir, what about the saucer—"

"Damn the saucer!"

• • •

Sentlent Bool, in his humongousness, had dented the side of the kilometer-high battle cruiser upon impact and spun into a tornado of limbs, then righted himself and attacked Giant Crash again. Like a bunch of Yankees heavy hitters batting at once, the octopus swung six tentacles and connected, again threatening to knock Crash to the ground and crush everything beneath him. Crash started to lose balance, shuffled his feet, and destroyed a giant fiberglass Mickey while the big rubbery bats connected with him in a barrage of pain.

Even as he was being pummeled by the tentacles, Crash torqued his body to absorb the blows and use them to keep himself upright. *I've got to get away from here or I'll kill everyone underground.*

But as big as Crash was, the octopus was bigger. And as powerful as Crash was, the octopus still had the edge. The giant naked man couldn't get a punch in, couldn't get a kick in, couldn't get a tackle in. With length twice his body's and slimy to boot, nothing Crash threw out made it past the tentacles. They. Just. Kept. Coming. Crash was burning all his energy on defense and futile offense.

Half a kilometer away, the battle cruiser roared to ignition and lifted off. Startled, Sentlent Bool turned for just a moment, and that was when Crash took his chance. A half-kilometer was only a few large steps for Giant Crash.

• • •

Second Sentlent Sarlz watched through the remotescope as the giant naked man with the perfect nose charged straight at them like a Rapsadian bull. *What does he think he's doing?* Sarlz thought.

With a few steps and a big leap, Crash threw a body tackle into the battle cruiser as it left the ground.

Unearthly screams filled the bridge as the ship creaked and groaned under the extra weight of the human's body and the crushing power of his arms. Crash held on with his arms and legs wrapped around the ship, squeezing as tight as possible. He felt the fuselage start to collapse like an old tin can.

Even with the extra baggage, the battle cruiser left solid ground, but its trajectory slipped to a forty-five-degree angle.

"Evasive maneuvers!" Second Sentlent Sarlz ordered.

"What evasive maneuvers, sir?"

"*Anything!*"

"We have no defense against this, sir! We're being pulled from the sky by a giant human!"

Sarlz cracked his beak, chipping off a small piece. His eyes widened as the gigantic naked man's genitals dangled across the remotescope's screen.

• • •

The ship creaked and groaned as it left solid ground, and Crash thought for the first time about how his plan might not have been the best idea. *Maybe this wasn't the right way to get that bastard's atten—*

Schwook. Tentacles grabbed Crash's ankles, trying to tear him from the ship. Crash kept his grip. Sentlent Bool also held tight, and was yanked violently from the surface.

With both giant creatures locked onto their respective targets and the ship tapping deep into its power source, the tangled mess of metal, human, and octopus dragged through the air north toward Los Angeles. With the added weight, the battle cruiser lost all possibility of gaining altitude and flew horizontally a kilometer above the ground. Wrapped tight around the middle of the ship was Crash. And hanging from Crash was Sentlent Bool, holding on by two tentacles, the rest of his appendages dangling and slapping across the tops of skyscrapers.

Earthlings screamed as the mass flew awkwardly overhead, and Grammeral Zeezak watched from the saucer as the battle cruiser and its hangers-on twisted shakily through the sky.

The octopus's weight was almost too much for Crash to carry. *Now or never,* he thought, and crushed his arms around the fuselage and scooted up, then torqued his body, causing the ship to spin slightly and the nose to dip. The Vyperian battle cruiser was going down. He winced in a realization. *Shit, I'm going down too.*

With a final heave and yank, he pulled the nose down past the tipping point and let go, dropping back to Earth and landing on top of Sentlent Bool in the thick of midtown Los Angeles.

Time seemed to crawl as the crushed chassis of the kilometer-high spaceship flew another few kilometers past Crash and the giant octopus and plunged nose-first into one of the countless old towers on the Miracle Mile. The ship's body gouged into the earth along the Wilshire Corridor, destroying miles of city and killing tens of thousands of Vyperians and humans alike in a burning and crushing mess of flesh and mortar. Dust from the impact kicked skyward and plunged the environment into blackness. Los Angeles was a dark, fiery cauldron.

Chapter 62

The two giant bodies were motionless, man on top of octopus. Crash had multiple broken bones, internal bleeding, and a nasty gash across his sternum. He came to first, finding himself face-down with his mouth open, and up under a tentacle. His lips were covered in slime. He groaned in pain, pushed himself up, and looked at the face of his enemy.

"Fuck you," he yelled while pulling back his fist. He landed his first punch into the side of the octopus's sac. Bool's eyes opened and, for a moment, the two warriors were face-to-face. All was silent as they gazed into each other's eyes with a shared rage. Well, silent except for the sound of the explosions from the battle cruiser, the countless sirens, people screaming, the helicopters flying overhead, and the buildings crumbling all around them.

Sentlent Bool wrapped his tentacles around Crash's body and squeezed as much life out as he could. "How does it feel to be crushed like my ship, earthling?"

"Eat shit," mumbled Crash, who whipped his head into Bool's face with as nasty a head butt as he could muster. But the grip didn't lessen. Like a half-dozen pythons, the tentacles tightened around Crash's body while his nanobots were put to the test to keep up. With his arms pinned to his sides, he had nothing to create leverage with. The two monsters writhed, crushing more buildings and killing more people while Crash himself fought to stay conscious. Bool constricted tighter. In his delirium, Crash almost hoped Sentlent Bool would bestow him with some poignant intergalactic wisdom as a parting gift, but the last thing he heard before he blacked out was simply, "Die."

• • •

When the jumbled mess of the ship and its giant hangers-on had taken flight, the force field dropped, and the wreckage that had been Disneyland and its surrounding parking lot became flooded with humans hoping to do whatever they thought they could do in such a time. Police were policing, firefighters were firefighting, and reporters were reporting. And the first person any of them approached was Senator Mike Horton.

"Senator Horton," all the reporters seemed to yell at once.

"Senator Horton. How did you get inside the force field?"

"What are you doing here?"

"How are you involved in all this?"

"Do you have any comment on the rumors of gay trysts?"

• • •

Grammeral Zeezak watched from the saucer as the battle cruiser exploded into a fireball. The battle cruiser they had lived on for years to get to Earth. The battle cruiser that became the final resting place for many of his warriors. The battle cruiser that had been their only hope to return to Sennat.

With the saucer only capable of inner-system flight, the truth sank in and burned Grammeral Zeezak at his core. While Los Angeles crumbled, he felt dread settle in. The Vyperians were earthlings now.

CHAPTER 63

The human had been rendered unconscious, and Sentlent Bool stood to his tentacles, making sure his grip remained tight around the naked man's body. The giant octopus loosened one appendage, and slid it upward and retightened it around Crash's neck. *I'm going to pull your head off. Then you'll be just like your friend.*

Squeezing with all his might, Bool heard the human's bones snap under the pressure. A few more twists and a yank, and Crash's head would pop off. Twist, twist, twist—

Splat.

What!

The giant octopus loosened his grip for a moment and spun his head around. Standing behind him was another human, the same size as Crash. And it was a female. And she was naked. And she had driven a giant metal girder into his shoulder.

"*Aaaarrrrggghhhh!*"

Sentlent Bool dropped Crash, flattening a city block in the process, and massaged his wound with one of his tentacles.

"I'm going to rip your arms off, you piece of shit!" the woman yelled.

Sentlent Bool snarled, even as he fought a lust building from deep inside. "I destroyed your companion! I'll destroy you!"

Tentacles out, he charged the woman. But instead of fighting back, she dodged out of the way, rolling across a grassy park and into a supermarket. Knowing she only needed to distract the giant octopus long enough for Crash's body to heal, Ahn followed through her roll to a standing position and wiped the rubble from her body. The octopus launched another attack, and this time a tentacle tip swiped the side of her face, ripping off the skin and causing her to scream in pain. *He better heal up fast.*

Moments earlier, Ahn had watched Crash become a giant, watched him move into an entirely different perspective than the one she was living in, and waited for whatever was supposed to happen to her to happen. After a few minutes of trying to avoid being crushed by the fighting giants, she chose to return to the safety of the underground freighter, dejection resting upon her shoulders.

She reached the entrance and found she no longer fit.

Oh, no.

As if reading her mind, Marnshoth's voice echoed out through the hidden passage.

"You have been given the same growth serum as earthling Jefferson. You don't have the nanotechnology to help you handle a concentrated dose, so a slower-acting formula was administered while you were unconscious. It was timed to match the arrival of the Vyperian mutation so you would be able to fight it together. Go."

Damn it all to hell, Ahn thought as her clothes ripped off her body and she shot skyward.

She knew she had to be careful. She was big, but she didn't have any nanotechnology to help her. Almost dead was might-as-well-be-dead for her.

Her nemesis raised two tentacles straight up into the air. *What the hell is that thing doing?* She glanced at Crash and saw movement. *C'mon, you son of a bitch. Get moving.* Bool dropped his two raised tentacles like hammers, missing Ahn by two lengths.

Ha. Is that all you got?

But the alien wasn't finished. He flipped over the top of his tentacles, using them to vault himself, and before Ahn could react, the giant octopus had flipped his entire body on top of her. The weight and mass came slamming down, smashing them both into a shopping center as tiny people ran screaming to escape out from underneath the behemoths. Pinned, Ahn squirmed as the octopus ran its slimy tentacles up her naked legs and across her breasts. *This,* she thought, *is the worst fucking thing I've felt in a long fucking time.* Suckers traced down her chest and stomach toward her naked femininity. "Oh, *hell* no," she screamed, and bit her attacker on the face as hard as she could. The beast screeched and pulled back as ooze sprayed from its wound, and Ahn saw a blur out of the corner of her eye: Crash, barreling at full speed.

Bool saw the woman's reaction. *Time for a surprise, human.*

The octopus stuck his rear end out and up into the air.

• • •

Crash shook off the cobwebs and felt his body healing. He had seen the two masses hit the ground, and hurried to get to his feet. Two big steps later, he leaped the rest of the way—right into a streaming jet of black fluid. *Ink!* he thought as he flew through the air, irreversibly committed to the leap. But the ink had caught him dead in the eyes and he landed not on the octopus, but in the rubble where it had just been.

Crash punched at the air in futility then wiped his eyes with his hands, but the ink was too thick, too viscous. He could hear the other two giants struggling around him, and could hear the sounds of the city while he stomped around blindly, no doubt crushing scores of his smaller brethren.

"Crash!" he heard Ahn yell in between pain-filled groans. "Water fountain!"

"What?"

"To your left!"

Crash remembered where he was—and the pond and water fountain in the middle of the shopping complex he'd just kicked over. He shuffled one step to the left, trying to kill as few fellow humans as possible, bent over, and felt around with his hands. Glass. Concrete. Tiny outdoor tables and chairs. Something squishy—Crash didn't want to know. Empty space ... *there.* He felt water and dunked his face into the pond and rubbed furiously, but the ink was potent and his head had been doused. *What was that trick Will taught me hunting spitting cobras?* He stopped rubbing, and instead held his eyes wide open and splashed and blinked until he could see again.

Will.

Crash thought of his friend as he stood. Sadness turned to anger and he wiped the last of the ink from his face and gathered his bearings. A half-kilometer stretch along Fairfax Avenue was black, coated with the giant space octopus's secretion. Ink had flooded the streets, and the faint sound of normal-sized humans struggling in the flash flood of dark, sticky fluid could be heard in Crash's ears hundreds of feet above the ground. But his attention was stolen by the sight of the octopus running across the city. Running with Rachel ensnared above him.

CHAPTER 64

"I am leaving your planet soon," Marnshoth told Faraday, "and unless you wish to travel with me, I suggest you make your exit."

"What about my son? And Jennica!?"

"Follow the lights, and you'll find them. Follow the lights back and you'll find the way out."

A track of lights illuminated, creating a line across the metal ceiling and out into the hallway. Faraday looked down at the Vyperian that had been Davis. "What about him?"

"That Vyperian still has work to do. Take the others and leave. Now."

Faraday looked one last time at the prone Vyperian and walked out, following the lights. The door to the holding room slid open and the video game screen went dark. Trevor and Jennica! both stared at the blank monitor for a moment longer, and then turned at the sound of approaching footsteps.

"Dad!"

Trevor ran into his father's arms, and Faraday scooped him up. Jennica! stood and watched the two hug, but was quickly pulled into the hug by Trevor.

"Can we leave now?" Trevor said.

"Yeah, kiddo. You've been playing that game long enough."

• • •

His eyes on the giant Vyperian and its captive, Crash sprinted across the city, covering entire blocks with each bounding step. He tried to stick to the main thoroughfares; that made it easier to see if any tiny humans were in danger of being stomped on. Not that he would notice anyway, but it made him feel better to think he was trying.

Where is that damn beast going?

Thundering across the Los Angeles Basin, Crash—as he had so many other times in his life—expertly chased down his target. Except this time was for real. There were no cameras to play to, no silly editing tricks to rely upon, no exaggerated dangers to entice viewers to stick around through another commercial break. Just a seven-hundred-foot-tall cephalopod with a four-hundred-foot-tall hostage running across the city and crushing everything in its path.

Crash closed in on the Vyperian as Ahn struggled to break free.

Bool had been zigzagging across the city and had made it downtown, where a few of the skyscrapers were actually taller than he was. The octopus swung around a taller building and disappeared. Crash watched the octopus dip for cover. *Not too many places he can hide, at least.*

Crash crashed across the 110 freeway and stomped through the convention center. The longer he remained big, the less he thought about the damage he was causing down below. People weren't people anymore; they were bugs. Buildings were paper, concrete was foam board, and Crash was Crash, as reckless as ever.

The roar of stomping monsters and buildings being

312

crushed thundered through the concrete canyons of downtown Los Angeles. Crash paused for a second to listen for his prey or its hostage, but the booming of his own machinations was all he could hear echoing back to him. Stepping over a city block and across Broadway, his foot came down on vendor after vendor of Mexican lingerie and bootleg DVDs. He reached the tall building where he lost sight of Bool and Ahn, and charged around it.

Right into the sights of the saucer.

• • •

Grammeral Zeezak watched through the remotescope while Crash barreled around the skyscraper and into view. "Fire."

Two death rays cut out through the front of the saucer as it floated at eye level in front of Crash. Still being carried by his forward momentum, the giant man couldn't react quickly enough to get out of the way as the beams carved into his naked torso and burned his flesh down to the ribs.

"Shit!" He stumbled to his knees. The spaceship was too far away to lunge for, and he knew he couldn't take much more from the death rays as they cut toward his heart, frying him faster than he could heal. He planted his fists into the ground like an ape and pushed himself up. The energy beams continued to target his chest, and the entire downtown Los Angeles financial district smelled like a pig roast.

The beams sliced across the front of Crash's body and he used the last of his strength to push and fall sideways instead of backward. The movement took him out of the path of the deadly rays and into the skyscrapers. He toppled into a bank

ATTACK OF THE VYPERIANS   TIM SAVAGE

building and brought the entire forty-five-story structure into the tower next to it, and they both collapsed to the ground under Crash's bulk. The earth shook as the streets and alleys filled with smoke and debris.

The deadly beams from the saucer followed the giant human as he stumbled, and then blasted into the buildings he fell behind.

• • •

"Awaiting your orders, my Lord."

Grammeral Zeezak was calm, but his reply was quick. "Attack from above. We end this now."

The saucer flitted up to the top of the skyline and into a giant cloud of dust that had erupted from the mayhem.

"Thermal imager on," Zeezak commanded.

The view on the remotescope changed from flat gray to an explosion of reds, oranges, blues, and greens.

"Take us over."

Zeezak watched the thermal image of the big human's broken body come into view a kilometer below, yellow legs half buried in blue rubble, bright red heart pumping bright red blood like waterfalls into the green streets.

"Take us in, and target the head."

"Yes, my Lord."

• • •

Crash couldn't see much farther than his hand in the sooty air, yet he knew the Vyperians were coming in for the kill. His body was shredded, he was pretty sure he had a collapsed lung, and his calf had been pierced clean through by a ten-meter splinter of stainless steel from some architectural masterpiece-turned-cause of excruciating pain.

Vision limited by the heavy dust, he strained his senses to catch any cue he could. He heard no sounds, smelled no scents. And then, squinting and staring, he saw it: a barely noticeable downdraft from the descending saucer in the thick, dirty air. Crash smirked at the revelation. *Just 'cause I can't see you, doesn't mean I don't know where you are.*

The beams locked on as he yanked the metal splinter from his calf. Screaming in agony, he whipped the giant needle of stainless steel into the void of dust. The metal, giving off no heat in the thermal image, appeared on screen as only a soft blue that blended in with the rest of the rubble. The big man's thermal movements merely suggested a flail for help.

Zeezak felt the saucer tilt and heard the screech of metal on metal before red alerts sounded, and the saucer wobbled off its axis as the spear plunged through the front quarter of the disk and stuck. In between the shrieks and hisses on the bridge, Zeezak managed to scream out for a damage report.

"The hull has been ruptured! We're being pulled down!"

"Counterbalance and retreat! *Now!*"

The spaceship wobbled down and then back up again, and was gone. Crash felt a whoosh as the air surrounding him was disturbed by the evacuating ship. His whole body felt like it was on fire. Like he had hot coals for blood. And then he felt the familiar deep tingle of that different burn. The warm burn that meant his body was getting fixed.

He took a breath and let his head settle for a moment on a

not particularly comfortable chunk of concrete and steel. He laughed. Laughed, because he'd lost track of how much pain he'd felt in the last few days. Laughed harder because he knew he would feel better than good in just a few minutes more. *I wonder if this is what God feels like.* He closed his eyes.

"*Craaaaaash!*"

Rachel. Crash sat up and groaned. *Maybe just another few seconds.*

"Crash! *Help!*"

Goddammit.

He pulled himself to his feet and climbed through the collapsed and crumbled buildings to find the Vyperian once again pinning Ahn down and running its tentacles up her legs.

"Hey, you son of a bitch! *Get off her.*"

The Vyperian looked up and snarled, but didn't stop.

"No more fucking around, alien. Time to die."

CHAPTER 65

Faraday led Trevor and Jennica! out of Marnshoth's elevator and into the bright California sunshine. The ground shook beneath them in a slow, long rumble.

"What is that?" asked Jennica!

"She's taking off. We need to get out of here. Move!"

Faraday picked Trevor up and the three humans ran across the rubble. Jennica! screamed and stopped when she saw the giant pile of salted Vyperians.

"What *is* that? What happened?"

"Food for her trip back home!" Dr. Faraday yelled back.

"Food? What about my princ—"

"Just run!"

Officials previously outside the force field converged on the three and an officer put his hand up as Faraday ran toward him.

"Sir, you need to come with us."

Faraday stopped and took the moment to catch his breath. "You need to get these people out of here right now," he gasped. "Or they're all going to die."

The officer looked around, felt the ground shake even more, and then thought best to heed the frantic man's advice. He clicked on his radio. "This is Officer Soderlund. We need to evacuate. Right now."

Faraday put his son down. "Trev, do you think you can

keep up?" he asked as Jennica! passed them both.

"I think so."

Without another word, father and son ran to catch up with Jennica! and the rest of the panicked humans who had turned around to run away.

• • •

Crash brought the pain, slamming down his fists like hammers of the gods and walloping the octopus. The Vyperian raised its rear ever so slightly, but Crash could sense what was coming next. A burst of hot octopus ink blasted into the sky, but Crash dropped and rolled under the spray. Bool released his grip on Ahn, and she twisted out and away from the slimy beast. Crash stared down his foe, and the Vyperian stood to its full height and taunted its human enemy. "Now we finish this, human."

The two bodies slammed into each other and the ground shook as each warrior grasped the other and crushed with all his might. Cars were smashed, buildings punched through, trees uprooted. Ahn tried her best to scramble away without destroying anything further, but she was far too hurt to worry about much more than her own safety. She looked around for something, anything that could help.

Her eyes fell to a gasoline tanker. She looked over at Crash and the octopus, still locked together in close combat. She stumbled, grasped her side with one hand, scooped up the tanker truck with the other, and yelled, "Crash! Get out of the way!"

Crash looked past Bool's writhing appendages, saw the tanker in her hand, and understood. He tightened his bear hug just long enough to know he had Bool gasping, and then used the octopus's own slime to slink down to ground level. As Crash dropped, Ahn hurled the gas truck as hard as her injured body would allow. It missed the alien.

"God *dammit!*"

The tanker did, however, land within reach of Crash. While the octopus struggled to catch its breath, Crash picked up the tanker, knocked the end off, and splashed the Vyperian's body with the fuel inside. Bool shrieked and hissed from the burn of the gasoline in his eyes. Ahn bent over and scooped up a chunk of burning wreckage.

"*Move,*" she screamed. Crash dove out of the way as the hobbling woman took careful aim and sidearmed the fireball at the octopus.

With a whoosh, flames engulfed the Vyperian's tubular body. Shrieks never heard before on Earth echoed across the Los Angeles Basin as the flaming octopus ran in a small circle, confused and tormented by the fire. Bool lunged toward Crash, and for a second Crash thought he was in serious trouble. But before the octopus could reach him the fire overwhelmed the cephalopod, and Bool's skin and flesh burned and crackled and the giant beast fell to the earth, burying a half kilometer of Los Angeles under flaming alien meat. The shrieks and hisses lessened, and as the beast cooked, the sounds of sizzling overtook the sounds of suffering.

CHAPTER 66

Jennica! ran her slender legs off as Faraday and Trevor caught up.

"How ... much ... more?" Trevor spat out through dry lips.

"Keep running!" was all Faraday said, all he could say with gasping breath.

The ground started to crack, and fissures opened here, there, everywhere. Faraday craned his neck to look back, and saw that the pile of dead, salted Vyperians was gone. *Fallen into an open hangar door.*

• • •

On board the buried freighter, Davis sat alone, unmasked, nursing his wounds as Marnshoth spoke to a mind long uncontrolled by its own consciousness.

Reset the life support systems....

Reset the automated feeding system....

Initialize navigation route to Sennat....

Leave me. Your final task awaits you on the surface....

• • •

Out of the corner of his eye, Faraday saw a flutter of movement as a bubble-shaped craft ascended and jetted away.

320

Trevor was starting to seriously lag behind, so Faraday yanked him up into his arms for the final stretch. They caromed around a crumbled brick wall to the Anaheim street where Crash's Ferrari had been sitting. *Please be there.* It was. But he had long since lost the keys.

Faraday searched his mind for instructions to hot-wire the sports car, but struck out. "Dammit."

"Oh my God, I got a car just like this for my sixteenth birthday! Is it yours?" squealed Jennica!

"No." Faraday didn't feel like explaining any further at the moment. He searched again with his super brain and found Ferrari electronics manuals. Cross-referenced. *Got it.* He threw a brick through the window, setting off the alarm. The scientist dove headfirst below the driver's seat, ducked under the already too-tight console, and ripped the panel off, while the ground shook so hard he could barely keep his hands still. Within a few seconds, he had a big fistful of wires out, and a few seconds after that the alarm shut off and the car started. He pulled his head out from under the steering wheel.

"All right, let's go. It's a good thing you two are small. My last trip in this thing was horrible."

· · ·

Licks of evening fog crept up over the saucer's rim and around the embedded metal spike as the craft hovered over the Pacific Ocean a hundred kilometers from the coast.

Grammeral Zeezak sat alone in his cabin under the dim lighting of the glowbats. The battle cruiser was burning wreckage. Most of the Vyperians under his command had been killed. The saucer was so badly damaged that Zeezak was on the verge of giving the evacuation command. And his princess was—he didn't know. All telepathy between him and the object of his desire was still blocked, and he was left unaware of her status or location.

Zeezak stared at the wall. Above his misting tent was a ceremonial scythe, crafted by the Lowest Slaves in the History of Time and gifted to him after his defeat of Marnshoth on Sennat so many years earlier. *I was so ambitious then. So powerful.* He rose from his throne and slowly scuttled to the weapon. *And now I have nothing. Not even pride. Even Sentlent Bool died a warrior, while I suffer a retreating coward's demise.* He ran a tentacle across the sharp edge of the blade, slicing a gash into his flesh. He closed his eyes and his ring turned pitch-black while he pulled the elongated blade from the wall and held it up to his own thick neck. The alien pulled slowly and felt the razor-sharp scythe warmly cut, deeper and deeper into his body. One more centimeter and it would sever the life vein completely, finalizing the mission's total failure.

The mission. *His* mission. The mission that saw the Second Tentacle of the Emperor tricked and destroyed by the schemes of an underestimated enemy long thought dead. But even imprisoned deep underground, she still got the better of every part of Grammeral Zeezak's strategy. The blade sank in deeper, and Q'Shin Zeezak leaned forward to finish the job. *Just a little farther and my failure will be complete—*

He stopped. *No. She hasn't won. Not yet.*

Zeezak lowered the weapon and gently placed it back on the display rack. He left it as it was, soiled with the oil and slime of his being. A reminder. His door chirped.

"Enter," he announced without turning around.

War Wager Kreev scuttled into the chamber.

"My Lord, Marnshoth's ship is attempting to leave its subterranean location."

Zeezak's ring turned bright red, leaving no trace of the absolute black it had just been. He continued to face the wall, not wanting to show his self-inflicted wounds. "Our status?"

"Weapons systems are disabled, my Lord."

"Can we make it to her before she clears the atmosphere?"

"The saucer doesn't have much power left, my Lord. We need to figure out our own plan—"

"Can we make it to *her*." Zeezak turned around, and the two stared at each other.

"Yes my Lord, we can make it."

Zeezak stroked his ring with his tips. Snapped his beak. "War Wager Kreev. You have stepped in admirably in the absence of Sentlent Bool."

"Thank you, my Lord."

"Set an intercept course for Marnshoth. She will not be returning home. Be ready to open the reactor cores. We're going to burn half the hemisphere off the face of this wretched planet while we're at it."

CHAPTER 67

"Shit." The asphalt buckled and shifted and caved under the Ferrari's right front tire, dropping the chassis to the street and showering the pavement with sparks. Faraday yanked the wheel and swerved to the left, keeping the rear wheel from slamming into the gaping hole but almost launching his son off Jennica!'s lap and out of the open-topped car.

"Shit!" Faraday yelled again as he grabbed Trevor by the shirt and pulled him back down.

"What's happening?" Jennica! screamed.

Faraday risked a look in the rearview, and saw a mountain of street rise up behind him.

"Marnshoth is trying to blast out of the ground!"

"Who's Man Sloth?" Jennica! screeched.

The asphalt rose and fell all around them as the Ferrari cut and slalomed through the street, narrowly missing parked cars and fresh holes in the ground. They kept moving, and the ground became more stable the farther away they got. Faraday shifted into third gear and allowed himself a short breath of relief.

"What are we gonna do now, Dad?"

Faraday glanced over at the passenger seat for the first time to make sure everyone was unhurt. "I don't know."

There was a moment of silence as the shock wore off. In the passenger seat, Jennica! choked back tears and Trevor hugged her tight. The pop star broke the silence. "Maybe we go find someplace safe."

Trevor squeezed tighter as Faraday responded. "Yeah."

• • •

The last of Disneyland heaved up and up like a new range of mountains being born, and when it seemed it couldn't rise any higher, it didn't, and instead the earth and everything that had been on it exploded outward as a gleaming, glowing starship slowly lifted from sight previously unseen.

Jennica! screeched and struggled to twist her body enough to see the spectacle behind her. At her excitement, Trevor also turned to look at the massive space freighter. The egg-shaped starship heaved under the dirt and rubble that hadn't yet fallen to the side.

"*Oh my God.* It's like a hundred miles long!" Jennica! yelled. Faraday guessed it was more like three, *but still. Incredible.* Kilometers away and surrounded by the throaty roar of the Ferrari 458, the three still were overwhelmed by the disturbingly deep rumble of Marnshoth's ship as it began its slow ascent to space.

"Dad! Look!"

Faraday followed his son's finger. Another craft had appeared in the distant sky. The saucer, headed straight toward Marnshoth's ship. Faraday looked away from the road again and squinted. "Is that a *spear* sticking out of it?"

• • •

Grammeral Zeezak left the anywherevator and scuttled to the front of the bridge. The red-alert alarm still blared intermittently, but otherwise his ship was deathly quiet. "Someone shut that thing off."

A few tense moments passed, and then all was silent. The saucer was flying on reserve power and barely held aloft, but the Grammeral knew that was all they needed. And the other Vyperians knew it as well. The freighter Marnshoth had been condemned to so long ago had no weapons, no defenses. A direct hit with the reactor cores open would send her to her death. And them to theirs.

The saucer cruised back over land. Dusk had settled, and the oval of starship lights in the distance appeared on the remotescope.

"How much time before intercept, Kreev?"

Grammeral Zeezak's failure to use Kreev's proper military title burned into the ears and hearts of the officers on the deck. To a species of such rank and file, it was truly a symbol of the end.

"Two Earth minutes, my Lord."

Zeezak turned his back to the remotescope and addressed his comrades. "Fellow Vyperians. It has been an honor to lead you. To the glimmering stars of space, I wish this could have ended differently. What logic could have predicted that pursuing the burning temptations of desire would have ended so disastrously?" Beaks snapped softly in saccharine agreement.

"However, we are not destined to perish without leaving a mark, and it shall be a mark that will forever leave the Vyperian imprint upon this planet. Kreev ... prepare to open the reactors."

"Yes, my Lord!"

"We shall show these humans that even in defeat, we are more powerful than they could possibly imagine."

War Wager Kreev traced his appendage across a thin touch tablet and enabled the Beledet crystals for detonation. "Reactors open and ready to detonate, my Lord."

"On my command."

Marnshoth's ship was gaining altitude. *But she isn't going to make it,* Zeezak thought. The interception was going to happen long before the Farceen queen would make it out of Earth's atmosphere. Grammeral Q'Shin Zeezak's ring flickered orange without his knowing. It was a color that rarely showed on Vyperians. It was the color of the acceptance of fate.

"My Lord."

Pulled out of his trance, Zeezak swiveled his upper body toward the voice. Two Vyperians stood before him.

"Speak."

"My Lord, this is Sivad, the only survivor from the battle cruiser. He returned on one of the bubblejets."

Zeezak extended his appendage and touched Sivad's ring, a motion reserved for only the rarest of occasions. "Welcome back, Sivad. Your service has been appreciated."

Sivad's face remained expressionless, even for a Vyperian. "The feeling is not mutual." Tension filled the bridge while Vyperians turned to look at the one that dared speak with such disrespect to the Grammeral, especially in time of darkness.

The Vyperian leader cautiously parried back. "You would dare speak that way to your Grammeral?"

"Thirty seconds until impact, my Lord!" said Kreev.

In the blink of an eye, Sivad whipped out a thermal grenade from his tangle of tentacles. The Vyperians on the bridge looked on in horror.

"What the snerch are you doing?" yelled Grammeral Zeezak.

Sivad's expression didn't change. "Marnshoth sends her regards. There will be no second meeting."

• • •

"Holy *shit*."

All eyes in the Ferrari were skyward when the saucer exploded into a fireball and flaming wreckage streaked like meteorites across the evening sky while fire rained down from above.

"What the hell happened?" yelled Jennica!

"Davis's final mission."

The three of them watched the giant egg-shaped starship blast straight up unmolested, accelerating faster as it ascended. Before long, it was a speck in the evening sky. And then it was gone.

"Where is my prince, do you think he's ... dead?" moaned Jennica!

Faraday tried to explain. "He wasn't your prince, it was a trap—"

"What are you *talking* about? He came here for me! He was gonna make me happy! Pull over! I've got to find him!"

Faraday scowled. There was no use. "We'll go look for him soon," he lied to get her to shut up. "Right now we need to find Crash and Rachel."

"Uh, Dad?" said Trevor. "Crash is the guy from TV, right?"

"Yeah."

"I found him."

Trevor's gaze was on the horizon off to the left.

In the distance, in the dusk, giant naked Crash was holding a giant moth by what could be called its throat while he punched it again and again with his free hand, knocking moth dust onto the city below with every landed swing.

Faraday slammed on the brakes. He'd been so overwhelmed by all the craziness around him, he'd tuned out all his media streams. He pulled into the fire lane of the freeway and he and Trevor and Jennica! watched the onslaught with unblinking eyes and open mouths.

"Why," Jennica! started, "why are they so ... so *big*. His ... it's *huge!*"

The three stared in amazement as Crash grabbed the moth's wings at the base, put a foot on its thorax, and ripped off the giant wings with his godlike strength. Giant Crash threw the wings to the ground and pumped his arms to the sky.

"That's it! I'm fuckin' done!" his voice thundered across the county.

EPILOGUE

Los Angeles was in ruins, but the ruiners had been vanquished. The Ferrari had broken down on the freeway near Beverly Hills, and Frank, Trevor, and Jennica! were picked up by the National Guard and brought to a hospital.

For the first time she could remember, Jennica! was in a room of regular people and no one gave much of a shit about her. And for the first time she could remember, much to her surprise, she almost liked the lack of attention. At least, until she craved a distraction to keep her from facing the all-too-familiar empty loneliness that was once again suffocating her heart. She flipped her hair and sighed loud enough to elicit stares.

"Does anyone have, like, an iPhone I can use?"

I'm glad we got her out, Faraday thought as he watched Jennica!'s antics from the other side of triage. *I'm also glad she's not my problem anymore.* He took in the scene around him. Nurses and doctors scurried about as casualties flooded the emergency room. He knew neither he nor his son needed medical attention before they had arrived at the hospital. "Come on, Trev. Let's let these guys work on the people who really need help." He got up, gently took Trevor's hand, and guided him through the chaos of injured civilians. The hospital doors slid open to the sight of a mob of people standing across the street, all staring up over the top of the hospital, gasping and gesturing and pointing wildly.

"What are they looking at?" asked Trevor.

Faraday thought about taking the safe route while Trevor yanked his hand toward the mass of excited people. "Wait a sec, Trev." He held his son back for but a moment, though. *There's a lot of me in him.* He looked again at the growing crowd of fervent Los Angelinos. Shook his head and smirked. *Curiosity might be the end of us all,* he thought as he let Trevor pull him toward the action. *But we've made it so far.*

• • •

James "Crash" Jefferson held Rachel Ahn in his arms for just a moment before collapsing onto her naked chest with exhaustion. The nanobots healed his ailments, but his energy was shot. And while *his* wounds had healed, hers were going to take much longer. But as broken and bruised as Ahn's body was, her spirit was still fighting strong.

She pushed Crash up off her chest. "C'mon, we can't rest here."

Crash took an exhausted breath. "Why not?"

But he got his answer not from Rachel, but from his own eyes when he opened them and saw they were resting on the side of a hill in the middle of the city. And more importantly, they were still the size of cruise ships. Crash tried to push up, but couldn't. He was too exhausted to move.

The two were silent for a minute before Ahn said what was on both their minds. "Does this wear off, or are we ..." she started, but couldn't finish. Tears pooled into her eyes. Crash held her closer, struggling to keep his own eyes open.

She nuzzled into his neck, suddenly becoming aware that everyone in Los Angeles was watching the two of them as they sat exposed, completely naked and vulnerable. She hid her face even more. "Tell me we're gonna get back to normal. Lie to me if you need to."

Crash swept her fine black hair back over her ear and whispered softly, booming his voice for a mile. "I can't. But I can tell you something else."

She looked up at him, fighting tears. "What?"

"That I'm glad you're big too. You know, in case I get lonely."

She ever so slightly smiled, then buried her face back into his neck as they settled into the hillside, causing boulders to tumble down and smash a row of cars along the street below. *He's a bastard, but he's all I've got till we figure this out. If we figure this out.*

And the two naked giants fell asleep while the world watched and wondered.

THE END